H . .

"N und
his beard could grow no whiter. He wanted to die.

"Miracle" by Connie Willis: "I'm the Spirit of Christmas Present... not Christmas Present. Christmas *Present*—Barbie dolls, ugly ties, cheese logs . . ."

"Icicle Music" by Michael Bishop: Not all holiday memories are welcome ones—and neither are all ghosts of Christmas Past . . .

"A Kidnapped Santa Claus" by L. Frank Baum: "The Daemons who live in the mountain caves grew to hate Santa Claus very much, and all for the simple reason that he made children happy . . ."

"Santa Claus vs. S.P.I.D.E.R." by Harlan Ellison: Kris Kringle is bringing peace and happiness to the world—even if that means he has to take out every politician in America to do it!

"How Santa Claus Came to Simpson's Bar" by Bret Harte: "Bedraggled, ragged, unshaven, and unshorn, with one arm hanging helplessly at his side, Santa Claus came to Simpson's Bar and fell fainting on the first threshold . . ."

"The Yattering and Jack" by Clive Barker: Deck the halls with demonic evil, falalalala lala lala . . .

. . . and many more.

Edited by Brian M. Thomsen

The American Fantasy Tradition

Shadows of Blue and Grey: The Civil War Writings of Ambrose Bierce

Oceans of Magic *(with Martin H. Greenberg)*

Anthologies available from Warner Aspect

Futures: Four Novels

by Peter F. Hamilton, Stephen Baxter, Paul McAuley, and Ian McDonald

A Dragon-Lover's Treasury of the Fantastic

edited by Margaret Weis

A Quest-Lover's Treasury of the Fantastic

edited by Margaret Weis

A Yuletide Universe

Sixteen Fantastical Tales

EDITED BY Brian M. Thomsen

An AOL Time Warner Company

Copyright information continued on page 256.

Warner Books, Inc., 1271 Avenue of the Americas, New York, NY 10020

Visit our Web site at www.twbookmark.com.

An AOL Time Warner Company

Book design by Fearn Cutler de Vicq
Printed in the United States of America
First Printing: November 2003
10 9 8 7 6 5 4 3 2 1

Library of Congress Cataloging-in-Publication Data
A yuletide universe : sixteen fantastical tales / edited by Brian M. Thomsen.
p. cm.
ISBN 0-446-69187-9
1. Christmas stories, American. 2. Fantasy fiction, American. 3. Science fiction, American. I. Thomsen, Brian.
PS648.C43Y85 2003
813'.0876008334—dc21 2003045069

For Arthur E. Thomsen, my father,
the man most responsible for this volume both directly and indirectly.

—BMT

Contents

Yuletide Greetings!

Deck the Halls and stuff the stockings!
Relax and enjoy some holiday cheer.
Santa's on board with disguises galore
It's a Yuletide Universe time of year.

So trim the tree with tinsel fresh from Connie's tinseltown
memories
While Clive has your favorite goose cooked
'Tis the season to be jolly
Read on and have a dickens of a time.

—Brian Thomsen

Santa Shorts

As every kid knows, big things sometimes come in small packages. (Just ask any parent who has had to assemble a multi-part toy on Christmas Eve only to find that it was never going to fit back in the box it came out of.)

Likewise these short shorts.

The Gaiman originated as a Christmas card for Neil's friends and acquaintances while the Gibson first appeared as a newspaper column.

No matter what the circumstances of their "nativity," all three are wonderful literary stocking stuffers.

Nicholas Was . . .

Neil Gaiman

Older than sin, and his beard could grow no whiter. He wanted to die.

The dwarfish natives of the Arctic caverns did not speak his language, but conversed in their own, twittering tongue, conducted incomprehensible rituals, when they were not actually working in the factories.

Once every year they forced him, sobbing and protesting, into Endless Night. During the journey he would stand near every child in the world, leave one of the dwarves' invisible gifts by its bedside. The children slept, frozen into time.

He envied Prometheus and Loki, Sisyphus and Judas. His punishment was harsher.

Ho.

Ho.

Ho.

Cyber-Claus

William Gibson

In the night of 12/24/07, though sensors woven through the very fabric of the house had thus far registered a complete absence of sentient bio-activity, I found myself abruptly summoned from a rare, genuine, and very expensively induced example of that most priceless of states, sleep.

Even as I hurriedly dressed, I knew that dozens of telepresent armed-response drones would already be sweeping in from the District, skimming mere inches above the chill surface of the Potomac. Vicious tri-lobed aeroforms that they were, they resembled nothing more than the Martian war machines of George Pal's 1953 epic, *The War of the Worlds.*

And while, from somewhere far above, now, came that *sound,* that persistent *clatter,* as though gunships disgorged whole platoons of iron-shod mercenaries, I could only wonder: who? Was it my estranged wife, the Lady Betsy-Jayne Motel-6 Hyatt, Chief Eco-trustee of the Free Duchy of Wyoming? Or was it Cleatus "Mainframe" Sinyard himself, president of the United States and perpetual co-chairman of the Concerned Smart People's Northern Hemisphere Co-prosperity Sphere?

"You're mumbling again, big guy," said Memory, shivering into hallucinatorily clear focus on the rumpled sheets, her thighs warm and golden against the Royal Stewart flannel. She adjusted the nosecones of her chrome bustier. "Also, you're on the verge of a major fashion crime."

I froze, the starched white tails of an Elmore of Shinjuku evening shirt, half-tucked into the waistband of a favorite pair of lovingly mended calfskin jodhpurs. She was right. Pearl buttons scattered like a flock of minuscule flying saucers as I tore myself out of the offending Elmore. I swiftly chose a classic Gap T-shirt and a Ralph Lauren overshirt in shotgun-distressed ochre corduroy. The Gap T's double-knit liquid crystal began to cycle sluggishly in response to body-heat, displaying crudely animated loops of once-famous televangelists of the previous century, their pallid flanks streaked with the sweat of illicit sexual exertion. Now that literally *everything* was digital, History and Image were no more than Silly Putty in the hands of anyone with a BFA and a backer in Singapore. But that was just the nature of Postmodernity, and, frankly, it suited me right down to the ground.

"Visitors upstairs, chief," she reminded me pointlessly, causing me to regret not having invested in that last chip-upgrade. "Like on the roof."

"How many?" And this was Samsung-Sears's idea of an *expert* system?

"Seventeen, assuming we're talking bipeds."

"What's that supposed to mean?"

"That Nintendo-Dow micropore sensor-skin you had 'em stretch over the RealistiSlate? After those Colombian bush ninjas from the Slunk Cartel tried to get in through the toilet-ventilators? Well, that stuff's registering, like, *hooves.* Tiny ones. Unless this is some kinda major Jersey Devil infestation, I make it eight quadrupeds—plus one *definite* biped."

"It can't be Sinyard then." I holstered a 3mm Honda and pocketed half a dozen spare ampules of gel. "He'd never come alone."

"So maybe that's the good news, but I gotta tell you, this guy weighs in at close to one-forty kilos. And wears size eleven-and-a-half boots. As an expert system, I'd advise you to use the Mossad & Wesson bullpup, the one with the subsonic witness-protection nozzles—" She broke off, as if listening to something only she could hear. "Uh-oh," she said, "I think he's coming down the *chimney* . . ."

Holiday

Richard Christian Matheson

It was sunset. The inn was settling into night and vacationers wandered up from the beach, tired and sunburned. It was very hot in Bermuda—like a desert with an azure sea seeping from one side.

The waiter brought my drink and I rested my feet on the patio wall overlooking the ocean. As the sea churned easily, wearily from its day, a man sat down next to me. His hair was white and there wasn't much of it. His skin was fair, almost pink, cheeks sunburned and high. About sixty to seventy, I figured.

"Mind?" he asked, half-finished drink in hand.

"I could use the company." He seemed harmless enough.

He settled down into the chaise, and together we watched the waves spreading over the sand and retreating. Birds with long, thin legs sprinted awkwardly over the sand and eventually lifted skyward.

"Flyin's a hell of a thing," he observed, after a long sip.

"I can't do it," I agreed, and he smiled.

"Where you from?" he asked, eyes sizing me.

"Los Angeles. Just down for some sun and free time." A waiter in penguin-proper sidled over and the man ordered us another round.

"My treat," he offered. "Makes me feel good."

I nodded thanks as he winked paternally.

"What's your name?" he asked, taking another swallow.

"Karl," I answered, ready for trouble. The way I saw it, paternal winkers always made trouble for you one way or another.

"Pretty nice," he appraised its sound. "Karl . . . yeah, pretty damn nice."

"Thanks," I said, growing less than fascinated with the exchange. I decided not to ask his name. Why wave the red cape.

"Say, Karl, do you mind if I ask you a personal question?"

No objection, so he went ahead.

"What did you get for Christmas last year?"

I swallowed a mouthful of ice after crushing it to bits.

"What?" I was starting to feel the liquor.

"For Christmas . . . what did you get?"

"You serious?" He was looking a bit sloshy himself, wiping his mouth with one hand, thoughtfully, drunkenly.

He gestured away my stinginess and I nodded unenthusiastically.

"Power saw from the wife, shirts and a record from the kids, binoculars from the folks, and a wine-making kit from the people in my department." I tinkled the ice around in my glass. "Oh, and this magazine I subscribe to, *Realtors Life,* sent me a barometer with an escrow chart. Helps you figure percentages."

The other round arrived and he paid the waiter. Tipped him good.

He sighed as he mumbled through my recitation of gifts. "What was the record?" he asked.

"Music from *Hatari.* Horrible stuff. Oboes imitating rhinos, you know?"

He nodded and swallowed half his new drink with a liquidy gobble. We didn't say anything else for a few minutes. Some of the inn workers came by, and lit the tiki torches and we watched them. Bugs were flying around, drawn to the glow. We swatted one or two.

"I love it down here," he said, voice blurry. "Just wish the hell I had the time to get away more often."

He looked at me with bloodshot eyes. "But in distribution . . . who has time to vacation?"

How the hell did I know? I sold condos and houses and made deals for closing costs and termite inspections. Dullest stuff in the world. Distribution was for pamphlets dropped from helicopters, as far as I could tell.

"Yeah," I answered, being polite. Why get a paternal winker mad if it could be avoided?

I shook my head no, feeling kind of sorry for him. Nuts, but sweet, I figured.

"Hey, sure you don't want to stay for another round?" I asked. No harm in *my* asking, I thought.

He smiled, glad we were getting along again.

"Nah . . . I should get back and get some sleep. Leaving in the morning, Karl."

I stood up to see him off.

"Well, nice meeting you, Santa."

That time it felt good.

"Same here, Karl," he said. "And like I said before, don't worry about this year." He winked at me, "I'll see to it you get something really nice; something you'll like."

I looked at him and smiled. "Thanks."

"Don't stay out too late, Karl," he said, and in a couple of seconds he was gone, tottering back to his room.

Well, I sat out there until midnight and thought a lot about Santa. His twinkling eyes and his fat stomach and his thin silver hair.

He sure did look like Santa Claus.

But, I mean really, truthfully, honestly, what was I supposed to think?

The man was clearly on a permanent holiday upstairs. No dial tone.

So, for another twenty minutes or so I watched the black Caribbean hissing over coral and finished off another drink.

Somehow, I finally made it back to my bungalow and thought for a little while in the dark. Sure, Santa Claus had looked like Santa Claus. But if looks were all it took, a lot of people could be a lot of people they weren't. The world would be crazy. Out of control.

And thinking sleepy thoughts along that line, I fell deeper into my pillow and nodded off.

The following morning, as I checked out, I peered at the desk clerk, going about his prissy duties. I lifted my voice slightly as I observed him tabulating my bill.

"I was chatting with a gentleman last night. A Mr. Claus." Why explain the whole thing? Only be setting myself up, I figured.

But in a surprise turn, the clerk lit up, his mouth turning into a silly-looking O.

"Oh," he cooed, "I'm so glad you reminded me, sir. Mr. Claus left this morning . . ." He turned and grabbed something from the mail slots as he continued chattering. "Flying north I believe he said."

Now there's a surprise, I thought.

Then he handed me something as he spun back, smiling all the while.

A manila envelope.

And so the plot thickened, I thought. I thanked him, paid the bill, and found myself a fat couch to sink into.

A few feet away, a wedding cake fountain dribbled as I unsealed the envelope. Maybe an apology, I thought. Although a wanted poster would have been more appropriate.

But as I slid what was inside all the way out, my heart smoked to a stop.

It was a picture of smiling Joe with a fat-ended slugger raised over one confident shoulder. And it was made out to me.

Clipped to it was a handwritten note:

Dear Karl,

Was up late last night and couldn't sleep. Really sorry about that Christmas. '39 was a bad year for me. The war was starting up, and my helpers' hearts just weren't in their work. The world wasn't in very good shape then, Karl, and I had my hands full. Hope this makes up for it. Have a Merry Christmas.

Your drinking pal, Santa

P.S. Maybe I'll see you around the 25th.

I'll be looking for you, I thought, as I read the note, trembling like some delighted kid.

I'll be looking for you.

Santa Substitutes

Everybody knows the jolly old elf.

Sometimes we've seen him at his North Pole workshop, other times at Thirty-fourth Street Macy's, and at another time we have even seen him on the planet Mars with a very young Pia Zadora.

But sometimes Santa is not what he seems.

He can turn up as his own evil twin, a gadget-laden secret agent from the early seventies, or even as a slightly confused mixed metaphor of holiday tropes.

(Sometimes Santa is just the disguise for a different holiday visitor with every bit as much of a claim to the day as the jolly old elf himself.)

Nackles

Donald E. Westlake

Did God create men, or does Man create gods? I don't know, and if it hadn't been for my rotten brother-in-law the question would never have come up. My *late* brother-in-law? Nackles knows.

It all depends, you see, like the chicken and the egg, on which came first. Did God exist before Man first thought of Him, or didn't He? If not, if Man creates his gods, then it follows that Man must create the devils, too.

Nearly every god, you know, has his corresponding devil. Good *and* Evil. The polytheistic ancients, prolific in the creation (?) of gods and goddesses, always worked up nearly enough Evil ones to cancel out the Good, but not quite. The Greeks, those incredible supermen, combined Good and Evil in *each* of their gods. In Zoroaster, Ahura Mazda, being Good, is ranged forever against the Evil one, Ahriman. And we ourselves know God and Satan.

But of course it's entirely possible I have nothing to worry about. It all depends on whether Santa Clause is or is not a god. He certainly *seems* like a god. Consider: He is omniscient; he knows every action of every child, for good or evil. At least on Christmas Eve he is omnipresent, everywhere at once. He administers justice tempered with mercy. He is superhuman, or at least non-human, though conceived of as having a human shape. He is aided by a corps of assistants who do *not* have completely human shapes. He rewards Good and punishes Evil. And, most important, he is believed in utterly by several million people, most of them under the age of ten. Is there any qualification for godhood that Santa Claus does not possess?

And even the non-believers give him lip-service. He has surely taken over Christmas; his effigy is everywhere, but where are the manger and the Christ child? Retired rather forlornly to the nave. (Santa's power is growing, too. Slowly but surely he is usurping Chanukah as well.)

Santa Claus *is* a god. He's no less a god than Ahura Mazda, or Odin, or Zeus. Think of the white beard, the chariot pulled through the air by a breed of animal which doesn't ordinarily fly, the prayers (requests for gifts) which are annually mailed to him and which so baffle the Post Office, the specially-garbed priests in all the department stores. And don't gods reflect their creators' (?) society? The Greeks had a huntress goddess, and gods of agriculture and war and love. What else would we have but a god of giving, of merchandising, and of consumption? Secondary gods of earlier times have been stout, but surely Santa Claus is the first fat primary god.

And wherever there is a god, mustn't there sooner or later be a devil?

Which brings me back to my brother-in-law, who's to blame for whatever happens now. My brother-in-law Frank is—or was—a very mean and nasty man. Why I ever let him marry my sister I'll never know. Why Susie *wanted* to marry him is an even greater mystery. I could just shrug and say Love Is Blind, I suppose, but that wouldn't explain how she fell in love with him in the first place.

Frank is—Frank was—I just don't know what tense to use. The present, hopefully. Frank is a very handsome man in his way, big and brawny, full of vitality. A football player; hero in college and defensive line-backer for three years in pro ball, till he did some sort of irreparable damage to his left knee, which gave him a limp and forced him to find some other way to make a living.

Ex–football players tend to become insurance salesmen, I don't know why. Frank followed the form, and became an insurance salesman. Because Susie was then a secretary for the same company, they soon became acquainted.

Was Susie dazzled by the ex-hero, so big and handsome? She's never been the type to dazzle easily, but we can never fully know what goes on inside the mind of another human being. For whatever reason, she decided she was in love with him.

So they were married, and five weeks later he gave her her first black eye. And the last, though it mightn't have been, since Susie tried to keep me from finding out. I was to go over for dinner that night, but at eleven in the morning she called the auto showroom where I work, to tell me she had a headache and we'd have to postpone the dinner. But she sounded so upset that I knew immediately something was wrong, so I took a demonstration car and drove over, and when she opened the front door there was the shiner.

I got the story out of her slowly, in fits and starts. Frank, it seemed, had a terrible temper. She wanted to excuse him because he was forced to be an insurance salesman when he really wanted to be out there on the gridiron again, but I want to be president and I'm an automobile salesman and *I* don't go around giving women black eyes. So I decided it was up to me to let Frank know he wasn't to vent his pique on my sister any more.

Unfortunately, I am five feet seven inches tall and weigh 134 pounds, with the Sunday *Times* under my arm. Were I just to give Frank a piece of my mind, he'd surely give me a black eye to go with my sister's. Therefore, that afternoon I bought a regulation baseball bat, and carried it with me when I went to see Frank that night.

He opened the door himself and snarled, "What do *you* want?"

In answer, I poked him with the end of the bat, just above the belt, to knock the wind out of him. Then, having unethically gained the upper hand, I clouted him five or six times more, and then stood over him to say, "The next time you hit my sister I won't let you off so easy." After which I took Susie home to *my* place for dinner.

And after which I was Frank's best friend.

People like that are so impossible to understand. Until the baseball bat episode, Frank had nothing for me but undisguised contempt. But once I'd knocked the stuffings out of him, he was my comrade for life. And I'm sure it was sincere; he would have given me the shirt off his back, had I wanted it, which I didn't.

(Also, by the way, he never hit Susie again. He still had the bad temper, but he took it out in throwing furniture out windows or punching dents in walls or going downtown to start a brawl in some bar. I offered to train him out of maltreating the house and furniture as I had trained him out of maltreating his wife, but Susie said no, that Frank had to let off steam and it would be worse if he was forced to bottle it all up inside him, so the baseball bat remained in retirement.)

Then came the children, three of them in as many years. Frank Junior came first, and then Linda Joyce, and finally Stewart. Susie had held the forlorn hope that fatherhood would settle Frank to some extent, but quite the reverse was true. Shrieking babies, smelly diapers, disrupted sleep, and distracted wives are trials and tribulations to any man, but to Frank they were—like everything else in his life—the last straw.

He became, in a word, worse. Susie restrained him I don't know how often from doing some severe damage to a squalling infant, and as the children grew toward the age of reason Frank's expressed attitude toward them was that their best move would be to find a way to become invisible. The children, of course, didn't like him very much, but then who did?

Last Christmas was when *it* started. Junior was six then, and Linda Joyce five, and Stewart four, so all were old enough to have heard of Santa Claus and still young enough to believe in him. Along around October, when the Christmas season was beginning, Frank began to use Santa Claus's displeasure as a weapon to keep the children "in line," his phrase for keeping them mute and immobile and terrified. Many parents, of course, try to enforce obedience the same way: "If you're bad, Santa Claus won't bring you any presents." Which, all things considered, is a negative and passive sort of punishment, wishy-washy in comparison with fire and brimstone and such. In the old days, Santa Claus would treat bad children a bit more scornfully, leaving a lump of coal in their stockings in lieu of presents, but I suppose the Depression helped to change that. There are times and situations when a lump of coal is nothing to sneer at.

In any case, an absence of presents was too weak a punishment for Frank's purposes, so last Christmastime he invented Nackles.

Who is Nackles? Nackles is to Santa Claus what Satan is to God, what Ahriman is to Ahura Mazda, what the North Wind is to the South Wind. Nackles is the new Evil.

I think Frank really *enjoyed* creating Nackles; he gave so much thought to the details of him. According to Frank, and as I remember it, this is Nackles: Very very tall and very very thin. Dressed all in black, with a gaunt gray face and deep black eyes. He travels through an intricate series of tunnels under the earth, in a black chariot on rails, pulled by an octet of dead-white goats.

And what does Nackles do? Nackles lives on the flesh of little boys and girls. (This is what Frank was telling his children; can you believe it?) Nackles roams back and forth under the earth, in his dark tunnels, pulled by the eight dead-white goats, and he searches for little boys and girls to stuff into his big black sack and carry away and eat. But Santa Claus won't let him have *good* boys and girls. Santa Claus is stronger than Nackles, and keeps a protective shield around little children, so Nackles can't get at them.

But when little children are bad, it hurts Santa Claus, and weakens the shield Santa Claus has placed around them, and if they keep on being bad pretty soon there's no shield left at all, and on Christmas Eve instead of Santa Claus coming down out of the sky with his bag of presents Nackles comes up out of the ground with his bag of emptiness, and stuffs the bad children in, and whisks them away to his dark tunnels and the eight dead-white goats.

Frank was proud of his invention, actually proud of it. He not only used Nackles to threaten his children every time they had the temerity to come within range of his vision, he also spread the story around to others. He told me, and his neighbors, and people in bars, and people he went to see in his job as insurance salesman. I don't know how many people he told about Nackles, though I would guess it was well over a hundred. And there's more than one Frank in this world; he told me from time to time of a client or neighbor or bar-crony who had heard the story of Nackles and then said, "By God, that's great. That's what *I've* been needing, to keep *my* brats in line."

Thus Nackles was created, and thus Nackles was promulgated. And would any of the unfortunate children thus introduced to Nackles believe in this Evil Being any less than they believed in Santa Claus? Of course not.

This all happened, as I say, last Christmastime. Frank invented Nackles, used him to further intimidate his already-intimidated children, and spread the story of him to everyone he met. On Christmas Day last year I'm sure there was more than one child in this town who was relieved and somewhat surprised to awaken the same as usual, in his own trundle bed, and to find the presents downstairs beneath the tree, proving that Nackles had been kept away yet another year.

Nackles lay dormant, so far as Frank was concerned, from December 25th of last year until this October. Then, with the sights and sounds of Christmas again in the land, back came Nackles, as fresh and vicious as ever. "Don't expect *me* to stop him!" Frank would shout. "When he comes up out of the ground the night before Christmas to carry you away in his bag, don't expect any help from *me!"*

It was worse this year than last. Frank wasn't doing as well financially as he'd expected, and then early in November Susie discovered she was pregnant again, and what with one thing and another Frank was headed for a real peak of ill-temper. He screamed at the children constantly, and the name of Nackles was never far from his tongue.

Susie did what she could to counteract Frank's bad influence, but he wouldn't let her do much. All through November and December he was home more and more of the time, because the Christmas season is the wrong time to sell insurance anyway and also because he was hating the job more every day and thus giving it less of his time. The more he hated the job, the worse his temper became, and the more he drank, and the worse his limp got, and the louder were his shouts, and the more violent his references to Nackles. It just built and built and built, and reached its crescendo on Christmas Eve, when some small or imagined infraction of one of the children—Stewart, I think—resulted in Frank's pulling all the Christmas presents from all the closets and stowing them all in the car to be taken back to the stores, because this Christmas for sure it wouldn't be Santa Claus who would be visiting this house, it would be Nackles.

By the time Susie got the children to bed, everyone in the house was a nervous wreck. The children were too frightened to sleep, and

Susie was too unnerved herself to be of much help in soothing them. Frank, who had taken to drinking at home lately, had locked himself in the bedroom with a bottle.

It was nearly eleven o'clock before Susie got the children all quieted down, and then she went out to the car and brought all the presents back in and ranged them under the tree. Then, not wanting to see or hear her husband any more that night—he was like a big spoiled child throwing a tantrum—she herself went to sleep on the living room sofa.

Frank Junior awoke her in the morning, crying, "Look, Mama! Nackles *didn't* come, he *didn't* come!" And pointed to the presents she'd placed under the tree.

The other two children came down shortly after, and Susie and the youngsters sat on the floor and opened the presents, enjoying themselves as much as possible, but still with restraint. There were none of the usual squeals of childish pleasure; no one wanted Daddy to come storming downstairs in one of his rages. So the children contented themselves with ear-to-ear smiles and whispered exclamations, and after a while Susie made breakfast, and the day carried along as pleasantly as could be expected under the circumstances.

It was a little after twelve that Susie began to worry about Frank's non-appearance. She braved herself to go up and knock on the locked door and call his name, but she got no answer, not even the expected snarl, so just around one o'clock she called me and I hurried on over. I rapped smartly on the bedroom door, got no answer, and finally I threatened to break the door in if Frank didn't open up. When I still got no answer, break the door in I did.

And Frank, of course, was gone.

The police say he ran away, deserted his family, primarily because of Susie's fourth pregnancy. They say he went out the window and dropped to the backyard, so Susie wouldn't see him and try to stop him. And they say he didn't take the car because he was afraid Susie would hear him start the engine.

That all sounds reasonable, doesn't it? Yet, I just can't believe Frank would walk out on Susie without a lot of shouting about it first. Nor that he would leave his car, which he was fonder of than his wife and children.

But what's the alternative? There's only one I can think of: Nackles.

I would rather not believe that. I would rather not believe that Frank, in inventing Nackles and spreading word of him, made him real. I would rather not believe that Nackles actually did visit my sister's house on Christmas Eve.

But did he? If so, he couldn't have carried off any of the children, for a more subdued and better-behaved trio of youngsters you won't find anywhere. But Nackles, being brand-new and never having had a meal before, would need *somebody.* Somebody to whom he was real, somebody not protected by the shield of Santa Claus. And, as I say, Frank was drinking that night. Alcohol makes the brain believe in the existence of all sorts of things. Also, Frank was a spoiled child if there ever was one.

There's no question but that Frank Junior and Linda Joyce and Stewart believe in Nackles. And Frank spread the gospel of Nackles to others, some of whom spread it to their own children. And some of whom will spread the new Evil to other parents. And ours is a mobile society, with families constantly being transferred by Daddy's company from one end of the country to another, so how long can it be before Nackles is a power not only in this one city, but all across the nation?

I don't know if Nackles exists, or will exist. All I know for sure is that there's suddenly a new level of meaning in the lyric of that popular Christmas song. You know the one I mean:

You'd better watch out.

Santa Claus vs. S.P.I.D.E.R.

Harlan Ellison®

☞ I ☜

It was half-past September when the red phone rang. Kris moved away from the warm and pliant form into which he had been folded, belly to back, and rubbed a hand across sticky eyes. The phone rang again. He could not make out the time on the luminous dial of his wrist watch. "What is it, honey?" mumbled the blond woman beside him. The phone rang a third time. "Nothing, baby . . . go back to sleep," he soothed her. She burrowed deeper under the covers as he reached for the receiver, plucking it out of the cradle in the middle of a fourth imperative.

"Yeah?" His mouth tasted unhappy.

A voice on the other end said, "The King of Canaan needs your service."

Kris sat up. "Wait a minute, I'll take it on the extension." He thumbed the HOLD button, slipped out of the bed even as he racked the receiver and, naked, padded across the immense bedroom in the dark. He found his way through the hall and into the front office, guiding his passage only by the barest touch of fingertips to walls. He pulled the bronze testimonial plaque from the little people away from the wall, spun the dial on the wall safe, and pulled it open. The red phone with its complex scrambler attachment lurked in the circular opening.

He punched out code on the scrambler, lifted the receiver and said, "The king fears the devil, and the devil fears the Cross." Code and counter-code.

"Kris, it's S.P.I.D.E.R.," said the voice on the other end.

"Shit!" he hissed. "Where?"

"The States. Alabama, California, D.C., Texas . . ."

"Serious?"

"Serious enough to wake you."

"Right, right. Sorry. I'm still half-asleep. What time is it?"

"Half-past September."

Kris ran a hand through his thick hair. "Nobody any closer for this one?"

"Belly Button was handling it."

"Yeah . . . and . . . ?"

"He floated to the top off the coast of Galveston. He must have been in the Gulf for almost a week. They packed plastic charges on his inner thighs . . ."

"Okay, don't describe it. I'm mad enough at being shook out of sleep. Is there a dossier?"

"Waiting for you at Hilltop."

"I'll be there in six hours."

He racked the receiver, slammed the safe port and spun the dial. He shoved the plaque back in place on the wall and stood with his balled fist lying against the bronze. Faint light from a fluorescent, left burning over one of the little people's drafting tables, caught his tensed features. The hard, mirthless lines of his face were the work of a Giacometti. The eyes were gun-metal blue, and flat, as though unseeing. The faintly cruel mouth was thinned to an incision. He drew a deep breath and the muscle-corded body drew up with purpose.

Then, reaching over to his desk, he opened a drawer and rang three times, sharply, on a concealed button set into the underside of the drawer. Down below, in the labyrinth, PoPo would be plunging out of his cocoon, pulling on his loincloth and earrings, tapping out the code to fill the egress chamber with water.

"Peace on Earth . . ." Kris murmured, starting back for the bedroom and his wet suit.

☞ II ☜

PoPo was waiting in the grotto, standing on a let-down shell beside the air tanks. Kris nodded to the little one and turned his back. PoPo helped him into his rig and, when Kris had cleared the mouthpiece, adjusted the oxygen mixture. "Keeble keeble?" PoPo inquired.

"Sounds like it," Kris replied. He wanted to be on his way.

"Dill-dill neat peemee," PoPo said.

"Thanks. I'll need it." He moved quickly to the egress chamber which had been filled and emptied. He undogged the wheel and swung the port open. A few trickles of Arctic water hit the basalt floor. He turned. "Keep the toy plant going. And look into that problem on tier 9 with CorLo. I'll be back in time for the holidays."

He put one foot over the sill, then turned and added, "If everything goes okay."

"Weeble zexfunt," said PoPo.

"Yeah, no war toys to you, too." He stepped inside the egress chamber, spun the wheel hard to dog it, and signaled through the lucite port. PoPo filled the chamber and Kris blew himself out.

The water was black and sub-zero. The homing light on the sub was his only comfort. He made it to the steel fish quickly, and within minutes was on his way. Once he had passed the outer extreme of the floe, he surfaced, converted to airborne, blew the tanks that extruded the pontoons, and taxied for a takeoff. Aloft, he made ramjet velocity and converted again.

Three hundred miles behind him, somewhere below the Arctic Ocean, PoPo was rousing CorLo from his cocoon and chiding the hell out of him for putting European threading on all the roller skates, thereby making all the American keys useless.

☞ III ☜

Hilltop was inside a mountain in Colorado. The peak of the mountain swung open, allowing Kris's VTOL (the sub, in its third conversion) to drop down onto the target pad.

He went quickly to the secret place.

The Taskmaster was waiting for him with the dossier. Kris flipped it rapidly: eidetic memory.

"S.P.I.D.E.R. again," he said softly. Then, with an inquiring tone, "It means

SOCIETY FOR
POLLUTION,
INFECTION AND
DESTRUCTION OF
EARTHMEN'S
RESOURCES

is that it?" The Taskmaster shook his head. Kris mmmm'ed. "Well, what are they up to this time? I thought we'd put them out of commission after that anthrax business in The Valley of The Winds."

The Taskmaster tilted back in his plastic chair. The multi-faceted eyeball-globes around the room picked up pinpoints of brilliance from the chair and cast them over the walls in a subtle light-show. "It's as you read there. They've taken over the minds of those eight. What they intend to do with them, as puppets, we have no idea."

Kris scanned the list again. "Reagan, Johnson, Nixon, Humphrey, Daley, Wallace, Maddox, and—who's this last one?—Spiro Agnew?"

"Doesn't matter. We can usually keep them out of trouble, keep them from hurting themselves . . . but since S.P.I.D.E.R. got into them, they've been running amuck."

"I've never even heard of most of these."

"How the hell could you, up there, making toys."

"It's the best cover I've ever had."

"So don't get crabby, just because you never see a newspaper. Take my word for it: these are the names this season."

"Whatever happened to that whatwashisname . . . Willkie?"

"Didn't pan out."

"S.P.I.D.E.R.," Kris said again. "Does it stand for

SPECIAL
POLITBURO
INTENT ON
DESTROYING
EVERYBODY'S
RACE

?" The Taskmaster shook his head again, a bit wearily.

Kris rose and pumped the Taskmaster's hand. "From the dossier, I suggest the best place to start is with this Daley, in Chicago."

The Taskmaster nodded. "That's what COMPgod said, too. You'd better stop down and see the Armorer before you leave. He's cobbled up a few swell new surprises for you."

"Will I be working that dumb red suit again?"

"As a spare, probably. It's a little early for the red suit."

"What time is it?"

"Half-past September."

☞ IV ☜

When Kris emerged from the dropshaft, Miss Seven-Seventeen's eyes grew round. He came toward her, with the easy, muscled stride that set him so far apart from the rest of the agents. (Most of them were little more than pudgy file-clerks; where had she ever gotten the idea that espionage was a line of work best suited to Adonises? Surely from the endless stream of bad spy novels that had glutted the newsstands; what a shock when she had discovered that pinching the trigeminal nerve to cause excruciating pain, or overpowering an enemy by cupping both hands and slapping both of his ears simultaneously were tactics as easily employed by men who resembled auks, as by beefcake contest winners. Tactics equally as effective when struck by gobbets of mud as by Rodin statues.) But Kris . . .

He came up to her desk, and stared down silently until she dropped her eyes. Then, "Hello, Chan."

She could not look at him. It was too painful. The Bahamas. That night. The gibbous moon hanging above them like an all-watching eye as the night winds played a wild accompaniment counterpoint to their insensate passion, the lunatic surf breaking around them on the silver sands. The goodbye. The waiting. The report from upstairs that he had been lost in Tibet. She could handle none of it . . . now . . . with him standing there . . . a thick, white scar across the breastbone, now hidden by his shirt, but known to her nonetheless, a scar made by Tibor Kaszlov's saber . . . she knew every inch of his flesh . . . and she could not answer. "Well, answer, stupid!" he said.

He seemed to understand.

She spoke into the intercom, "Kris is here, sir." The red light flashed on her board, and without looking up she said, "The Armorer will see you now."

He strode past her, seemingly intent on walking into the stone wall. At the last possible instant it slid back smoothly and he disappeared into the Armorer's workshop. The wall slid back and Seven-Seventeen suddenly realized she had been fisting so tightly that her lacquered nails had drawn blood from her palm.

The Armorer was a thickset, bluff man given to tweeds and pipes. His jackets were made specially for him on Savile Row, with many pockets, to hold the infinitude of gadgets and pipe tools he constantly carried.

"Kris, good to see you." He took the agent's hand and pumped it effusively. "Mmm. Harris tweed?"

"No, as a matter of fact it's one of those miracle fibers," Kris replied, turning smoothly to show the center-vent, depressed-waist, Edwardian-styled, patch-pocket jacket. "Something my man in Hong Kong whipped up. Like it?"

"Elegant," the Armorer said. "But we aren't here to discuss each other's sartorial elegance, are we?"

They had a small mutual laugh at that. Divided evenly, it took less than ten seconds. "Step over here," the Armorer said, moving toward a wall-rack where several gadgets were displayed on pegboard. "I think you'll find these most intriguing."

"I thought I wasn't supposed to use the red suit this time," Kris said tartly. The red suit was hung neatly on a teakwood valet near the wall.

The Armorer turned and gave him a surprised look. "Oh? Who told you that?"

Kris touched the suit, fingered it absently. "The Taskmaster."

The Armorer's mouth drew down in a frown. He pulled a pipe from a jacket pocket and thrust it between his lips. It was a Sasieni Fantail with an apple bowl shape, seriously in need of a carbon-cake scraping. "Well, let us just say the Taskmaster occasionally fails to follow his own lines of communication." He was obviously distressed, but Kris was in no mood to become embroiled in inter-office politics.

"Show me what you've got."

The Armorer pulled a small penlight-shaped gadget off one of the pegboards. There was a clip on its upper end for attaching to a shirt pocket. "Proud of this one. I call it my deadly nightshade." He lit the pipe with a Consul butane lighter, turning up the flame till it was blue, just right for soldering.

Kris took the penlight-shaped gadget and turned it over and over. "Neat. Very compact."

The Armorer looked like a man who has just bought a new car, about to ask a neighbor to guess how much he had paid for it. "Ask me what it does."

"What does it do?"

"Spreads darkness for a radius of two miles."

"Great."

"No, really. I mean it. Just twist the clip to the right—no, no, don't do it now, for Christ's sake! you'll blot out all of Hilltop—when you get in a spot, and you need an escape, just twist that clip and pfizzzz you've got all the cover you need for an escape." The Armorer blew a dense cloud of pipe smoke: It was Murray's Erinmore Mixture, very aromatic.

Kris kept looking at the suit. "What's new with *that?*"

The Armorer pointed with the stem of the pipe. It was a mannerism. "Well, you've got the usual stuff: the rockets, the jet-pack, the napalm, the mace and the Mace, the throwing knives, the high-pressure hoses, the boot-spikes, the .30 caliber machine guns, the acid, the flammable beard, the stomach still inflates into a raft, the flamethrower, the plastic explosives, the red rubber nose grenade, the belt tool-kit, the boomerang, the bolo, the *bolas*, the machete, the derringer, the belt-buckle time bomb, the lockpick equipment, the scuba gear, the camera and Xerox attachment in the hips, the steel mittens with the extensible hooks, the gas mask, the poison gas, the shark repellent, the Sterno stove, the survival rations and the microfilm library of one hundred great books."

Kris fingered the suit again. "Heavy."

"But in addition," the Armorer said happily, "this time we've really extended ourselves down here in Armor—"

"You're doing a helluva job."

"Thanks, sincerely, Kris."

"No, I mean *really*!"

"Yes, well. In addition, this time the suit has been fully automated, and when you depress this third button on the jacket, the entire suit becomes inflatable, airborne, and seals for high-level flight."

Kris pulled a sour face. "If I ever fall over I'll be like a turtle on its back."

The Armorer gave Kris a jab of camaraderie, high on the left biceps. "You're a great kidder, Kris." He pointed to the boots. "Gyroscopes. Keep you level at all times. You *can't* fall over."

"I'm a great kidder. What else have you got for me?"

The Armorer stepped to the pegboard and pulled off an automatic pistol. "Try this."

He depressed a button on the control console and the east wall of the Armory dropped, revealing a concealed firing range behind it. Silhouette targets were lined up at the far end of the tunnel.

"What happened to my Webley?" Kris asked.

"Too bulky. Too unreliable. Latest thing, you're holding: a Lassiter-Krupp laser explosive. Sensational!"

Kris turned, showing his thinnest side to the mute silhouettes. He extended and locked his right arm, bracing it with left hand around right wrist, and squeezed the trigger. A beam of light and a sibilant hiss erupted from the muzzle of the weapon. At the same instant, down the tunnel, all ten of the silhouettes vanished in a burst of blinding light. Shrapnel and bits of stone wall ricocheted back and forth in the tunnel. The sound of their destruction was deafening.

"Jesus God in Heaven," Kris murmured, turning back to the Armorer, who was only now removing the glare-blast goggles. "Why didn't you warn me about this stupid thing! I can't use one of these . . . I have to be surreptitious, circumspect, unnoticed. This bloody thing would be fine to level Gibraltar, but it's ridiculous for hand-to-hand combat. Here, take it!"

He thrust the weapon at the Armorer.

"Ingrate!"

"Give me my Webley, you lunatic!"

"Take it, it's there on the wall, you short-sighted slave of the Establishment!"

Kris grabbed the automatic, and the deadly nightshade. "Send the suit care of my contact in Montgomery, Alabama," he said, hurrying toward the door.

"Maybe I will, and maybe I won't, you moron!"

Kris stopped and turned. "Listen, man, dammit, I can't stand here and argue with you about firepower. I've got to save the world!"

"Melodrama! Lout! Reactionary!"

"Cranky bastard! And I hate your damned blunderbuss, that's what . . . I *hate* the stupid loud thing!"

He reached the wall, which slid back, and dashed through. Just before it closed completely, the Armorer threw down his pipe, smashed it with his foot and screamed, "And I hate that faggy jacket of yours!"

☞ V ☜

Daley: Chicago, Illinois

Chicago, from the Shore Drive, looked like one immense burning garbage dump. They were rioting again on the South Side. And from the direction of Evanston and Skokie could be seen twin spiraling arms of thick, black smoke. In Evanston the D.A.R. was looting and burning; in Skokie the D.A.R. had joined with the women of the

W.C.T.U. from Evanston, and the offices of a paperback pornographer were being razed. The city was going insane.

Kris drove the rental birdcage Maserati into Ohio Street, turned right onto the underground ramp of the motel, and let the attendant take it. Carrying only his attaché case, he made for the fire exit leading up to the first floor of the motel. Once inside the stairwell, however, he turned to the blank wall, used his sonic signaler, and the wall pivoted open. He hurried inside, closed the wall, and threw the attaché case onto the double bed. The

WAITING

light was glowing on the closed-circuit television. He flicked the set on, stood in front of the camera, and was pleased to see that his Chicago contact, Freya, was wearing her hair long again.

"Hello, Ten-Nineteen," he said.

"Hello, Kris. Welcome to the Windy City."

"You've got big troubles."

"How soon do you want to start? I've got Daley pinpointed."

"How soon can I get to him?"

"Tonight."

"Soon enough. What are you doing at the moment?"

"Not much."

"Where are you?"

"Down the hall."

"Come on over."

"In the after*noon*!?!"

"A healthy mind in a healthy body."

"See you in ten minutes."

"Wear the *Réplique.*"

☞ VI ☜

Dressed entirely in black, the Webley in an upside-down breakaway rig, its butt just protruding from his left armpit, Kris pulled himself across the open space between the electrified fence and the dark, squat powerhouse, his arms and legs crablike in the traditional infantryman's crawl.

Inside that building, Daley had been pinpointed by Ten-Nineteen's tracking equipment. He had been there for almost two days, even through the riots.

Kris had asked Freya what he was up to, there in the powerhouse. She had not known. The entire building was damped, impenetrable to any sensors she had employed. But it was S.P.I.D.E.R. business, whatever it was—that had to be for dead certain. For a man in his position to be closeted away like that, while his city went up in flames—that had to be for *dead* certain.

Kris reached the base of the powerhouse. He slid along its face till he could see the blacked-over windows of the el above him. They were nearly a foot over his head. No purchase for climbing. He had to pull a smash&grab. He drew three deep breaths, broke the Webley out of its packet and pulled the tape wound round the butt. It came loose, and he taped the weapon into his hand. Then three more deep breaths. Digging hard he dashed away from the building, thirty feet into the open, sucked in breath again, spun, and dashed back for the powerhouse. Almost at the face of the building he bent deeply from the knees, pushed off, and crossed his arms over his head as he smashed full into the window.

Then he was through, arching into the powerhouse, performing a tight somersault and coming down with knees still bent, absorbing the impact up through his hips. Glass tinkled all around him, his blacksuit was ripped raggedly down across the chest. His right arm came out, straight, the Webley extended.

Light suddenly flooded the powerhouse. Kris caught the scene in one total impression: everything.

Daley was hunched over an intricate clockwork mechanism, set high on a podiumlike structure at the far end of the room. Black-light equipment throughout the room still glowed an evil rotting purple. Three men, wearing skintight outfits of pale green, were starting toward him, pulling off black-light goggles. A fourth man still had his hand on the knife-switch that had raised the interior lights. There was more.

Kris saw great serpentine connections running from Daley's clockwork mechanism, snaking across the floor to hookups on the walls. A blower system, immense and bulky, dominated one entire wall. Vats of some bubbling dark substance, almost like liquid smoke, ranked behind the podium.

"Stop him!" Daley screamed.

Kris had only a moment as the three men in green came for him. And in that instant he chose to firm his resolve for what was certainly to come. He always had this instant, on every assignment, and he had to prove to himself that it was right, what he must do, however brutal. He chose, in that instant, to look at Daley; and his resolve was firmed more eloquently than he could have hoped. This was an evil old man. What might have been generous old age in another man, had been cemented into lines of unspeakable ugliness. This man was evil incarnate. Totally owned by S.P.I.D.E.R.

The three green men lumbered forward. Big men, heavily muscled, faces dulled with malice. Kris fired. He took the first one in the stomach, spinning him back and around, into one of his companions, who tried to sidestep, but went down in a twist of arms and legs as the first green man died. Kris pumped three shots into the tangle and the arms and legs ceased moving, save for an occasional quiver. The third man broke sidewise and tried to tackle Kris. He pulled back a step and shot him in the face. The green man went limp as a Raggedy Andy doll and settled comically onto his knees, then tumbled forward onto the meat that had been his head.

As though what had happened to his companions meant nothing to the fourth man, he stretched both arms out before him—zombielike—and stumbled toward Kris. The agent disposed of him with one shot.

Then he turned for Daley.

The man was raising a deadly-looking hand weapon with a needle-muzzle. Kris threw himself flat-out to the side. It was only empty space that Daley's weapon burned with its beam of sizzling crimson energy. Kris rolled, and rolled, and rolled right up to the blower system. Then he was up, had the Webley leveled and yelled, "Don't make me do it, Daley!"

The weapon in Daley's hand tracked, came to rest on Kris, and the agent fired at that moment. The Webley barked ferociously. The needle-nosed weapon shattered under the impact of the steel-jacketed round, and Daley fell backward off the podium.

Kris was on him in a moment.

He had him up on his feet, thrust against the podium, and a two-fingered paralyzer applied to a pressure point in the clavial depression before Daley could regain himself. Daley's mouth dropped open with the pain, but he could not speak. Kris hauled him up on the podium, a bit more roughly than was necessary, and threw him down at the foot of the clockwork mechanism.

It was incredibly complex, with timers and chronographs hooked in somehow between the vats of bubbling smoke and the blower system on the wall. Kris was absorbed in trying to understand precisely what the equipment *did,* when he heard the sigh at his feet. He glanced down just in time to see something so hideous he could not look at it straight on—emerge from Daley's right ear, slither and scuttle onto the floor of the podium, and then explode in a black puff of soot and filth. When Kris looked again, all that remained was a dusty smear; what might be left should a child set fire to a heap of powdered magnesium and potassium nitrate.

Daley stirred. He rolled over on his back and lay gasping. Then he tried to sit. Kris knelt and helped him to a sitting position.

"Oh, my God, my God," Daley mumbled, shaking his head as if to clear it. The evil was gone from his face. Now he was little less than a kindly old gentleman who had been sick for a very very long time. "Thank you, whoever you are. Thank you."

Kris helped Daley to his feet, and the old man leaned against the clockwork mechanism.

"They took me over . . . years ago," he said.

"S.P.I.D.E.R., eh?" Kris said.

"Yes. Slipped inside my head, inside my mind. Evil. Totally evil. Oh, God, it was awful. The things I've done. The rotten, unconscionable things! I'm so ashamed. I have so much to atone for."

"Not you, Your Honor," said Kris, "S.P.I.D.E.R. *They're* the ones who'll pay. Even as this one did." The black splotch.

"No, no, no . . . *me*! I did all those terrible things, now *I* have to clean it all up. I'll tear down the South Side slums, the Back o' the Yards squalor. I'll hire the best city planners to make living space for all those black people I ignored, that I used shamefully for my own political needs. Not soulless high-rises wherein people stifle and lose their dignity, but decent communities filled with light and laughter. And I'll free the Polacks! And all the machine politics I used to use to assign contracts to inadequate builders . . . I'll tear down all those unsafe buildings and have them done right! I'll disband the secret gestapo I've been gathering all these years, and hire only those men who can pass a stringent police exam that will take into account how much humanitarianism they have in them. I'll landscape everything so this city will be beautiful. And then I'll have to give myself up for trial. I hope I don't get more than fifty years. I'm not that young any more."

Kris sucked on a tooth reflectively. "Don't get carried away, Your Honor."

Then he indicated the clockwork machine.

"What was this all about?"

Daley looked at the machine with loathing. "We'll have to destroy it. This was my part of the eight-point plan S.P.I.D.E.R. put into operation twenty-four years ago, to . . . to . . ."

He stumbled to a halt; a confused, perplexed look spread over his kindly features. He bit his lower lip.

"Yes, go on," Kris urged him, "to do what? What's S.P.I.D.E.R.'s master plan? What is their goal?"

Daley spread his hands. "I—I don't know."

"Then tell me . . . who *are* they? Where do they come from? We've battled them for years, but we have no more idea of who they are than when we started. They always self-destruct themselves like that one—" he nodded toward the sooty smear on the podium, "—and we haven't been able to capture one. In fact, you're the first pawn of theirs that we've ever captured alive."

Daley kept nodding all through Kris's unnecessary explanation. When the agent was finished, he shrugged. "All I remember—whatever it was in my head there, it seems to have kept me blocked off from learning anything very much—all I remember is that they're from another planet."

"Aliens!" Kris almost shouted, instantly grasping what Daley had said. "An eight-point plan. The other seven names on the list, and yourself. Each of you taking one phase of a master plan whose purpose we do not as yet understand."

Daley looked at him. "You have a genuine gift for stating the obvious."

"I like to synthesize things."

"Amalgamate."

"What?"

"Nothing. Forget it. Go on."

Kris looked confused. "No, as a matter of fact, *you* go on. Tell me what this equipment here was supposed to do."

"It's still doing it. We haven't shut it off."

Kris looked alarmed. "How do we shut it off?"

"Push that button."

Kris pushed the button, and almost immediately the vats stopped bubbling, the smokelike substance in the vats subsided, the blowers ceased blowing, the clockwork machine slowed and stopped, the cuckoo turned blue and died, the hoses flattened, the room became silent. "What *did* it do?" Kris asked.

"It created and sowed smog in the atmosphere."

"You're kidding."

"I'm *not* kidding. You don't really think smog comes from factories and cars and cigarettes, do you? It cost S.P.I.D.E.R. a fortune to dummy up reports and put on a publicity campaign that it was cars and such-like. In actuality, I've been spreading smog into the atmosphere for twenty-four years."

"Sonofagun," Kris said, with awe. Then he paused, looked cagey, and asked, "Tell me, since we now know that S.P.I.D.E.R. are aliens from outer space, does it mean

SCABROUS,
PREDATORY
INVADERS
DETERMINED TO
ELIMINATE
RATIONALITY

?" Daley stared at him. "Don't ask *me;* no one tells me anything."

Then he jumped down off the podium and started for the door to the powerhouse. Kris looked after him, then picked up a crowbar, and set about destroying the smog machine. When he had finished, sweating, and surrounded by crushed and twisted wreckage, he looked up to see Daley standing by the open door leading outside.

"Something I can do for you?" he asked.

Daley smiled wistfully. "No. Just watching. Now that I'm a nice fellah again, I wanted to see my last example of random, brutal violence. It's going to be so quiet in Chicago."

"Tough it out, baby," Kris said, with feeling.

☞ VII ☜

The eight-point plan seemed to tie together in Alabama. Wallace. But Wallace was off campaigning for something or other, and apparently the eight-point plan needed his special touch (filtered through the even gentler touch of a S.P.I.D.E.R. operative, inside his head) to be tied together. Kris decided to save Wallace for the last. Time was important, but Freya was covering for Daley and the death of the smog machine in Chicago, and frankly, time be hanged! This looked like the last showdown with S.P.I.D.E.R., so Kris informed Hilltop he was going to track down and eradicate the remaining seven points of the plan, with Wallace coming under his attention around Christmastime. It would press Kris close, but he was sure PoPo was on the job at the factory; and what had to be done . . . had to be done. It was going to be anything but easy. He thought wistfully of his Arctic home, the happily buzzing toy factory, the way Blitzen, particularly, nuzzled his palm when he brought the sugar cubes drenched in LSD, and the way the little mothers flew when they got loaded.

Then he pulled his thoughts away from happier times and cooler climes, setting out to wreck S.P.I.D.E.R. He took the remaining seven in order . . .

☞ VIII ☜
Reagan: Camarillo, California

Having closed down all the state mental institutions on the unassailable theory that nobody was really in need of psychiatric attention ("It's all in their heads!" Reagan had said at a $500-a-plate American Legion dinner only six months earlier), Kris found him in the men's toilet on the first floor of the abandoned Camarillo state facility, combing his pompadour.

Reagan spun around, seeing Kris's reflection in the mirror, and screamed for help from one of his zombie assistants, a man in green, who was closeted in a pay toilet. (Inmates had been paid a monthly dole in Regulation Golden State Scrip, converted from monies sent to them by married children who didn't want their freako-devo-pervo relatives around; this Scrip could be used to work the pay toilets. Reagan had always believed in a pay-as-you-go system of state government.)

Kris hit the booth with a savate kick that shattered the door just as the man in green was emerging, the side of his shoe collapsing the man's spleen. Then the agent hurled himself on Reagan, in an attempt to capture him, subdue him, and somehow keep the S.P.I.D.E.R. symbiote within Reagan's head from self-destructing. But the devilishly handsome Reagan abruptly pulled away and as Kris watched, horrified, he began to shimmer and change shape.

In moments it was not Reagan standing before Kris, but a seven-headed Hydra, breathing from its seven mouths a) fire, b) ammonia clouds, c) dust, d) broken glass, e) chlorine gas, f) mustard gas and g) a combination of halitosis and rock music.

Three of the heads (c, e, & f) lunged forward on their serpentine necks, and Kris flattened against the toilet wall. His hand darted into his jacket and came out with a ball-point pen. He shook it twice, anticlockwise, and the pen converted into a two-handed sword. Wielding the carver easily, Kris lay about him with vigor, and in a few minutes the seven heads had been severed.

Kris aimed true for the heart of the beast, and ran it through. The great body thumped over on its side, and lay still. It shimmered and changed back into Reagan. Then the black thing scampered out of his ear, erupted and smeared the floor tiles with soot.

Later, Reagan combed his hair and applied pancake makeup to the glare spots on his nose and cheekbones, and moaned piteously about the really funky things he had done under the stupefying and incredibly evil direction of S.P.I.D.E.R. He swore he didn't know what the letters of the organization's name stood for. Kris was depressed.

Reagan then showed him around the Camarillo plant, explaining that *his* part of the eight-point plan was to use the great machines on the second and third floors to spread insanity through the atmosphere. They broke up the machines with some difficulty: much of the equipment was very hard plastic.

Reagan assured Kris he would work with Hilltop to cover the demise of the second phase of the eight-point plan, and that from this day forward (he raised a hand in the Boy Scout salute) he would be as good as good could be: he would bring about much-needed property tax reform, he would stop *nuhdzing* the students at UCLA, he would subscribe to the *L.A. Free Press*, *The Avatar*, *The East Village Other*, the *Berkeley Barb*, *Horseshit*, *Open City* and all the other underground newspapers so he could find out what was *really* happening; and within the week he would institute daily classes in folk dancing, soul music and peaceful coercion for members of the various police departments within the state.

He was smiling like a man who has regained that innocence of childhood or nature that he had somehow lost.

☞ IX ☜
Johnson: Johnson City, Texas

Kris found him eating mashed potatoes with his hands, sitting apart from the rest of the crowd. He looked like hell. He looked weary. There was half an eaten cow on a spit, turning lazily over charcoal embers. Kris settled down beside him and passed the time of day. He thought Kris was with the party. He belched. Then Kris snapped a finger against his right temple, and dragged his unconscious form into the woods.

When Johnson came around, he knew it was all over. The S.P.I.D.E.R. symbiote scuttled, erupted, smeared on the dead leaves—it was now the middle of October—and Johnson said he had to hurry off to stop the war. Kris didn't know which war he was referring to, but it sounded like a fine idea.

"Tell me," said Kris, earnestly, "does S.P.I.D.E.R. mean

SECRET
PREYERS
INVOLVED IN
DEMOLISHING
EVERYTHING
RIGHT-MINDED

or is it something even more obscure?"

Johnson spread his hands. He didn't know.

Johnson told him his part of the eight-point plan was fomenting war. And butchering babies. But now that was all over. He would recall the troops. He would let all the dissenters out of prison. He would retool for peace. He would send grain to needy nations. He would take elocution lessons. Kris shrugged and moved on.

☞ X ☜

Humphrey & Nixon: Washington, D.C.

It was a week after the election. One of them was president. It didn't matter. The other one was shilling for the opposition, and between them they'd divided the country down the middle. Nixon was trying to get a good shave, and Humphrey was trying to learn to wear contact lenses that would make his eyes look bigger.

"You know, Dick, the trouble is, basically, I got funny little eyes, like a bird, y'know?"

Nixon turned from the mirror on the office wall and said, "You should complain. I've got five o'clock shadow and it's only three-thirty. Hey, who's that?"

Humphrey turned in the easy chair and saw Kris.

"Goodbye, S.P.I.DE.R.," Kris said, and fired sleep-darts at each of them.

Before the darts could hit, the black things scuttled, erupted and smeared. "Damn!" Kris said, and left the office without waiting for Nixon and Humphrey to regain consciousness. It would be a week or two before that happened, in any case. The Armorer wasn't yet on-target when it came to gauging how long people stayed under with these darts. Kris left, because he knew their parts of the eight-point plan were to confuse issues, to sow confusion and dissension in the atmosphere. Johnson had told him that much. Now they would become sweet fellahs, and the president would play like he had a watchbird watching him, saying no-no.

Christmas was fast a-coming. Kris was homesick.

☞ XI ☜

S.P.I.D.E.R. tried to kill Kris in Memphis, Detroit, Cleveland, Great Falls and Los Angeles. They missed.

☞ XII ☜
Maddox: Atlanta, Georgia

It was too ugly to describe. It was the only S.P.I.D.E.R. pawn that Kris had to kill. With a little gold ax-handle: a souvenir of Maddox's famous restaurant. Kris destroyed the nigger-hating machine, Maddox's part in the eight-point plan, and ate fried chicken all the way to Montgomery, Alabama.

☞ XIII ☜
Wallace: Montgomery, Alabama

The red-suited Santa Claus trudged across the open square in front of the Montgomery state building, clanging his little brass bell. The Santa Claus was fat, jolly, bearded, and possibly the deadliest man in the world.

Kris looked around him as he plowed through the ankle-deep

snow. The state buildings were clustered around the perimeter of the circular square, and he had a terrible prickling feeling up and down his spine. It might have been the cumbersome suit with all its equipment, so confining it made him sweat even in the midst of December 24th cold and whiteness. His boots were soaking wet from the snow, his pace measured, as he climbed the State House steps . . . watching.

Everything was closed down for the holidays. All Alabama state facilities. Yet there was movement inside the city . . . last-minute shoppers hurrying to fulfill their quotas as happy consumers . . . children scurrying here and there, seeming to be going somewhere, but probably just caroming. (Kris always smiled when he saw the kids; they were truly the only hope; they had to be protected; not cut off from reality, but simply protected; and the increasing cynicism in the young had begun to disturb him; yet it seemed as though the young activists were fighting against everything S.P.I.D.E.R. stood for, unconsciously, but doing a far better job than their elders.)

A man, hurrying past, down the steps, bundled to the chin in a heavy topcoat, glanced sidewise, squinting, and ignored the outstretched donation cup the Santa Claus proffered. Kris continued on up.

The tracking devices inside the fur-tasseled hat he now wore bleeped and the range-finding trackers were phasing higher as Kris neared Wallace. It was going to be a problem getting into the building. But then, if it weren't for problems making it necessary to carry such a surfeit of equipment in the red suit, Santa Claus would be a thin, svelte figure. "Ho ho ho," Kris murmured, expelling puffs of frosty air.

As he reached the first landing of the State House, Kris began the implementation of his plan to gain access. Fingertipping the suit controls in the palm of his right mitten, he directed the high-pressure hoses toward a barred window on the left wing of the State House. Once they had locked-in directionally, Kris coded the tubes to run acid and napalm, depressed the firing studs, and watched as the hoses sprayed the window with acid, dissolving bars and glass alike. Then the napalm erupted from the hoses in a burning spray, arcing over the snow and striking the gaping hole in the face of the State House. In moments the front of the State House was burning.

Kris hit the jet-pack and went straight up. When he was hovering at two hundred feet, he cut in the rockets and zoomed over the State House. The rockets died and Kris settled slowly, then cut out the jet-pack. He was on the roof . . . unseen. The fire would keep their attention. At this stage in the eradication of the eight-point plan they would be expecting him, but they wouldn't know it would be this formidable an assault force.

The geigers were giving a hot reading from the North Wing of the State House. His seven-league boots allowed him to leap over in three strides, and he packed plastic charges along the edges of the roof, damping them with implosion spray so the force of their blast would be directed straight down. Then he set the timer and leaped back to the section of roof where his trackers gave him the strongest Wallace reading. Extending the hooks in his mittens, he cut a circular patch in the roof, then burned it out with acid. It hung in its place. Suddenly, the plastic charges went off on the roof of the North Wing, and under cover of the tumult, he struck! He used the boot-spikes to kick in the circular patch he'd cut in the roof. The circular opening had cut through the roofing material; now he used the flamethrower to burn through the several layers of lath and plaster and beaming, till all that stood between him and entrance was the plaster of the ceiling. He withdrew a grenade from the inner pockets of the capacious suit, pulled the pin, released the handle, and dropped it into the hole. There was a sharp, short explosion, and when the plaster dust cleared he was free to leap down inside the Alabama State House.

Kris jumped, setting the boots for light bounce.

He jumped into a readily waiting group of green-suited zombies. "Ho ho ho!" Kris chortled again, opening up with the machine guns. Bodies spun and flopped and caromed off walls, and seconds later the reception squad was stacked high in its own seepage of blood.

They had barricaded the doors to the room. Kris now had no time for lockpicks. He pulled off his red rubber nose and hurled it. The doors exploded outward in a cascading shower of splintered toothpickery. He plunged through the smoke and still-flying wreckage, hit the hallway, turned to follow the pinging urgency of his trackers. Wallace was moving. Trying to get away? Not unlikely.

Hauling out the bolo knife, he dashed forward again. Green-suited zombies came at him from a cross-corridor and he hacked his way through them without pause. A shot spanged off the wall beside his ear and he half-turned, letting a throwing-knife drop into his hand from its oiled sheath. The marksman was half-in, half-out of a doorway down the corridor. Kris let the knife slide down his palm, caught it by the tip, and in one quicksilver movement overhanded it. The knife just scored the edge of the doorjamb and buried itself in the zombie's throat. He disappeared inside the room.

The trackers were now indicating a blank wall at the end of a cul-de-sac. Kris came on at it, full out, his suit's body armor locked for ramming. He hit the wall and went right through. Behind the blank face of the cul-de-sac was a stone stairway, leading down into the darkness. Zombies lurked on those stairs. The .30 cal's were good enough for them; Kris fled down the stairs, firing ahead of him. The zombies peeled away and fell into darkness.

At the bottom he found the underground river, and saw the triangular black blades of shark dorsals.

Still murmuring ho ho ho, Kris dove headfirst into the stygian blackness. The water closed over him, and nothing more could be seen, save the thrashing of sharks.

Less than an hour later, the entire Alabama State House and much of the public square went straight up in a hellfire explosion of such ferocity that windows were knocked out in slat-back houses of po' darkies in Selma.

☞ XIV ☜

She was lightly scraping her long painted fingernails down his naked back. He lay prone on the bed, occasionally reaching to the nightstand for a pull on the whiskey and water. The livid scars that still pulsed on his back seemed to attract her. She wet her full lips, and her naked, large-nippled breasts heaved as she surveyed his body.

"He fought to the end. The sonofabitch was the only one of the eight who really *liked* that black thing in his head. Really, genuinely evil. Worst of the bunch; no wonder S.P.I.D.E.R. picked him to ramrod the eight-point plan." He buried his face in the pillow, as though trying to blot out the memory of what had gone before.

"I waited three and a half months for you to come back," the blonde said, tidying her bosom. "The least you could do is tell me where you *were*!"

He turned over and grabbed her. He pulled her down to him and ran his hands over her lush flesh. She seemed to burn with a special heat. Much, much later, some time in mid-January, he released her, and said, "Baby, it's just too goddam ugly to talk about. All I'll say is that if there had been *any* chance of saving that Wallace mother from his own meanness, I'd have taken it."

"He was killed?"

"When the underground caverns blew. Sank half the state of Alabama. Funny thing was . . . it sunk mostly Caucasian holdings. All the ghettos are still standing. The new governor—Shabbaz X. Turner—has declared the entire state a disaster area, and he's got the Black Cross organized to come in and help all the poor white folks who were refugee'd by the explosion. That bastard Wallace must have had the entire state wired."

"Sounds dreadful."

"Dreadful? You know what that fink had as his part of the eight-point plan?"

The girl looked at him wide-eyed.

"I'll tell you. It was his job—through the use of tremendously sophisticated equipment—to harden the thought-processes of the young, to age them. To set their concepts like concrete. When we exploded all that devil's machinery, suddenly everyone started thinking freely, digging each other, turning to one another and realizing that the world was in a sorry state, and that what they'd been sure of, a moment before, might just possibly be in question. He was literally turning the young into old. And it was causing aging."

"You mean we don't age naturally?"

"Hell no. It was S.P.I.D.E.R. that was making us get older and older, and fall apart. Now we'll all stay the way we are, reach an age physically of about thirty-six or -seven, and then coast on out for another two or three hundred years. And oh yeah, no cancer."

"That too?"

Kris nodded.

The blonde lay on her back, and Kris traced a pattern on her stomach with his large, scarred hands. "Just one thing," the blonde said.

"Yeah, what's that?"

"What was S.P.I.D.E.R.'s eight-point plan all about? I mean, aside from the individual elements of making everyone hate everyone else, what were they trying for?"

Kris shrugged. "That, and what the name S.P.I.D.E.R. means, we may never know. Now that their organization has been broken up. Shame. I would've liked to've known."

And you will know, a voice suddenly said, inside Kris's head. The blonde rose up, off the bed, and withdrew a deadly stinger pistol from beneath the pillows. *Our agents are everywhere,* she said, telepathically.

"You!" Kris ejaculated.

Since the moment you returned, after Christmas. While you were recuperating from your wounds, lying there unconscious, I slipped in—having trailed you from Alabama—that's why you never found evidence that Wallace's symbiote had self-destructed—I slipped in and invaded this poor husk. What made you think you had beaten us, fool? We are everywhere. We came to this planet sixty years ago—check your history; you'll find the exact date. We are here, and here we stay. For the present to wage a terrorist war, but soon—to take everything for ourselves. The eight-point plan was our most ambitious to date.

"Ambitious!" Kris sneered. "Hate, madness, cancer, prejudice, confusion, subservience, smog, corruption, aging . . . what kind of filth are you?"

We are S.P.I.D.E.R., the voice said, while the blonde held the needle on him. *And once you know what S.P.I.D.E.R. stands for, you will know what our eight-part plan was intended to do to you poor, weak Earthmen.*

Watch! The voice was jubilant.

And the S.P.I.D.E.R. symbiote crawled out of her ear and darted for Kris's throat. He reacted instantly, spinning off the bed. The symbiote missed his throat by micro-millimeters. Kris hit the wall, shoved off with a bare foot and dove back onto the bed, scrambling around the blonde, grabbing her hand, and directing the needle of the weapon at the symbiote. It scuttled for cover, even as the lethal blast seared across the bedsheets. Then Kris grabbed for the deadly nightshade, on the bedstand beside him, and hurled it.

Instantly, all of the underground toy-making complex was awash in darkness.

He felt the blonde jerk in his grasp, and he knew that the S.P.I.D.E.R. symbiote had fled back to its one place of safety. Inside her. He had no choice but to kill her. But she threw the needle away, and he was locked there in eternal darkness, on the bed, holding her body as it struggled to free itself; and he was forced by his nakedness to kill her using the one weapon God had given him when he came into the world.

It was a special weapon, and it took almost a week to kill her.

But when it was over, and the darkness had cleared, he lay there thinking. Exhausted, ten pounds lighter, weak as a kitten, and thinking.

Now he knew what S.P.I.D.E.R. meant.

The symbiote was small, black, hairy, and scuttled on many little legs. The eight-point plan was intended to make people feel bad. That simple. It was to make them feel simply crummy. And crummy people kill each other. And people who kill each other leave a world intact enough for S.P.I.D.E.R.

All he had to do was delete the periods.

☞ XV ☜

The time/motion studies came in the next week. They said that the deliveries this past holiday had been the sloppiest on record. Kris and PoPo shuffled the reports and smiled. Well, it would be better next year. No wonder it was so sloppy this year . . . how effective was a Santa Claus who was really an imposter? How effective could Santa Claus be when he was PoPo and CorLo, the one standing on the other's shoulders, wearing a red suit three sizes too big for them? But with Kris laid up from saving the world, they had had no choice.

There were complaints coming in from all over.

Even from Hilltop.

"PoPo," Kris said, when the phones refused to cease clanging, "I'm not taking any calls. They want me, they can reach me at Antibes. I'm going off to sleep for three months. They can reach me in April sometime."

He started out of the office just as CorLo ran in, a wild expression on his face. "Geeble gip freesee jim jim," CorLo said. Kris slumped back into his seat.

He dropped his head into his hands.

Everything went wrong.

Dasher had knocked up Vixen.

"The shits just won't let you live," Kris murmured, and began crying, softly yet manfully.

Historical Note: The astute reader will be quick to notice that though Mr. Ellison's story was written prior to November 1968, and was published early in 1969, it has only one small flaw in it. The insidious eight-point plan totally ignores the Republican vice-presidential candidate at the time, Mr. Spiro Agnew who, though elected, was later sentenced to prison for criminous acts, left office in disgrace, and has since become an icon for mendacity. Apparently the author forgot him. Apparently the author was not the only one. Go figure.

O Come Little Children . . .

Chet Williamson

"It even *smells* like Christmas," the boy told his mother, as they strolled down the narrow aisles of the farmer's market. That it looked and sounded like that happiest of holidays went without saying. Carols blared everywhere, from the tiniest of the stand-holder's transistor radios to the brass choir booming from the market's PA system. Meat cases were framed with strings of lights, a myriad of small trees adorned a myriad of counters across which bills the color of holly were pushed and goods and coins returned, and red and green predominated above all other hues. But it was the odors that entranced: the pungency of gingerbread, the sweet olfactory sting of fresh Christmas cookies. There were mince pies and pumpkin pudding, and a concoction of cranberry sauce and dried fruit in syrup whose aroma made the boy pucker and salivate as though a fresh lemon had brushed his tongue. The owner of the sandwich stand was selling small, one-dollar, Styrofoam plates of turkey and stuffing to those too rabid to wait until Christmas, three long days away. The smell was intoxicating, and the line was long.

The boy's mother, smiling and full of the spirit, bought many things that would find their way to their own Christmas table, and the sights and sounds and smells kept the boy from being bored, as he usually was at the Great Tri-County Farmer's and Flea Market.

It was on the way out, as he and his mother walked through the large passage that divided the freshness of the food and produce stands from the dusty tawdriness of the flea market, that the boy saw the man dressed as Santa Claus. At first glance he did not seem a very *good* Santa Claus. He was too thin, and instead of a full, white, cottony, fake beard, his own wispy mass of facial hair had been halfheartedly lightened, as though he'd dipped a comb in white shoe polish and given it a few quick strokes. "There," the boy's mother remarked, "is one of Santa's *lesser* helpers."

The boy was way past the point where every Santa was the *real* Santa. In truth, he was just short of total disbelief. TV, comic books, and the remarks of older friends had all taken their toll, and he now thought that although the existence of the great man was conceivable, it was not likely, and to imagine that any of these kindly, red-suited men who smiled wearily in every department store and shopping mall was the genuine article was quite impossible.

Even if he had believed fully, he doubted if anyone under two would have accepted the legitimacy of the Santa he saw before him. Aside from the thinness of both beard and frame, the man's suit was threadbare in spots, the black vinyl boots scuffed and dull, and the white ruffs at collar and cuffs had yellowed to the color of old piano keys. His lap was empty. The only person nearby was a cowboy-hatted man sitting on a folding chair identical to that on which the Santa sat. A Polaroid Pronto hung from his neck, and next to him a card on an easel read YOUR PICTURE WITH SANTA—$3.00. The $3.00 part was printed much smaller than the words. The boy and his mother were nearly by the men when the one in the red suit looked at them.

The boy stopped. "Mom," he said, loud enough for only his mother to hear. "May I sit on his lap?"

She gave an impatient sigh. "Oh, Alan . . ."

"Please?"

"Honey, do you really *want* your picture taken with . . . ?"

"I don't want a picture. I just want to sit on his lap."

"No, sweetie," she said, looking at the man looking at the boy. "I don't think so."

They were in the parking lot by the time she looked at her son once more. To her amazement, huge tears were running down his face. "What's wrong, honey?"

"I wanted to sit on his *lap,*" the boy choked out.

"Oh, Alan, he's not Santa, he's just a helper. And not a very good one either."

"Can't I? Please? Just for a minute . . ."

She sighed and smiled, thinking that it would do no harm, and that she was in no hurry. "All right. But no picture."

The boy shook his head, and they went back inside. The man in the red suit smiled as he saw the boy approach without hesitation, and patted his thigh in an unspoken invitation for the boy to sit. The man in the cowboy hat stood up, but before he could bring the camera to eye level, the boy said, "No picture, please," and the man, with a look of irritation directed at the boy's mother, sat down again.

The boy remained on the man's lap for less than a minute, talking so quietly that his mother could not hear. When he started to slide off he stopped suddenly, as though caught, and his mother saw that the metal buckle of the boy's loose-hanging coat belt had become entangled in the white plush of the man's left cuff. The man tried unsuccessfully to extricate it with the fingers of his gloved right hand, then put the glove in his mouth and yanked his hand free. With his long, thin fingers he freed the boy, who hopped smiling onto the floor and waved a hand, enclosed in his own varicolored mitten. When he rejoined his mother, he was surprised to find her scowling. "What's wrong?"

"Nothing," she answered. "Let's go."

But he knew something was wrong and found out later at dinner. "*I* think he must have been *on* something."

"Oh, come on," his father said, taking a second baked potato. "Why?"

His mother went on as though he were not there. "He just *looked* it. He had these real hollow eyes, like he hadn't slept in days. Really thin. The suit just hung on him. And, uh . . ." She looked at the boy, who pretended to be interested in pushing an unmelted piece of margarine around on his peas.

"What?"

"His hand. He took off his glove and his hand was all bruised, like he'd been shooting into it or something."

"Shooting what?" the boy asked.

"Drugs," his father said, before his mother could make something up.

"What's that? Like what?"

His mother smiled sardonically at his father. "Go ahead, Mr. Rogers. Explain."

"Well . . . *drugs.* Like your baby aspirin, only a lot stronger. People take some drugs just to make them feel good, but then later they feel real bad, so you shouldn't ever take them at all."

"What's the shooting part?"

"Like a shot, when the doctor gives you a shot."

"Like Mommy's diabetes."

"Yeah, like that. Only people who take too many *bad* drugs have their veins . . ." He saw the question on the boy's face. ". . . their little blood hoses inside their skin collapse on them. So they might stick the needles in their legs, or in the veins in the backs of their hands, or even their feet or the inside of their mouth, or . . ."

"That's fine, thank you," his mother said sharply. "I think we've learned enough tonight."

"He wouldn't do *that,"* the boy said. "He was too *nice."*

His father shook his head. "Aw, honey, you never know. Nice people can have problems too." And then his mother changed the subject.

The next day the boy told his mother that he wished he could see Santa Claus again. "Santa Claus?" she asked.

"At the market. *You* know."

"Oh, Alan, *him?* Honey, you saw him yesterday. You told him what you wanted then, didn't you?"

"I don't want to tell him what I want. I just want to see him because he's *nice.* I *liked* him."

After the boy was in bed, his father and mother sat in the living room, neither of them paying attention to the movie on cable. "He say anything to you about Santa today?" he asked her.

She nodded. "Couple of times. You?"

"Yeah. He really went for this guy, huh?"

"I don't know why."

"Oh, Alan can be so compassionate—probably felt sorry for the guy."

She shook her head. "No, it wasn't like that. He really seemed drawn by him, almost as though . . ." She paused.

"As though he really thought the guy was Santa Claus?" her husband finished.

"I don't know," she answered, looking at the car crash on the TV screen but not really seeing it. "Maybe."

She turned off the movie with no complaints from her husband, and began to go over the final list of ingredients for their Christmas dinner. "Uh-oh," she murmured, and went out to the kitchen. In a minute she returned; frowning lovingly at her husband. "Well, it's not that I don't appreciate your making dinner tonight, but I just realized your oyster stew used the oysters for the Christmas casserole."

"You're kidding."

"Nope." She was amused to see that there was actually panic in his face.

"What'll we *do*?"

"Do without."

"But . . . but oyster casserole's a tradition."

"Some tradition—just because we had it last year."

"I liked it."

"And where are we going to find oysters on a Sunday?"

"It's not the day, it's the month. And December has an *R* in it."

"Sure. But Sunday doesn't have *oysters* in it. The IGA's closed, Acme, Weis . . ."

His face brightened. "The farmer's market! They have a fish stand, and they're open tomorrow. You could run out and . . ."

"Me? I didn't cook the oyster stew."

"You ate it."

She put her left hand over his head and pounded it gently with her right. "Sometimes you are a real sleazoid."

"Now, Mrs. Scrooge," he said, pulling her onto his lap, "where's that Christmas spirit, that charity?"

"Good King Wenceslas I ain't."

"How about if I vacuum while you're gone so my mother doesn't realize what a slob you are?"

"How many pounds of oysters do you want?"

It started to snow heavily just before midnight and stopped at dawn. The snow was light and powdery, easy for the early morning trucks to push from the roads. The family went to church, then came home for a simple lunch, as if afraid to ingest even a jot too much on the day before the great Christmas feast. "Well," the boy's mother said after they'd finished cleaning up the dishes, "I'm off for oysters. Anyone want to come?"

"To the farm market?" asked the boy. His mother nodded. "Can I see Santa?"

His father and mother exchanged looks. "I don't think so," she replied. "Do you want to go anyway?"

He thought for a moment. "Okay."

The parking lot was still covered with snow, although the cars had mashed most of it down to a dirty gray film. Only the far end of the parking lot, where a small, gray trailer sat attached to an old, nondescript sedan, was pristine with whiteness. It was typical, the boy's mother thought, of the management not to pay to have the lot plowed—anyone who'd hire a bargain basement Santa like that one and then charge three bucks for a thirty-five-cent picture with him.

The seafood stand was out of oysters, but its owner said that the small grocery shop at the market's other end might still have some. "Could I see Santa?" the boy asked as they walked.

"Alan, I told you no. Besides, he's probably gone by now. He's got a busy night tonight." She knew it sounded absurd even as she said it. If *that* Santa was going to be busy, it wouldn't be delivering toys—it would probably be looking for a fix. Repulsion crossed her face as she thought again of those hollow eyes, that pale skin, the telltale bruises on his bare hand, and she wondered what her son could possibly see in that haggard countenance.

She thought she would ask him, but when she looked down, he was gone. In a sharp, reflexive motion, she looked to the other side, then behind her, but the boy was not there. She strained to see him through the forest of people, then turned and retraced her steps, as her heart beat faster and beads of cold sweat touched her face. "Alan!" she called, softly but high, to pierce the low, murmuring din around her. "Alan!"

It took some time for the idea to occur that her son had disobeyed her and had set out to find the market's Santa Claus on his own. She had not thought him capable of such a thing, for he knew and understood the dangers that could face a small child alone in a public place, especially a place like a flea market that had more than its share of transients and lowlifes. She told herself that he would be all right, that nothing could happen to a little boy the day before Christmas, that someone she knew would see him and stop him and take care of him until she could find him, or that he would be there on Santa Claus's lap, smiling sheepishly and guiltily when he spotted her.

She was running now, jostling shoppers, their arms loaded with last-minute thoughts. Within a minute, she entered the large open area between the markets. The chairs and the sign were there, the Santa and his photographer were not. Neither was her son.

For a long moment she stood, wondering what to do next, and finally decided to find the manager and ask him to make an announcement on the PA system. But first she called her husband, for she could no longer bear to be alone.

By the time he met her in the manager's office, the announcement had been made four times without a response. The boy's father held his mother, who was by this time crying quietly, very much afraid. "Where was he going?" the manager, a short, elderly man with a cigarette in one hand and a can of soda in the other, asked.

"I thought it was to see Santa, but he wasn't there when I got there."

The manager nodded. "Yeah, he quit at noon. I wanted him to work through five, but he wouldn't. Said he hadda meet somebody."

The boy's father looked at the manager intently over his wife's head. "Who is this guy?"

"Santa? Don't know his name. Just breezed in about a week ago and asked if I wanted a Santa cheap."

"What do you mean you don't know his name? You *pay* him, don't you?"

"Cash. Off the books. You'll keep that quiet now. And Riley, my helper, he got a Polaroid, so we made enough to pay him outta the pictures."

The boy's father took his arms from around his wife. "Where is this guy?"

"He's got a trailer the other side of the lot."

"All right," the father nodded. "We're going to talk to him. And if he can't give us any answers, we're calling the police."

The manager started to protest, but the couple walked out of the office and down the aisles, trying hard not to run and so admit their panic to themselves. "It'll be all right," the boy's father kept saying. "We'll find him. It'll be all right."

And they did. When they walked into the open area where Santa had been, their son was standing beside the gold aluminum Christmas tree. He smiled when he saw them, and waved.

They ran to him, and his mother scooped him up and hugged him, crying. His father placed a hand on his head as if to be certain he was really there, then tousled his hair, swallowing heavily to rid his throat of the cold lump that had been there since his wife's call.

"Where *were* you?" the boy's mother said, holding him ferociously. "Where did you *go?*"

"I wanted to see him," he said, as if that were all the explanation necessary.

"But I told you *no.* You know better, Alan. Anything could've happened. We were worried sick."

"I'm sorry, Mom. I just *had* to see him."

"But you didn't," his father said. "So where *were* you? Why didn't you answer the announcements?"

"Oh, I saw him, Dad. I was *with* him."

"You . . . *where?*"

"He was here. He said he was waiting for me, that he'd been hoping I'd come again. He looked really different, he didn't have on his red suit or anything."

His mother shook her head. "But . . . I *looked* here."

"Oh, I *found* him here okay. But then we went to his place."

"*What?*" they both asked at once.

"His trailer. It's sort of like the one Grandpa and Grandma have."

"Why . . . did you go out there?" his mother asked, remembering the trailer and the car at the end of the lot.

"He asked me to."

"Alan," his father said, "I've told you never, *never* to go with anyone for *any* reason."

"But it was all right with him, Dad. I knew I'd be safe with *him.* He told me when we were walking. Out to his trailer."

"Told you *what?*"

"How he always looks for somebody."

"Oh, my God. . . ."

"What's the matter, Mom?"

"Nothing. Nothing. What else did this . . . man say?"

"He just said he always comes back this time of year, just to see if people still believe in him. He said lots of people *say* they do, but they don't, not really. He said they just say so because they want their *kids* to believe in him. But if he finds one person who really believes, and knows who he really is, then it's all gonna be okay. Till next Christmas. He said it's almost always kids, like me, but that that's okay. As long as there's somebody who believes in him and trusts him enough to go with him."

The boy's father knelt beside him and put his big hands on the boy's thin shoulders. "Alan. Did he touch you? Touch you anywhere at all?"

"Just here." He held up his mitten-covered hands. "My hands."

"Alan, this man played a mean joke on you. He let you think that he's somebody that he really isn't."

"Oh no, Dad, you're wrong."

"Now listen. This man was *not* Santa Claus, Alan."

The boy laughed. "*I* know *that!* I haven't believed in Santa Claus for almost a whole *month!*"

His mother barely got the words out. "Then who . . . ?"

"And you were wrong too, Mom. He didn't have any little needle holes in his hands. Just the big ones. Straight through. Just like he's supposed to."

Her eyes widened, and she put her fist to her mouth to hold in a scream. Her husband leaped to his feet, his face even paler than before. "Where's this trailer?" he asked in a voice whose coldness frightened the boy.

They strode out the door together into the late afternoon darkness. Street lights illuminated every part of the parking lot. "It . . . was there," she said, staring across at white emptiness.

"The *bastard.* Got out while the getting was good. He . . ." The father paused. "There?" he said, pointing.

"Yes. It was right over there." The boy nodded in agreement with his mother.

"It couldn't've been." He started to walk toward the open space, and his family followed. "There are no tracks. It hasn't snowed. And there's no wind." He looked at the unbroken plain of powdered snow.

"Hey! Hey, you folks!" They turned and saw the manager laboring toward them, puffs of condensation roaring from his mouth. "That your kid? He okay?"

The boy's father nodded. "Yeah. He seems to be. We were trying to find that man. Your Santa Claus. But he's . . . gone."

"Huh! You believe that? And I still owe him fourteen bucks." He turned back toward the warmth of the market, shaking his head. "Left without his money. Some people . . ."

"Never mind," his wife said. "He's all right. Let him believe." She touched her husband's shoulder. "Maybe we should all believe. It's almost easier that way."

When they got home, the boy took off his mittens, and his father and mother saw the pale red marks, one in each palm, where he said the man's fingers had touched him. They were suffused with a rosy glow, as if the blood pulsed more strongly there. "They'll go away," the boy's father said. "In time, they'll go away." But they did not.

It's a Wonderful Miracle on 34th Street's Christmas Carol

Brian Thomsen

The shrink on the golf course said . . .
The elf said . . .
Then this elf said . . .
So this other shrink says . . .

The portly patient continued with his protestations, but eventually lay back on the couch and tried to relax, nervously stroking his snow-white and bushy beard.

"I know you're a bit uncomfortable," Dr. Ahmet offered. "Most people are on their first visit."

"I guess I never thought I would wind up on some Upper East Side shrink's couch," Kris replied, quickly adding, "No offense intended. Over the 'shrink,' I mean."

"None taken. So why don't you tell me why you are here?"

"Beyond the fact that you're covered by my HMO?" Kris kidded with a chuckle.

"Yes, beyond that particularly rewarding reason."

Kris sighed and began his confession.

"I guess I'm just having a problem dealing with who I am now."

"As compared to who you were?" Dr. Ahmet inquired.

"Yes."

"And that was?"

Kris fidgeted and sat up, and replied with a sigh, "Kris Kringle."

Dr. Ahmet was puzzled. He didn't recognize the name.

"Come again," he re-inquired.

"Kris Kringle."

"Never heard of him," Dr. Ahmet said with a shake of the head. "Sorry."

Kris sighed again.

"That's the problem," Kris confessed. "But maybe I should start at the beginning. Bear with me for a few minutes. This might sound kind of strange."

Dr. Ahmet looked at his watch and replied, "You have forty minutes left of our fifty-minute hour. You talk, I'll listen."

The formerly jolly old elf began his tale.

* * *

It was an unseasonably warm November first, and Santa was really beginning to feel the year-end holiday pressures.

Let me digress for a moment.

Santa Claus, who also goes by such monikers as Saint Nick, Father Christmas, and even Kris Kringle, was up to a while ago the most beloved figure on the face of the earth. He lived at the North Pole at his enchanted toyshop where elves worked all year round to make toys for all of the world's good little girls and boys. Then on Christmas Eve, that was December 24th, he would load up his sleigh and hitch up his flying reindeer and take to the heavens to deliver them to deserving darlings all over the world.

Don't interrupt just yet.

Anything that defied logic worked by magic.

Humor me.

I had just taken my morning post-breakfast break. Mrs. Claus's bacon was a little greasier than usual and I decided to give the newspapers a quick scan while waiting for nature to take its course.

I quickly became depressed.

Seventy-five percent of the papers were devoted to advertising that made the crass commercialism of *Return of the Jedi* look like a Sunday sermon by Mother Teresa, and if that wasn't bad enough—

SALEMART TRADEMARKS SANTA CLAUS

Walt Saleton III announced yesterday that he and his organization—the number-one retail chain in the U.S.A.—had just signed an exclusive license with the heirs of famed illustrator/political cartoonist Thomas Nast for all rights—for a period of not less than seventy-five years—to the image/likeness/character/persona of Santa Claus for an undisclosed sum thought to be well into seven figures.

Saleton has assured all concerned that he has no desire to restrict the presence of the jolly old elf from the public but hastened to add that adequate legal notice of permission will be required.

Such legal notice will read: *Used by permission of Salemart the nation's number-one retail chain—When you want to shop smart, shop Salemart!*

To say that I became more depressed was an understatement tantamount to saying that Rudolph's nose was a bit shiny or that in general elves might not be very tall.

But I had been depressed before.

(Who can forget the downer of having David Huddleston playing you in an eponymous bomb where Lithgow and Moore got top billing?)

This time was different.

I was also angry.

I spoke without thinking.

"Dammit they can have their Santa Circle C Claus TM," I swore, and then with a vehemence wished, "And to quote George Bailey, 'I wish I had never been born at all.' That would show them. No real Santa at all, just a two-bit caricature by a political cartoonist turned into everyone's favorite commercial holiday buffoon! Merry Christmas and shop again."

I had not even finished my rant when I noticed the strange stares I was receiving from unknown faces, and that I was standing in front of a huge discount department store on Thirty-fourth Street in Manhattan.

* * *

Dr. Ahmet looked at his watch, and observed, "So you, Kris Kringle, are really Santa Claus."

The jolly old elf became defensive for a moment.

"Now let me continue for a bit more. Everything will become clear shortly."

"Just proceed," Ahmet replied, making a mental note that this was the first Santa for his golf circle. Drs. Levin and Shapiro had already told him about two Ronald McDonald's and a Colonel Sanders, while Dr. Martin seemed to specialize in rockstar wannabes and a five-time-a-weeker who thought he was on alternate weeks Orson Welles and Ethel Merman.

His would be the first Santa.

* * *

It doesn't take a genius to understand what had happened.

The North Pole, the flying reindeer, the magic toyshop, the whole shebang runs on the energy of magic as fueled by the power of wishes, and as Father Christmas—Santa by another name—I was the custodian of that power, all of which fueled my foolish wish, which thus changed the world.

* * *

"And?"

"And?"

"You still have twenty minutes."

"Oh. Well, the first thing I did was to find my place in this world and, as you might have guessed, it wasn't much of a surprise."

"You are a holiday greeter at . . ."

"Yes, but I digress, and I know time is running out."

"For this session."

"This session?"

"Yes," Ahmet explained, "you're covered for a maximum of twenty sessions a year under your policy. More if you're incarcerated."

"Incarcerated?"

"Committed."

* * *

Now being a greeter at the Thirty-fourth Street Salesmart wasn't bad, but it just wasn't the same as life at the North Pole, and besides the world still needed a "real Santa Claus."

I had to do something to make things right.

I remembered my short list.

* * *

"Short list?"

"Those children who offered to return my kindness with like kindness. You know, if there was ever anything they could do for me, if you're ever in the Bronx look me up, that sort of thing."

"Oh."

"Unfortunately, most of them seemed to have gotten off on the wrong track and had gotten jobs as lobbyists in Washington . . . not exactly the gift giving I had in mind. There were a few, though, who had not succumbed to such political diversions."

* * *

Mickey Darden Rivera was always looking for the big break. He had missed out on being part of O.J.'s dream team because of a Springer appearance, which had yet to yield him his own Fox show, and I think he knew that my case would do it for him.

This was a case that Court TV just wouldn't be able to pass on . . . or at least that was what Mickey said.

I really didn't care about going to trial, I told him, all I wanted was to get things back the way they should be. I then explained about the North Pole and the wish thing and . . .

He put up his hand and told me to stop talking.

It might damage our case.

He told me he didn't care about the facts.

If I said that I wasn't just some Salesmart greeter and that I was the real Santa Claus that was good enough for him.

The problem was that the copyright and trademarks were all very legal and really rather difficult to challenge at this point (I assume that getting control of the copyrights and trademarks was the first step in getting back my original identity), and that the old post office ploy that had worked in the Macy's case was a bit too risky at the present time.

But then he came up with what he called a Dickens of an idea.

* * *

"Which was . . . ?" Ahmet inquired, getting ready to close off the session.

* * *

We snuck into the house of Walt Saleton III and convinced him that we were the ghosts of Christmas and that he would have to sign over . . .

* * *

"Wait, " Ahmet interrupted. "Snuck in?"

"Well, since going down the chimney was no longer an option given my loss of magic powers . . ."

"Of course."

"We jimmied the lock at the back door, and . . ."

"Enough," Dr. Ahmet said, standing up. "I'm afraid our session is over for this week. I think that we have made some progress, but things are going to take some time, so how about next week at the same time? We can finish up this story and maybe start to talk about your childhood."

Kris got to his feet and shook the doctor's hand.

"You know," the jolly elf said, "being a greeter at Salesmart really isn't so bad. The employee benefits are great and they have already guaranteed me a post-holiday position, and there still is a Christmas, and the children don't seem to mind, and . . ."

"Next week," Dr. Ahmet assured.

"Next week," Kris agreed, and left the office.

* * *

"So did you have him committed?"

* * *

"Thought about it . . . but then I got a call from Walt Saleton III. Seems that he was being troubled by bad dreams and hallucinations and was willing to pay triple the rates for some holiday season counseling. So how could I commit that old loon after such a lovely Christmas present with year-end taxes and all."

* * *

"You want to sub for me twice a week on Orson/Ethel?"

* * *

"Just hit the ball, or the gynecologists behind us are going to want to play through."

* * *

. . . at least that's the way I heard it.

Variations on the Holiday Theme

When you think about Christmas what comes to mind?

- The debate over best Christmas film (*Miracle on 34th Street* versus *It's a Wonderful Life* or *A Christmas Story*)
- The favorite version of Dickens's *A Christmas Carol* (and the argument over whether *Scrooged* and *Mister Magoo* have to be excluded)
- A memory of a Christmas past or perhaps a past Christmas present

Whether your tastes lie post-modern or Dickensian Victorian, have we got a holiday tale for you.

The Yattering and Jack

Clive Barker

Why the powers (long may they hold court; long may they shit light on the heads of the damned) had sent it out from Hell to stalk Jack Polo, the Yattering couldn't discover. Whenever he passed a tentative inquiry along the system to his master, just asking the simple question, "What am I doing here?" it was answered with a swift rebuke for its curiosity. None of its business, came the reply, its business was to do. Or die trying. And after six months of pursuing Polo, the Yattering was beginning to see extinction as an easy option. This endless game of hide and seek was to nobody's benefit, and the Yattering's immense frustration. It feared ulcers, it feared psychosomatic leprosy (condition lower demons like itself were susceptible to), worst of all it feared losing its temper completely and killing the man outright in an uncontrollable fit of pique.

What was Jack Polo anyway?

A gherkin importer; by the balls of Leviticus, he was simply a gherkin importer. His life was worn out, his family was dull, his politics were simple-minded and his theology non-existent. The man was a no-account, one of nature's blanket little numbers—why bother with the likes of him? This wasn't a Faust: a pact-maker, a soul-seller. This one wouldn't look twice at the chance of divine inspiration: he'd sniff, shrug and get on with his gherkin importing.

Yet the Yattering was bound to that house, long night and longer day, until he had the man a lunatic, or as good as. It was going to be a lengthy job, if not interminable. Yes, there were times when even psychosomatic leprosy would be bearable if it meant being invalided off this impossible mission.

For his part, Jack J. Polo continued to be the most unknowing of men. He had always been that way; indeed his history was littered with the victims of his naïveté. When his late, lamented wife had cheated on him (he'd been in the house on at least two of the occasions, watching the television) he was the last one to find out. And the clues they'd left behind them! A blind, deaf and dumb man would have become suspicious. Not Jack. He pottered about his dull business and never noticed the tang of the adulterer's cologne, nor the abnormal regularity with which his wife changed the bed-linen.

He was no less disinterested in events when his younger daughter Amanda confessed her lesbianism to him. His response was a sigh and a puzzled look.

"Well, as long as you don't get pregnant, darling," he replied, and sauntered off into the garden, blithe as ever.

What chance did a fury have with a man like that?

To a creature trained to put its meddling fingers into the wounds of the human psyche, Polo offered a surface so glacial, so utterly without distinguishing marks, as to deny malice any hold whatsoever.

Events seemed to make no dent in his perfect indifference. His life's disasters seemed not to scar his mind at all. When, eventually, he was confronted with the truth about his wife's infidelity (he found them screwing in the bath) he couldn't bring himself to be hurt or humiliated.

"These things happen," he said to himself, backing out of the bathroom to let them finish what they'd started.

"Che sera, sera."

Che sera, sera. The man muttered that damn phrase with monotonous regularity. He seemed to live by that philosophy of fatalism, letting attacks on his manhood, ambition and dignity slide off his ego like rainwater from his bald head.

The Yattering had heard Polo's wife confess all to her husband (it was hanging upside down from the light-fitting, invisible as ever) and the scene had made it wince. There was the distraught sinner, begging to be accused, bawled at, struck even, and instead of giving her the satisfaction of his hatred, Polo had just shrugged and let her say her piece without a word of interruption, until she had no more to unbosom. She'd left, at length, more out of frustration and sorrow than guilt; the Yattering had heard her tell the bathroom mirror how insulted she was at her husband's lack of righteous anger. A little while after she'd flung herself off the balcony of the Roxy Cinema.

Her suicide was in some ways convenient for the fury. With the wife gone, and the daughters away from home, it could plan for more elaborate tricks to unnerve its victim, without ever having to concern itself with revealing its presence to creatures the powers had not marked for attack.

But the absence of the wife left the house empty during the days, and that soon became a burden of boredom the Yattering found scarcely supportable. The hours from nine to five, alone in the house, often seemed endless. It would mope and wander, planning bizarre and impractical revenges upon the Polo-man, pacing the rooms, heartsick, companioned only by the clicks and whirrs of the house as the radiators cooled, or the refrigerator switched itself on and off. The situation rapidly became so desperate that the arrival of the midday post became the high point of the day, and an unshakeable melancholy would settle on the Yattering if the postman had nothing to deliver and passed by to the next house.

When Jack returned the games would begin in earnest. The usual warm-up routine: it would meet Jack at the door and prevent his key from turning in the lock. The contest would go on for a minute or two until Jack accidentally found the measure of the Yattering's resistance, and won the day. Once inside, it would start all the lampshades swinging. The man would usually ignore this performance, however violent the motion. Perhaps he might shrug and murmur: "Subsidence," under his breath, then, inevitably, *"Che sera, sera."*

In the bathroom, the Yattering would have squeezed toothpaste around the toilet seat and have plugged up the shower-head with soggy toilet paper. It would even share the shower with Jack, hanging unseen from the rail that held up the shower curtain and murmuring obscene suggestions in his ear. That was always successful, the demons were taught at the Academy. The obscenities in the ear routine never failed to distress clients, making them think they were conceiving of these pernicious acts themselves, and driving them to self-disgust, then to self-rejection and finally to madness. Of course, in a few cases the victims would be so inflamed by these whispered suggestions they'd go out on the streets and act upon them. Under such circumstances the victim would often be arrested and incarcerated. Prison would lead to further crimes, and a slow dwindling of moral reserves—and the victory was won by that route. One way or another insanity would win out.

Except that for some reason this rule did not apply to Polo; he was unperturbable: a tower of propriety.

Indeed, the way things were going the Yattering would be the one to break. It was tired; so very tired. Endless days of tormenting the cat, reading the funnies in yesterday's newspaper, watching the game shows: they drained the fury. Lately, it had developed a passion for the woman who lived across the Street from Polo. She was a young widow, and seemed to spend most of her life parading around the house stark naked. It was almost unbearable sometimes, in the middle of a day when the postman failed to call, watching the woman and knowing it could never cross the threshold of Polo's house.

This was the Law. The Yattering was a minor demon, and his soul-catching was strictly confined to the perimeters of his victim's house. To step outside was to relinquish all powers over the victim: to put itself at the mercy of humanity.

All June, all July and most of August it sweated in its prison, and all through those bright, hot months Jack Polo maintained complete indifference to the Yattering's attacks.

It was deeply embarrassing, and it was gradually destroying the demon's self-confidence, seeing this bland victim survive every trial and trick attempted upon him.

The Yattering wept.

The Yattering screamed.

In a fit of uncontrollable anguish, it boiled the water in the aquarium, poaching the guppies.

Polo heard nothing. Saw nothing.

* * *

At last, in late September, the Yattering broke one of the first rules of its condition, and appealed directly to its masters.

Autumn is Hell's season; and the demons of the higher dominations were feeling benign. They condescended to speak to their creature.

"What do you want?" asked Beelzebub, his voice blackening the air in the lounge.

"This man . . ." the Yattering began nervously.

"Yes?"

"This Polo . . ."

"Yes?"

"I am without issue upon him. I can't get panic upon him, I can't breed fear or even mild concern upon him. I am sterile, Lord of the Flies, and I wish to be put out of my misery."

For a moment Beelzebub's face formed in the mirror over the mantelpiece.

"You want *what*?"

Beelzebub was part elephant, part wasp. The Yattering was terrified.

"I—want to die."

"You cannot die."

"From this world. Just die from this world. Fade away. Be replaced."

"You will not die."

"But I can't break him!" the Yattering shrieked, tearful.

"You must."

"Why?"

"Because we tell you to." Beelzebub always used the Royal "we," though unqualified to do so.

"Let me at least know why I'm in this house," the Yattering appealed. "What is he? Nothing! He's nothing!"

Beelzebub found this rich. He laughed, buzzed, trumpeted.

"Jack Johnson Polo is the child of a worshipper at the Church of Lost Salvation. He belongs to us."

"But why should you want him? He's so dull."

"We want him because his soul was promised to us, and his mother did not deliver it. Or herself, come to that. She cheated us. She died in the arms of a priest, and was safely escorted to—"

The word that followed was anathema. The Lord of the Flies could barely bring himself to pronounce it.

"—Heaven," said Beelzebub, with infinite loss in his voice.

"Heaven," said the Yattering, not knowing quite what was meant by the word.

"Polo is to be hounded in the name of the Old One, and punished for his mother's crimes. No torment is too profound for a family that has cheated us."

"I'm tired," the Yattering pleaded, daring to approach the mirror. "Please. I beg you."

"Claim this man," said Beelzebub, "or you will suffer in his place."

The figure in the mirror waved its black and yellow trunk and faded.

"Where is your pride?" said the master's voice as it shriveled into distance. "Pride, Yattering, pride."

Then he was gone.

In its frustration the Yattering picked up the cat and threw it into the fire, where it was rapidly cremated. If only the law allowed such easy cruelty to be visited upon human flesh, it thought. If only. If only. Then it'd make Polo suffer such torments. But no. The Yattering knew the laws as well as the back of its hand; they had been flayed on to its exposed cortex as a fledgling demon by its teachers. And Law One stated: "Thou shalt not lay palm upon thy victims."

It had never been told why this law pertained, but it did.

"Thou shalt not . . ."

So the whole painful process continued. Day in, day out, and still the man showed no sign of yielding. Over the next few weeks the Yattering killed two more cats that Polo brought home to replace his treasured Freddy (now ash).

The first of these poor victims was drowned in the toilet bowl one idle Friday afternoon. It was a petty satisfaction to see the look of distaste register on Polo's face as he unzipped his fly and glanced down. But any pleasure the Yattering took in Jack's discomfiture was canceled out by the blithely efficient way in which the man dealt with the dead cat, hoisting the bundle of soaking fur out of the pan, wrapping it in a towel and burying it in the back garden with scarcely a murmur.

The third cat that Polo brought home was wise to the invisible presence of the demon from the start. There was indeed an entertaining week in mid-November when life for the Yattering became almost interesting while it played cat and mouse with Freddy the Third. Freddy played the mouse. Cats not being especially bright animals the game was scarcely a great intellectual challenge, but it made a change from the endless days of waiting, haunting and failing. At least the creature accepted the Yattering's presence. Eventually however, in a filthy mood (caused by the remarriage of the Yattering's naked widow) the demon lost its temper with the cat. It was sharpening its nails on the nylon carpet, clawing and scratching at the pile for hours on end. The noise put the demon's metaphysical teeth on edge. It looked at the cat once, briefly, and it flew apart as though it had swallowed a live grenade.

The effect was spectacular. The results were gross. Cat-brain, cat-fur, cat-gut everywhere.

Polo got home that evening exhausted, and stood in the doorway of the dining room, his face sickened, surveying the carnage that had been Freddy III.

"Damn dogs," he said. "Damn, damn dogs."

There was anger in his voice. Yes, exulted the Yattering, anger. The man was upset: there was clear evidence of emotion on his face.

Elated, the demon raced through the house, determined to capitalize on its victory. It opened and slammed every door. It smashed vases. It set the lampshades swinging.

Polo just cleaned up the cat.

The Yattering threw itself downstairs, tore up a pillow. Impersonated a thing with a limp and an appetite for human flesh in the attic, and giggling.

Polo just buried Freddy III, beside the grave of Freddy II, and the ashes of Freddy I.

Then he retired to bed, without his pillow.

The demon was utterly stumped. If the man could not raise more than a flicker of concern when his cat was exploded in the dining room, what chance had it got of ever breaking the bastard?

There was one last opportunity left.

It was approaching Christ's Mass, and Jack's children would be coming home to the bosom of the family. Perhaps they could convince him that all was not well with the world; perhaps they could get their fingernails under his flawless indifference, and begin to break him down. Hoping against hope, the Yattering sat out the weeks to late December, planning its attacks with all the imaginative malice it could muster.

Meanwhile, Jack's life sauntered on. He seemed to live apart from his experience, living his life as an author might write a preposterous story, never involving himself in the narrative too deeply. In several significant ways, however, he showed his enthusiasm for the coming holiday. He cleared his daughters' rooms immaculately. He made their beds up with sweet-smelling linen. He cleaned every speck of cat's blood out of the carpet. He even set up a Christmas tree in the lounge, hung with iridescent balls, tinsel and presents.

Once in a while, as he went about the preparations, Jack thought of the game he was playing, and quietly calculated the odds against him. In the days to come he would have to measure not only his own suffering, but that of his daughters, against the possible victory. And always, when he made these calculations, the chance of victory seemed to outweigh the risks.

So he continued to write his life, and waited.

Snow came, soft pats of it against the windows, against the door. Children arrived to sing carols, and he was generous to them. It was possible, for a brief time, to believe in peace on earth.

Late in the evening of the twenty-third of December the daughters arrived, in a flurry of cases and kisses. The younger, Amanda, arrived home first. From its vantage point on the landing the Yattering viewed the young woman balefully. She didn't look like ideal material in which to induce a breakdown. In fact, she looked dangerous. Gina followed an hour or two later; a smoothly polished woman of the world at twenty-four, she looked every bit as intimidating as her sister. They came into the house with their bustle and their laughter; they rearranged the furniture; they threw out the junk food in the freezer; they told each other (and their father) how much they had missed each other's company. Within the space of a few hours the drab house was repainted with light, and fun and love.

It made the Yattering sick.

Whimpering, it hid its head in the bedroom to block out the din of affection, but the shock-waves enveloped it. All it could do was sit, and listen, and refine its revenge.

Jack was pleased to have his beauties home. Amanda so full of opinions, and so strong, like her mother. Gina more like *his* mother: poised, perceptive. He was so happy in their presence he could have wept; and here was he, the proud father, putting them both at such risk. But what was the alternative? If he had canceled the Christmas celebrations, it would have looked highly suspicious. It might even have spoiled his whole strategy, wakening the enemy to the trick that was being played.

No; he must sit tight. Play dumb, the way the enemy had come to expect him to be.

The time would come for action.

At 3:15 a.m. on Christmas morning the Yattering opened hostilities by throwing Amanda out of bed. A paltry performance at best, but it had the intended effect. Sleepily rubbing her bruised head, she climbed back into bed, only to have the bed buck and shake and fling her off again like an unbroken colt.

The noise woke the rest of the house. Gina was first in her sister's room.

"What's going on?"

"There's somebody under the bed."

"What?"

Gina picked up a paperweight from the dresser and demanded the assailant come out. The Yattering, invisible, sat on the windowseat and made obscene gestures at the women, tying knots in its genitalia.

Gina peered under the bed. The Yattering was clinging to the light fixture now, persuading it to swing backwards and forwards, making the room reel.

"There's nothing there—"

"There is."

Amanda knew. Oh yes, she knew.

"There's something here, Gina," she said. "Something in the room with us, I'm sure of it."

"No." Gina was absolute. "It's empty."

Amanda was searching behind the wardrobe when Polo came in.

"What's all the din?"

"There's something in the house, Daddy. I was thrown out of bed."

Jack looked at the crumpled sheets, the dislodged mattress, then at Amanda. This was the first test: he must lie as casually as possible.

"Looks like you've been having nightmares, beauty," he said, affecting an innocent smile.

"There was something under the bed," Amanda insisted.

"There's nobody here now."

"But I felt it."

"Well I'll check the rest of the house," he offered, without enthusiasm for the task. "You two stay here, just in case."

As Polo left the room, the Yattering rocked the light a little more.

"Subsidence," said Gina.

It was cold downstairs, and Polo could have done without padding around barefoot on the kitchen tiles, but he was quietly satisfied that the battle had been joined in such a petty manner. He'd half-feared that the enemy would turn savage with such tender victims at hand. But no: he'd judged the mind of the creature quite accurately. It was one of the lower orders. Powerful, but slow. Capable of being inveigled beyond the limits of its control. Carefully does it, he told himself, carefully does it.

He traipsed through the entire house, dutifully opening cupboards and peering behind the furniture, then returned to his daughters, who were sitting at the top of the stairs. Amanda looked small and pale, not the twenty-two-year-old woman she was, but a child again.

"Nothing doing," he told her with a smile. "It's Christmas morning and all through the house—"

Gina finished the rhyme.

"Nothing is stirring; not even a mouse."

"Not even a mouse, beauty."

At that moment the Yattering took its cue to fling a vase off the lounge mantelpiece.

Even Jack jumped.

"Shit," he said. He needed some sleep, but quite clearly the Yattering had no intention of letting them alone just yet.

"Che sera, sera," he murmured, scooping up the pieces of the Chinese vase, and putting them in a piece of newspaper. "The house is sinking a little on the left side, you know," he said more loudly. "It has been for years."

"Subsidence," said Amanda with quiet certainty, "would not throw me out of my bed."

Gina said nothing. The options were limited. The alternatives unattractive.

"Well maybe it was Santa Claus," said Polo, attempting levity. He parceled up the pieces of the vase and wandered through into the kitchen, certain that he was being shadowed every step of the way. "What else can it be?" He threw the question over his shoulder as he stuffed the newspaper into the wastebin. "The only other explanation—" here he became almost elated by his skimming so close to the truth, "the only other possible explanation is too preposterous for words."

It was an exquisite irony, denying the existence of the invisible world in the full knowledge that even now it breathed vengefully down his neck.

"You mean poltergeist?" said Gina.

"I mean anything that goes bang in the night. But, we're grown-up people aren't we? We don't believe in Bogeymen."

"No," said Gina flatly, "I don't, but I don't believe the house is subsiding either."

"Well, it'll have to do for now," said Jack with nonchalant finality. "Christmas starts here. We don't want to spoil it talking about gremlins, now, do we?"

They laughed together.

Gremlins. That surely bit deep. To call the Hellspawn a gremlin.

The Yattering, weak with frustration, acid tears boiling on its intangible cheeks, ground its teeth and kept its peace.

There would be time yet to beat that atheistic smile off Jack Polo's smooth, fat face. Time aplenty. No half-measures from now on. No subtlety. It would be an all out attack.

Let there be blood. Let there be agony.

They'd all break.

* * *

Amanda was in the kitchen, preparing Christmas dinner, when the Yattering mounted its next attack. Through the house drifted the sound of King's College Choir, "O Little Town of Bethlehem, how still we see thee lie . . ."

The presents had been opened, the G and T's were being downed, the house was one warm embrace from roof to cellar.

In the kitchen a sudden chill permeated the heat and the steam, making Amanda shiver; she crossed to the window, which was ajar to clear the air, and closed it. Maybe she was catching something.

The Yattering watched her back as she busied herself about the kitchen, enjoying the domesticity for a day. Amanda felt the stare quite clearly. She turned round. Nobody, nothing. She continued to wash the Brussels sprouts, cutting into one with a worm curled in the middle. She drowned it.

The Choir sang on.

In the lounge, Jack was laughing with Gina about something.

Then, a noise. A rattling at first, followed by a beating of somebody's fists against a door. Amanda dropped the knife into the bowl of sprouts, and turned from the sink, following the sound. It was getting louder all the time. Like something locked in one of the cupboards, desperate to escape. A cat caught in the box, or a—

Bird.

It was coming from the oven.

Amanda's stomach turned, as she began to imagine the worst. Had she locked something in the oven when she'd put in the turkey? She called for her father, as she snatched up the oven cloth and stepped towards the stove, which was rocking with the panic of its prisoner. She had visions of a basted cat leaping out at her, its fur burned off, its flesh half-cooked.

Jack was at the kitchen door.

"There's something in the oven," she said to him, as though he needed telling. The stove was in a frenzy; its thrashing contents had all but beaten off the door.

He took the oven cloth from her. This is a new one, he thought. You're better than I judged you to be. This is clever. This is original.

Gina was in the kitchen now.

"What's cooking?" she quipped.

But the joke was lost as the stove began to dance, and the pans of boiling water were twitched off the burners on to the floor. Scalding water seared Jack's leg. He yelled, stumbling back into Gina, before diving at the stove with a yell that wouldn't have shamed a Samurai.

The oven handle was slippery with heat and grease, but he seized it and flung the door down.

A wave of steam and blistering heat rolled out of the oven, smelling of succulent turkey-fat. But the bird inside had apparently no intentions of being eaten. It was flinging itself from side to side on the roasting tray, tossing gouts of gravy in all directions. Its crisp brown wings pitifully flailed and flapped, its legs beat a tattoo on the roof of the oven.

Then it seemed to sense the open door. Its wings stretched themselves out to either side of its stuffed bulk and it half hopped, half fell on to the oven door, in a mockery of its living self. Headless, oozing stuffing and onions, it flopped around as though nobody had told the damn thing it was dead, while the fat still bubbled on its bacon-strewn back.

Amanda screamed.

Jack dived for the door as the bird lurched into the air, blind but vengeful. What it intended to do once it reached its three cowering victims was never discovered. Gina dragged Amanda into the hallway with her father in hot pursuit, and the door was slammed closed as the blind bird flung itself against the paneling, beating on it with all its strength. Gravy seeped through the gap at the bottom of the door, dark and fatty.

The door had no lock, but Jack reasoned that the bird was not capable of turning the handle. As he backed away, breathless, he cursed his confidence. The opposition had more up its sleeve than he'd guessed.

Amanda was leaning against the wall sobbing, her face stained with splotches of turkey grease. All she seemed able to do was deny what she'd seen, shaking her head and repeating the word "no" like a talisman against the ridiculous horror that was still throwing itself against the door. Jack escorted her through to the lounge. The radio was still crooning carols which blotted out the din of the bird, but their promises of goodwill seemed small comfort.

Gina poured a hefty brandy for her sister and sat beside her on the sofa, plying her with spirits and reassurance in about equal measure. They made little impression on Amanda.

"What *was* that?" Gina asked her father, in a tone that demanded an answer.

"I don't know what it was," Jack replied.

"Mass hysteria?" Gina's displeasure was plain. Her father had a secret: he knew what was going on in the house, but he was refusing to cough up for some reason.

"What do I call: the police or an exorcist?"

"Neither."

"For God's sake—"

"There's *nothing* going on, Gina. Really."

Her father turned from the window and looked at her. His eyes spoke what his mouth refused to say, that this was war.

Jack was afraid.

The house was suddenly a prison. The game was suddenly lethal. The enemy, instead of playing foolish games, meant harm, real harm to them all.

In the kitchen the turkey had at last conceded defeat. The carols on the radio had withered into a sermon on God's benedictions.

What had been sweet was sour and dangerous. He looked across the room at Amanda and Gina. Both, for their own reasons, were trembling. Polo wanted to tell them, wanted to explain what was going on. But the thing must be there, he knew, gloating.

He was wrong. The Yattering had retired to the attic, well-satisfied with its endeavours. The bird, it felt, had been a stroke of genius. Now it could rest awhile: recuperate. Let the enemy's nerves tatter themselves in anticipation. Then, in its own good time, it would deliver the coup de grâce.

Idly, it wondered if any of the inspectors had seen his work with the turkey. Maybe they would be impressed enough by the Yattering's originality to improve its job prospects. Surely it hadn't gone through all those years of training simply to chase half-witted imbeciles like Polo. There must be something more challenging available than that. It felt victory in its invisible bones: and it was a good feeling.

The pursuit of Polo would surely gain momentum now. His daughters would convince him (if he wasn't now quite convinced) that there was something terrible afoot. He would crack. He would crumble. Maybe he'd go classically mad: tear out his hair, rip off his clothes; smear himself with his own excrement.

Oh yes, victory was close. And wouldn't his masters be loving then? Wouldn't it be showered with praise, and power?

One more manifestation was all that was required. One final, inspired intervention, and Polo would be so much blubbering flesh.

Tired, but confident, the Yattering descended into the lounge.

Amanda was lying full-length on the sofa, asleep. She was obviously dreaming about the turkey. Her eyes rolled beneath her gossamer lids, her lower lip trembled. Gina sat beside the radio, which was silenced now. She had a book open on her lap, but she wasn't reading it.

The gherkin importer wasn't in the room. Wasn't that his footstep on the stair? Yes, he was going upstairs to relieve his brandy-full bladder.

Ideal timing.

The Yattering crossed the room. In her sleep Amanda dreamt something dark flitting across her vision, something malign, something that tasted bitter in her mouth.

Gina looked up from her book.

The silver balls on the tree were rocking, gently. Not just the balls. The tinsel and the branches too.

In fact, the tree. The whole tree was rocking as though someone had just seized hold of it.

Gina had a very bad feeling about this. She stood up. The book slid to the floor.

The tree began to spin.

"Christ," she said. "Jesus Christ."

Amanda slept on.

The tree picked up momentum.

Gina walked as steadily as she could across to the sofa and tried to shake her sister awake. Amanda, locked in her dreams, resisted for a moment.

"Father," said Gina. Her voice was strong, and carried through into the hall, it also woke Amanda.

Downstairs, Polo heard a noise like a whining dog. No, like two whining dogs. As he ran down the stairs, the duet became a trio. He burst into the lounge half expecting all the hosts of Hell to be in there, dog-headed, dancing on his beauties.

But no. It was the Christmas tree that was whining, whining like a pack of dogs, as it spun and spun.

The lights had long since been pulled from their sockets. The air stank of singed plastic and pine-sap. The tree itself was spinning like a top, flinging decorations and presents off its tortured branches with the largesse of a mad king.

Jack tore his eyes from the spectacle of the tree and found Gina and Amanda crouching, terrified, behind the sofa.

"Get out of here," he yelled.

Even as he spoke, the television sat up impertinently on one leg and began to spin like the tree, gathering momentum quickly. The clock on the mantelpiece joined the pirouetting. The pokers beside the fire. The cushions. The ornaments. Each object added its own singular note to the orchestration of whines which were building up, second by second, to a deafening pitch. The air began to brim with the smell of burning wood, as friction heated the spinning tops to flashpoint. Smoke swirled across the room.

Gina had Amanda by the arm, and was dragging her towards the door, shielding her face against the hail of pine needles that the still-accelerating tree was throwing off.

Now the lights were spinning.

The books, having flung themselves off the shelves, had joined the tarantella.

Jack could see the enemy, in his mind's eye, racing between the objects like a juggler spinning plates on sticks, trying to keep them all moving at once. It must be exhausting work, he thought. The demon was probably close to collapse. It couldn't be thinking straight. Over-excited. Impulsive. Vulnerable. This must be the moment, if ever there was a moment, to join battle at last. To face the thing, defy it, and trap it.

For its part, the Yattering was enjoying this orgy of destruction. It flung every movable object into the fray, setting everything spinning.

It watched with satisfaction as the daughter twitched and scurried; it laughed to see the old man stare, pop-eyed, at this preposterous ballet.

Surely he was nearly mad, wasn't he?

The beauties had reached the door, their hair and skin full of needles. Polo didn't see them leave. He ran across the room, dodging a rain of ornaments to do so, and picked up a brass toasting fork which the enemy had overlooked. Bric-a-brac filled the air around his head, dancing around with sickening speed. His flesh was bruised and punctured. But the exhilaration of joining battle had overtaken him, and he set about beating the books, and the clocks, and the china to smithereens. Like a man in a cloud of locusts he ran around the room, bringing down his favorite books in a welter of fluttering pages, smashing whirling Dresden, shattering the lamps. A litter of broken possessions swamped the floor, some of it still twitching as the life went out of the fragments. But for every object brought low, there were a dozen still spinning, still whining.

He could hear Gina at the door, yelling to him to get out, to leave it alone.

But it was so enjoyable, playing against the enemy more directly than he'd ever allowed himself before. He didn't want to give up. He wanted the demon to show itself, to be known, to be recognized.

He wanted confrontation with the Old One's emissary once and for all.

Without warning the tree gave way to the dictates of centrifugal force, and exploded. The noise was like a howl of death. Branches, twigs, needles, balls, lights, wire, ribbons, flew across the room. Jack, his back to the explosion, felt a gust of energy hit him hard, and he was flung to the ground. The back of his neck and his scalp were shot full of pine-needles. A branch, naked of greenery, shot past his head and impaled the sofa. Fragments of tree pattered to the carpet around him.

Now other objects around the room, spun beyond the tolerance of their structures, were exploding like the tree. The television blew up, sending a lethal wave of glass across the room, much of which buried itself in the opposite wall. Fragments of the television's innards, so hot they singed the skin, fell on Jack, as he elbowed himself towards the door like a soldier under bombardment.

The room was so thick with a barrage of shards it was like a fog. The cushions had lent their down to the scene, snowing on the carpet. Porcelain pieces: a beautifully-glazed arm, a courtesan's head, bounced on the floor in front of his nose.

Gina was crouching at the door, urging him to hurry, her eyes narrowed against the hail. As Jack reached the door, and felt her arms around him, he swore he could hear laughter from the lounge. Tangible, audible laughter, rich and satisfied.

Amanda was standing in the hall, her hair full of pine-needles, staring down at him. He pulled his legs through the doorway and Gina slammed the door shut on the demolition.

"What is it?" she demanded. "Poltergeist? Ghost? Mother's ghost?"

The thought of his dead wife being responsible for such wholesale destruction struck Jack as funny.

Amanda was half smiling. Good, he thought, she's coming out of it. Then he met the vacant look in her eyes and the truth dawned. She'd broken, her sanity had taken refuge where this fantastique couldn't get at it.

"What's in there?" Gina was asking, her grip on his arm so strong it stopped the blood.

"I don't know," he lied. "Amanda?"

Amanda's smile didn't decay. She just stared on at him, through him.

"You do know."

"No."

"You're lying."

"I think . . ."

He picked himself off the floor, brushing the pieces of porcelain, the feathers, the glass, off his shirt and trousers.

"I think . . . I shall go for a walk."

Behind him, in the lounge, the last vestiges of whining had stopped. The air in the hallway was electric with unseen presences. It was very close to him, invisible as ever, but so close. This was the most dangerous time. He mustn't lose his nerve now. He must stand up as though nothing had happened; he must leave Amanda be, leave explanations and recriminations until it was all over and done with.

"Walk?" Gina said, disbelievingly.

"Yes . . . walk . . . I need some fresh air."

"You can't leave us here."

"I'll find somebody to help us clear up."

"But Mandy."

"She'll get over it. Leave her be."

That was hard. That was almost unforgivable. But it was said now.

He walked unsteadily towards the front door, feeling nauseous after so much spinning. At his back Gina was raging.

"You just can't leave! Are you out of your mind?"

"I need the air," he said, as casually as his thumping heart and his parched throat would permit. "So I'll just go out for a moment."

No, the Yattering said. No, no, no.

It was behind him, Polo could feel it. So angry now, so ready to twist off his head. Except that it wasn't allowed, *ever*, to touch him. But he could feel its resentment like a physical presence.

He took another step towards the front door.

It was with him still, dogging his every step. His shadow, his fetch; unshakable. Gina shrieked at him, "You sonofabitch, look at Mandy! She's lost her mind!"

No, he mustn't look at Mandy. If he looked at Mandy he might weep, he might break down as the thing wanted him to, then everything would be lost.

"She'll be all right," he said, barely above a whisper.

He reached for the front door handle. The demon bolted the door, quickly, loudly. No temper left for pretense now.

Jack, keeping his movements as even as possible, unbolted the door, top and bottom. It bolted again.

It was thrilling, this game; it was also terrifying. If he pushed too far surely the demon's frustration would override its lessons?

Gently, smoothly, he unbolted the door again. Just as gently, just as smoothly, the Yattering bolted it.

Jack wondered how long he could keep this up for. Somehow he had to get outside: he had to coax it over the threshold. One step was all that the law required, according to his researches. One simple step.

Unbolted. Bolted. Unbolted. Bolted.

Gina was standing two or three yards behind her father. She didn't understand what she was seeing, but it was obvious her father was doing battle with someone, or something.

"Daddy—" she began.

"Shut up," he said benignly, grinning as he unbolted the door for the seventh time. There was a shiver of lunacy in the grin, it was too wide and too easy.

Inexplicably, she returned the smile. It was grim, but genuine. Whatever was at issue here, she loved him.

Polo made a break for the back door. The demon was three paces ahead of him, scooting through the house like a sprinter, and bolting the door before Jack could even reach the handle. The key was turned in the lock by invisible hands, then crushed to dust in the air.

Jack feigned a move towards the window beside the back door but the blinds were pulled down and the shutters slammed. The Yattering, too concerned with the window to watch Jack closely, missed his doubling back through the house.

When it saw the trick that was being played it let out a little screech, and gave chase, almost sliding into Jack on the smoothly polished floor. It avoided the collision only by the most balletic of maneuvers. That would be fatal indeed: to touch the man in the heat of the moment.

Polo was again at the front door and Gina, wise to her father's strategy, had unbolted it while the Yattering and Jack fought at the back door. Jack had prayed she'd take the opportunity to open it. She had. It stood slightly ajar: the icy air of the crisp afternoon curled its way into the hallway.

Jack covered the last yards to the door in a flash, feeling without hearing the howl of complaint the Yattering loosed as it saw its victim escaping into the outside world.

It was not an ambitious creature. All it wanted at that moment, beyond any other dream, was to take this human's skull between its palms and make a nonsense of it. Crush it to smithereens, and pour the hot thought out on to the snow. To be done with Jack J. Polo, forever and forever.

Was that so much to ask?

Polo had stepped into the squeaky-fresh snow, his slippers and trouser-bottoms buried in chill. By the time the fury reached the step Jack was already three or four yards away, marching up the path towards the gate. Escaping. Escaping.

The Yattering howled again, forgetting its years of training. Every lesson it had learned, every rule of battle engraved on its skull was submerged by the simple desire to have Polo's life.

It stepped over the threshold and gave chase. It was an unpardonable transgression. Somewhere in Hell, the powers (long may they hold court; long may they shit light on the heads of the damned) felt the sin, and knew the war for Jack Polo's soul was lost.

Jack felt it too. He heard the sound of boiling water, as the demon's footsteps melted to steam the snow on the path. It was coming after him! The thing had broken the first rule of its existence. It was forfeit. He felt the victory in his spine, and his stomach.

The demon overtook him at the gate. Its breath could clearly be seen in the air, though the body it emanated from had not yet become visible.

Jack tried to open the gate, but the Yattering slammed it shut.

"*Che sera, sera,*" said Jack.

The Yattering could bear it no longer. He took Jack's head in his hands, intending to crush the fragile bone to dust.

The touch was its second sin, and it agonized the Yattering beyond endurance. It bayed like a banshee and reeled away from the contact, sliding in the snow and falling on its back.

It knew its mistake. The lessons it had beaten into it came hurtling back. It knew the punishment too, for leaving the house, for touching the man. It was bound to a new lord, enslaved to this idiot-creature standing over it.

Polo had won.

He was laughing, watching the way the outline of the demon formed in the snow on the path. Like a photograph developing on a sheet of paper, the image of the fury came clear. The law was taking its toll. The Yattering could never hide from its master again. There it was, plain to Polo's eyes, in all its charmless glory. Maroon flesh and bright lidless eye, arms flailing, tail thrashing the snow to slush.

"You bastard," it said. Its accent had an Australian lilt.

"You will not speak unless spoken to," said Polo, with quiet, but absolute, authority. "Understood?"

The lidless eye clouded with humility.

"Yes," the Yattering said.

"Yes, Mister Polo."

"Yes, Mister Polo."

Its tail slipped between its legs like that of a whipped dog.

"You may stand."

"Thank you, Mr. Polo."

It stood. Not a pleasant sight, but one Jack rejoiced in nevertheless.

"They'll have you yet," said the Yattering.

"Who will?"

"You know," it said, hesitantly.

"Name them."

"Beelzebub," it answered, proud to name its old master. "The powers. Hell itself."

"I don't think so," Polo mused. "Not with you bound to me as proof of my skills. Aren't I the better of them?"

The eye looked sullen.

"Aren't I?"

"Yes," it conceded bitterly. "Yes. You are the better of them."

It had begun to shiver.

"Are you cold?" asked Polo.

It nodded, affecting the look of a lost child.

"Then you need some exercise," he said. "You'd better go back into the house and start tidying up."

The fury looked bewildered, even disappointed, by this instruction.

"Nothing more?" it asked incredulously. "No miracles? No Helen of Troy? No flying?"

The thought of flying on a snow-spattered afternoon like this left Polo cold. He was essentially a man of simple tastes: all he asked for in life was the love of his children, a pleasant home, and a good trading price for gherkins.

"No flying," he said.

As the Yattering slouched down the path towards the door it seemed to alight upon a new piece of mischief. It turned back to Polo, obsequious, but unmistakably smug.

"Could I just say something?" it said.

"Speak."

"It's only fair that I inform you that it's considered ungodly to have any contact with the likes of me. Heretical even."

"Is that so?"

"Oh yes," said the Yattering, warming to its prophecy. "People have been burned for less."

"Not in this day and age," Polo replied.

"But the Seraphim will see," it said. "And that means you'll never go to that place."

"What place?"

The Yattering fumbled for the special word it had heard Beelzebub use.

"Heaven," it said triumphant. An ugly grin had come on to its face; this was the cleverest maneuver it had ever attempted; it was juggling theology here.

Jack nodded slowly, nibbling at his bottom lip.

The creature was probably telling the truth: association with it or its like would not be looked upon benignly by the Host of Saints and Angels. He probably *was* forbidden access to the plains of paradise.

"Well," he said, "You know what I have to say about that, don't you?"

The Yattering stared at him frowning. No, it didn't know. Then the grin of satisfaction it had been wearing died, as it saw just what Polo was driving at.

"What do I say?" Polo asked it.

Defeated, the Yattering murmured the phrase.

"Che sera, sera."

Polo smiled. "There's a chance for you yet," he said, and led the way over the threshold, closing the door with something very like serenity on his face.

Icicle Music

Michael Bishop

Chimes on the roof, like icicles being struck in sequence by a small silver mallet.

Wind whistled away the icicle shards, hurled them back together somewhere above Danny's bedroom, turned their disconcerting chimes into a hair-raising electronic drone, then boomed so fiercely over cottonwood grove and nearby river that he had to suppose he'd only imagined the eerie icicle music.

Or had he? It was Christmas Eve, 1957 (to be exact, very early Christmas morning), and maybe those unearthly chimes were coming from another Soviet space shot, a beep-beep-beeping *Sputnik* passing over Van Luna, polluting Kansas's atmosphere with Commie radiation and a sanity-sabotaging barrage of high-frequency sound pulses. Who could say?

Danny got up. Careful not to rouse his mother (who ordinarily commuted thirty-plus miles, round-trip, to her job in personnel at McConnell Air Force Base in Wichita), he crept barefoot into the boxy little house's living room. He let the Christmas tree in the corner—light strings unplugged, foil tinsel agleam, fragile glass ornaments minutely rotating—emerge from the gloom.

Had Santa come yet? *Ha!* Danny wasn't misled. He was twelve, had been for more than a month. And even if he hadn't just had his birthday, he hadn't believed in Santa for three or four years. And he hadn't really bought Jolly Saint Nick's year-end gift-giving since the year Esther Jane Onions let him take her bubble gum in a "kiss exchange"—a double-dare-you bet with Freddie DeVore—in the bushes behind the grain elevator off Depot Street.

Danny'd been, yeah, nine that year. The kiss exchange—Esther Jane's breath smelling just like her last name—had made him feel really funny. He would never do *that* again. It had destroyed his faith in Freddie DeVore's friendship, the inevitability of girls, and, in fact, the reliability of nearly everyone. (Even Ike, with that famous grin of his, for which his folks had voted in '56, was probably a cheat in some ways, fudging golf scores and "forgetting" to report on his taxes all the money he'd won.) Anyway, E.J.'s breath, Freddie's refusal to ante up the agreed-upon Eddie Yost baseball card, Ike's secret sins, and three more disappointing years had forever numbed the kid in him.

Nine Ten. Eleven.

And—*wham!*—he was illusion-free, a twelve-year-old dreaming of his driver's license, his first legal beer, and the full assumption of Daddy Pitts's role as head of household and chief provider. The rotten skid-out. In fact, Danny hoped his dad was in jail somewhere this Christmas, or in a cardboard box over a steam grate in K.C. or Topeka, or even—sucks to him, anyhow—in a wooden one under a pile of gooey black Kansas dirt. It'd serve the bum right.

Actually, "Santa"—Milly, Danny's mom—had already come. His main present, unwrapped, lay on the green flannel tree skirt under the scrawny pine he'd chopped down on Mr. Arno's place. It glinted there like the sword of a medieval Turk.

It was the shotgun he'd begged for, a gas-operated "automatic" 12-gauge, the kind that absorbed some of its recoil instead of kicking back like a colicky mule. Even in the darkness, Danny could tell that it was beautiful. His mom must have set aside ten—no, *fifteen*—bucks a month for the better part of this past year to buy it for him. He approached the tree, lifted and cradled the gun, and let his fingers roam it from red velvet-edged butt plate to the evil-looking shark-fin notch of its front head, dumbstruck by the deadly power in his arms.

Two small packages, wrapped, lay beside the shotgun, and Danny guessed that they contained shells. Kneeling and hefting one of these boxes, he confirmed his guess. Now he could go dove hunting with Brad Selley. Not *now*, of course—but in the morning, after he and Mom had had their Christmas together.

His immediate problem was that morning, even if Mom got up at six or so, was still a good four hours away. The wall clock in the kitchen (designed to resemble the pilot's wheel on an old-fashioned clipper ship) said so. Figuring himself safe for a time, Danny sat down Buddha style, the shotgun in his lap, and meticulously removed the slick red paper from one of the boxes of shells. Then, holding his breath, he loaded the gun, aimed it at the cockeyed angel atop the tree, faked pulling the trigger, and faked, too, the 12-gauge's rumbling discharge: Ka-SHOOOOOOOM! An imaginary explosion sloshed back and forth in his mouth and throat.

Then, upon lowering the shotgun, Danny heard the wind die. He heard a faint, panicky pawing overhead and the same dreamy icicle music that had called him from sleep. Dad had built their place near Van Luna's riverside dump, on a muddy patch of land inherited from Mom's grandparents. It was two miles from the city limits, a mile from their nearest neighbors, and the boy began to wonder if a crook—or a couple of crooks, a whole *army* of them—had cased their house, decided it was an easy hit, and showed up tonight (Christmas morning) to break in, hag up all their silverware and presents, and then skedaddle, booty-laden, into Arkansas or Oklahoma.

Danny, holding the 12-gauge, got up and backed away to the door of his own bedroom. The popping icicle music continued, as did the agitated scrabbling on the rooftop shingles. Then both the chimes and the pawing ceased, and there was only a hushed curling of wind—and Danny's heartbeat, like acorns falling into a rusted gasoline drum—to suggest that God had ever created sound waves or that the universe had ever before experienced them.

The living room had a fireplace. Dad had built it (lopsidedly, Mom accused, and the catawampus fireplace supported this gripe) of river stones and second-rate mortar. He'd put in no damper. When it rained, huge drops whistled down the flue, hit the inner hearth, and splattered the living room rug with inky soot. Disgusted, Mom had stopped trying to use it. In fact, she'd stuffed the throat of the chimney with wadded-up sheets of the *Wichita Beacon* to keep the oily rain from further staining the hearth rug.

Now, to Danny's dismay, the crinkled ball of newspaper fell out of the chimney into the firebox. A second sheet cascaded down, and a third, and a fourth.

Then a pair of booted feet appeared in the firebox, dangling down uncertainly, both boots as worn as harness leather. *Whumpf!* The boots crashed through the crumpled newspaper to the hearth. A pair of skinny legs in mud-fouled khaki materialized in the shadows above them. With a grunt and a muttered curse, a man in a heavy red-plaid coat kicked away the papers, ducked out of the firebox, and hobbled over to the tree, carrying what looked like a grungy World War II duffel bag.

Santa Claus? wondered Danny. Father Christmas? Kriss Kringle? Saint Nick? Or just a chimney-shinnying thief?

The man's duffel *looked* empty. It hung down his back like a collapsed parachute. His greasy white hair squeezed out from under the roll of his red woolen sailor's cap to tickle the frayed collar of his jacket. In spite of the darkness, Danny could see the man clearly, as if his unexpected arrival had triggered an explosion of ghostly amber light.

Then, turning, the intruder looked straight at him.

Danny ducked out of sight. A moment later, though, he peered back around and saw that Klepto Kriss Kringle had a pale, stubbly beard and a pair of bleak, ever-moving eyes.

What if he weren't just a thief? What if he were a rapist or a murderer? What if he had his sights on the shotgun now in Danny's arms? Assuming, as seemed likely, that he'd staked out their house and watched Mom bring it home. . . .

Danny (Danny told himself), you've waited too long. You should *do* something. You've got the draw on him, don't you? Why are you being so wishy-washy?

"Hold it, mister!" Danny said, stepping out of the doorway and leveling the twin barrels of his shotgun on the intruder. Santa—no, the lousy burglar—twisted an ornament off the tree and hurled it all the way across the room. It struck the lintel over Danny's head, showering pieces of feathery, mirror plastic. A flashing, quicksilver rain of tiny knives.

Ducking, Danny thumbed the safety off and shot. The blast spat flames, a burst of orange and blue that knocked Danny backward into his bedroom.

Klepto Kriss howled.

The Christmas tree toppled, like a bombed pagoda bringing down all the bamboo chimes, hammered-tin animals, and folded-up paper fish hanging from its dozens of eaves. The noise was *loud.* The entire house shook. Had there been an earthquake?

Golly, Danny thought, struggling to his feet. My shotgun's a gas-powered job. It's not supposed to kick.

"Danny!" his mother shouted from her own bedroom. *"Danny, hon, are you all right?"* She sounded panicked, downright rattled. For a moment, Danny regretted squeezing off a pellet pattern in reply to a desperately flung Christmas tree ornament. But all he'd done was issue a command—a reasonable command, given the circumstances—and Klepto had tried to take his head off. If the 12-gauge had been in the other guy's hands, Danny knew, *he'd* be dead now. Gut-shot by a stinking burglar on Jesus's birthday.

He met his mom outside their bedroom doors, which were across the hall from each other. At first, Klepto seemed not to be there any longer, as if he'd simply vanished, but then Mom saw a rotting boot dangling down from the throat of the chimney. *"What's that?"* She grabbed Danny's shotgun, rushed to the tree, kicked its fallen branches aside, found a box of shells, expertly loaded the shotgun, and ran to the fireplace.

Danny was already there, reaching repeatedly for the toe of the visible boot, as if it were the persnickety beak of a cottonmouth. Each time he grabbed for it, it struck back. So Danny reached and pulled away, reached and pulled away.

Who wanted to get booted in the kisser? And why (now that he thought of it) had Mom taken his shotgun? He had more right to it than she did. After all, blood dripping into the wadded-up pages of the *Beacon* proved that he'd hit his target.

Then the boot withdrew, a storm of soot whirled from the smoke chamber above the missing damper, and both he and Mom were fitfully coughing, waving their hands and colliding with each other in their attempts to back away.

When the soot storm subsided, Mom knelt and pointed the barrels of Danny's shotgun up the angled flue.

"Come down here, you snake! Who do you think you are, stealing our Christmas?"

The burglar's soot-dislodging climb went on.

Mom, fiery-eyed, shouted, "Come down or I'll shoot!"

"Don't do it," Danny warned her. "You'll hit him in the butt, maybe, but most of the pellets'll come back on us."

That was good enough for Mom. Flicking on a light as she ran, she headed through the kitchen to the back door. Danny followed, still aching to get the shotgun back, but no longer conscious of the biting cold. Mom hit the porch light, ran down the steps into the yard, gimped barefoot over the brown grass to a spot from which she and Danny could see the black jut of the chimney, and reached out a hand to halt Danny beside her.

Danny gaped.

No moon sailed the indigo velvet of the Sedgwick County sky, but every star visible from the Northern Hemisphere had winked into being up there. He was dazzled. It was hard to make out if the smear on the roof—the bundled silhouette of the man he'd shot—was a living thing or merely a phantom of starlight, wind, and jittery shadows. Danny saw this figure hoist itself out of their chimney, stumble over a lofty plain of shingles, and fall atop a four-legged shape with a white flag for a tail and two black branches of horn for headgear.

Unless he was imagining things, there was a *deer* on their roof, a buck with twelve to fifteen points. The guy who'd tried to steal their Christmas was mounting the jumpy creature. He encouraged it—*"Up, Blitzen, up!"*—to fly him to safety over both the riverside dump and the rooftops of their sleeping town.

"Stop!" Mom shouted. "Stop or I'll shoot!" She sounded just like a sheriff on a TV cowboy show.

"No, Milly!" the man on the roof pleaded. "Don't!"

"Clifton?" Mom murmured. Then, louder: *"Clifton?"*

The compact little buck (a courser, Danny thought, like in "The Night Before Christmas," which Mrs. French had read them on the day before their holidays) soared up from the house. It lifted like a dream creature, pawing the night air and defining both itself and its desperate, neck-clutching rider against a blowing purple scrim of stars. All Danny could do was marvel. There should have been seven other reindeer (if the words of that silly poem counted for anything), but one was about all Danny could handle.

The deer—the courser—drew an invisible circle over their backyard. Mom and he looked up to see its glinting hooves and white belly. Then the thief sprawled across the deer took a shiny ball from the pocket of his coat and nearly unseated himself sidearming it with all his wounded strength at Mom and him.

"Here's something for you, Milly!" And the stolen ornament—a second one, Danny realized—shattered on Mom's forehead.

"Ouch!"

"Merry Christmas to both you and the brat, bitch! And to all a good ni—"

Mom brushed fragments from her hair, raised the shotgun, took aim at the departing courser, and fired. Rider and mount received the ripping impact of the pellets. A cry from the man. A brief, anguished bleating from the reindeer.

The man fell headlong into the yard. The animal veered toward the dump, legs flailing, but crashed onto the barbed-wire fence Mom had put up to keep rabbits and stray dogs out of their vegetable garden. Its body crumpled the rusty strands of the fence, slicing itself open on the barbs.

Meanwhile, Mom fought painfully up from the frozen earth. (The 12-gauge's recoil had thrown her down.) She thrust the weapon into Danny's hands and ran to the shotgunned intruder. Danny ran to see whatever he could see. The man—the would-be reindeer pilot—was dead, his neck broken and his head tilted away from his coat as if it wanted nothing to do with the hobo corpse to which it still so obviously belonged.

"Clifton," Mom said. "You stupid fool."

At his mother's direction, Danny hauled the deer off the fence, gutted it, and spent the remainder of that unending Christmas dawn rendering the deer on the back porch. They could use the venison, Mom said, and if 1958 wasn't any better than 1957 had been, they'd need a *lot* of it.

Meanwhile, Mom dragged the dead man into the dump; planted him in the cottony guts of a hide-a-bed sofa; wrestled the sofa into a mountain of ancient tires, mushy cardboard boxes, splintered orange crates, and broken tool handles; doused the heap with lighter fluid from her Ronco and a gallon of gasoline siphoned from her pink-and-charcoal Rambler station wagon; and threw a burning Winston into all that jumbled trash to light it.

The pyre burned all night, a surrealistic flickering that Danny could see through the screened-in porch on which he was processing the carcass of the flying deer. Later Mom helped him wrap all the different cuts of meat in smooth butcher paper—steaks, roasts, spare ribs, reindeer burgers. Then they washed their hands, limped into the living room, and sat down cross-legged next to the toppled tree to hunt for their presents.

"Was that Dad?" Danny said, avoiding Mom's eyes.

"Yeah."

"It didn't look like him."

"He'd changed a lot."

"Why?"

"I don't know. You'd have to ask him. Which, I guess, isn't possible anymore."

"He called that deer Blitzen. It flew."

"Yeah, well, Papa didn't always tell the truth." Mom dug the boy's only gift to her out from under the waterfall of tinsel, "Ah, this is great. How did you know I wanted a handmade ashtray? The way the colors swirl together—pretty."

"Thanks," said Danny, rubbing his shoulder.

"I'll exchange the gun for one with less kick. You've got my word on it. Please don't let it ruin your Christmas."

Mom leaned over and kissed Danny on the nose.

Then she handed him his other presents: a complete set of the plays of William Shakespeare, and a book of poetry by somebody Mom called William Butler Yeats. Danny didn't think he'd get to them very soon.

* * *

"I am—I mean, I *was*—the boy in that story," Danny Pitts told Philip, the worried young man sitting next to his bed in a hospital room in Denver. The blinds on the only window had been hoisted; the icicles on the exterior cornice hung down like the barrels of a glass-blower's panpipe.

"You don't mean me to take it as true, do you?" said Philip.

Once upon a time Daniel had known Philip's surname. Tonight—Christmas Eve, 1987—he couldn't recall it. His memory did better with events of a decade, two decades, even thirty-plus years ago. Ancient history.

"Why not?" There were tubes in Daniel's nose. The plastic bag of an IV drip hung over him like a disembodied lung.

"Your mother killed an intruder, then burned his corpse in the Van Luna dump?"

"Yes."

"O.K., Daniel, if you say so. What about 'Blitzen'?"

"See Moore, Clement Clarke. *I* didn't name the creature."

"The creature's name's a red herring." Philip grimaced. "What about its reality?"

"Specious, I guess. At least as a courser. Mom probably shot my dad as he was flying into the cottonwoods. She bagged the poor deer purely by accident."

"There *was* a deer?"

"I rendered it. I used a hacksaw, a hammer, a dozen different knives. We had venison for months."

"Not a talent we'd've ever attributed to you, Daniel." Philip meant the actors and aspiring playwrights in the theater projects that Daniel raised money for and directed.

"Meat processing?" Daniel said.

Philip gave him a faint smile. "Your mother wasn't prosecuted for the slaying?"

"It was self-defense. Or property defense, call it. Besides, no one ever found out."

"Your dad's bones are still out there in the dump?"

"I guess. But even if his bones are still there, his surviving aura isn't. Not always, anyway."

Philip wanted an explanation. Or *pretended* to want one. He was trying to be kind. Daniel was grateful. At this crucial pass, he thought it important to narrate the fallout of what had happened on that long-ago Christmas morning.

"My father—his ghost, anyway—appeared to me ten years later. To the day, Christmas 1967."

"In Van Luna?"

"No. I left there after graduating high school. I vowed never to go back, Philip. A vow I've kept."

"So where were you?"

"Cross-country skiing over a meadow of snow- and ice-laden trees in the northwestern corner of Yellowstone Park. A scene out of *The Empire Strikes Back,* Philip. Unearthly. Alien. Some of the trees had gusted together, and then frozen, in architectures of special-effect weirdness. The sky looked nickel-plated, but with a light behind it like thousands of smeared-out coals.

"And your dad—the ghost?"

"Hold on, O.K.?" Daniel opened his eyes as fully as he could, given all the plastic tubing. "I had a hemispherical tent. On Christmas Eve, I pitched it near a fountain of spruces. I snuggled deep into my sleeping bag. I listened to the crazy-lady arias of the wind. A super feeling. Peaceful. Exhilarating."

"Yeah. Alone on Christmas. Thirty-five below."

Toward morning, before dawn, icicle music woke me. (If you've never heard it, I can't explain it.) A guy in a red-plaid coat was quivering like geyser steam outside my tent."

"Klepto Kriss?"

"A.k.a. Clifton Pitts. He—it—sort of modulated in and out of existence with the moaning of the wind. Then he retreated, backing away toward the mountains. I had to throw on my coat and boots and go after him."

"Just what I do when I see a ghost: I chase it."

Daniel, taking his time now, breathing as if invisible crystals of ice had interthreaded the air, told Philip (who, he remembered, almost always ran lights for him) that his pursuit of his father's aura had been successful: he had caught up with it.

The ghost had questioned him, wondering why Daniel was alone on Christmas Day, what he'd done with his life, and how, at his young age, he'd escaped taking up an M-16 in the war against the Reds in Southeast Asia. A Pitts—a strapping kid like Danny—should have volunteered.

"Did you tell him how you'd 'escaped'?" Philip asked.

"I told him. And he—it—retreated, fading away into the wind so that I wasn't able to follow it any longer. A bit later, after eating, I began to think I'd hallucinated the wraith's visit. The cold, the high, thin air. It wasn't unlikely, the possibility my mind had played tricks."

"Sounds good to me. Better than a visitation."

"Except—"

"Yeah?"

"Right after thinking I'd hallucinated my dad's visit, I looked around and saw my sleeping bag was gone. My father—his ghost—had taken it."

"An animal dragged it off, Daniel. Some other outdoorsy dude stole it while you were chasing your mirage."

"No. There'd've been signs. Tracks. Footprints. Something. And I hadn't been gone that long."

"What would a ghost want with your sleeping bag?"

"To kill me, Philip. As soon as I recollected that it had come on an anniversary—the tenth anniversary of Clifton Pitts's death—I knew why it had come. An eye for an eye, a tooth for a tooth. On Jesus's birthday."

"A sleeping bag?"

"Not just that. As soon as I'd realized what was happening, my tent blew away. It flipped back, beat against the trees, whirled off into the clouds. I was miles from the nearest town. Without my tent or sleeping bag, I was screwed."

"But you got out O.K."

"I followed some elk tracks to a hay bale left out for them by a tender-hearted rancher. Pure luck."

"But you did get out."

"No thanks to Papa Pitts."

"Who's haunted you every Christmas?"

"No. Only on ten-year anniversaries of that reindeer shoot in Van Luna."

Philip cocked his head. "What happened last time?"

"In '77 he materialized in an intensive care unit in Wichita. On which occasion he stole my mother."

"You saw it?"

"It began with icicle music—this time, though, from a hospital cart turning over in a hall. Test tubes shattering." Daniel shut his eyes. "Festively."

"You'd returned to Kansas to be at your mom's bedside?"

"Yes. Dad showed too. It annoyed him, how well I was doing. Healthy-hedonistic, looking contented. Mom's lung cancer was a nice counter-balance for him—proof that the woman who'd killed him wasn't immortal. And that her son—*his* son as well—might also be vulnerable. In fact, after taking Mom's soul, he assured me that my heyday was over. *Our* heyday."

Daniel remembered that he had received this news while staring perplexedly at his mother's waxen face. Then the ghost (an unseen mirage to all the medical folk traipsing in and out) had begun to fade, Milly's soul—the ghost had kissed her—fading with it. How did it feel to be swallowed by a mirage?

"He told you that?" Philip said. " 'Our heyday is over'?"

Daniel blinked a yes.

"How do you suppose he knew?"

"Who can say? Maybe he guessed. Or maybe it was just redneck spleen. A cartoon of 'Rudolph the Red-Nosed Reindeer' on a TV in a seventh-floor waiting room rubbed him wrong; he wasn't happy about the way the war'd turned out; he didn't like the peanut farmer in Washington. Grievances, grievances."

Philip got up, walked around the sick man's bed to the window.

He seemed agitated. "This is another ten-year anniversary. To the day, Daniel. He's due again."

"Right. Maybe you'd better split, Philip."

"I'll drop in tomorrow. With Mario and Trent."

"Gary," Daniel said. "I want Gary to drop in."

"Gary was a sweet man, Daniel. But he's gone. We can't recall him to us. You know that."

"I know that."

"Hang on, O.K.? Just hang on." Philip leaned down, touched his lips to Daniel's brow, and murmured, "Goodbye." Then, finally, finally, he exited.

The radio at the nurses' station down the hall was broadcasting carols. An intern and a candy striper were dancing together just outside Daniel's room. Someone at the other end of the floor blew a raspberry on a noise-maker. The intern peeked in, sporting a cap with plastic reindeer antlers. Daniel waved feebly to let him know his getup was amusing. Satisfied, the intern backed out.

Fa-la-la-la-*la*, la-la-la-*la*.

* * *

Outside Daniel's window, faint icicle music. The glassblower's panpipe hanging from the cornice had begun to melt, releasing long-pent melodies.

"Come on," Daniel murmured. "Come on."

He couldn't wait. He wanted his father's bitter ghost to get a move on. If it materialized in the room and stole his soul, that would be a welcome violation: a theft and a benediction, the first Christmas present his daddy had given him in over thirty years.

Come quickly, Father. Come.

Miracle

Connie Willis

There was a Christmas tree in the lobby when Lauren got to work, and the receptionist was sitting with her chin in her hand, watching the security monitor. Lauren set her shopping bag down and looked curiously at the screen. On it, Jimmy Stewart was dancing the Charleston with Donna Reed.

"The Personnel Morale Special Committee had cable piped in for Christmas," the receptionist explained, handing Lauren her messages. "I love *It's a Wonderful Life,* don't you?"

Lauren stuck her messages in the top of her shopping bag and went up to her department. Red and green crepe paper hung in streamers from the ceiling, and there was a big red crepe paper bow tied around Lauren's desk.

"The Personnel Morale Special Committee did it," Cassie said, coming over with the catalog she'd been reading. "They're decorating the whole building, and they want us and Document Control to go caroling this afternoon. Don't you think PMS is getting out of hand with this Christmas spirit thing? I mean, who wants to spend Christmas Eve at an office party?"

"I do," Lauren said. She set her shopping bag down on the desk, sat down, and began taking off her boots.

"Can I borrow your stapler?" Cassie asked. "I've lost mine again. I'm ordering my mother the Water of the Month, and I need to staple my check to the order form."

"The water of the month?" Lauren said, opening her desk drawer and taking out her stapler.

"You know, they send you bottles of a different one every month. Perrier, Evian, Calistoga." She peered in Lauren's shopping bag. "Do you have Christmas presents in there? I hate people who have their shopping done four weeks before Christmas."

"It's four *days* till Christmas," Lauren said, "and I don't have it all done. I still don't have anything for my sister. But I've got all my friends, including you, done." She reached in the shopping bag and pulled out her pumps. *"And* I found a dress for the office party."

"Did you buy it?"

"No." She put on one of her shoes. "I'm going to try it on during my lunch hour."

"If it's still there," Cassie said gloomily. "I had this echidna toothpick holder all picked out for my brother, and when I went back to buy it, they were all gone."

"I asked them to hold the dress for me," Lauren said. She put on her other shoe. "It's gorgeous. Black off-the-shoulder. Sequined."

"Still trying to get Scott Buckley to notice you, huh? I don't do things like that anymore. Nineties women don't use sexist tricks to attract men. Besides, I decided he was too cute to ever notice somebody like me." She sat down on the edge of Lauren's desk and started leafing through the catalog. "Here's something your sister might like. The Vegetable of the Month. February's okra."

"She lives in Southern California," Lauren said, shoving her boots under the desk.

"Oh. How about the Sunscreen of the Month?"

"No," Lauren said. "She's into New Age stuff. Channeling and stuff. Last year she sent me a crystal pyramid mate selector for Christmas."

"The Eastern philosophy of the month," Cassie said, "Zen, sufism, tai chi—"

"I'd like to get her something she'd really like," Lauren mused. "I always have a terrible time figuring out what to get people for Christmas. So this year, I decided things were going to be different. I wasn't going to be tearing around the mall the day before Christmas, buying things no one would want and wondering what on earth I was going to wear to the office party. I started doing my shopping in September, I wrapped my presents as soon as I bought them, I have all my Christmas cards done and ready to mail—"

"You're disgusting," Cassie said. "Oh, here, I almost forgot." She pulled a folded slip of paper out of her catalog and handed it to Lauren. "It's your name for the Secret Santa gift exchange. PMS says you're supposed to bring your present for it by Friday so it won't interfere with the presents Santa Claus hands out at the office party."

Lauren unfolded the paper, and Cassie leaned over to read it. "Who'd you get? Wait, don't tell me. Scott Buckley."

"No, Fred Hatch. And I know just what to get him."

"Fred? The fat guy in Documentation? What is it, the Diet of the Month?"

"This is supposed to be the season of love and charity, not the season when you make mean remarks about someone just because he's overweight," Lauren said sternly. "I'm going to get him a videotape of *Miracle on 34th Street.*"

Cassie looked uncomprehending.

"It's Fred's favorite movie. We had a wonderful talk about it at the office party last year."

"I never heard of it."

"It's about Macy's Santa Claus. He starts telling people they can get their kids toys cheaper at Gimbel's, and then the store psychiatrist decides he's crazy—"

"Why don't you get him *It's a Wonderful Life*? That's *my* favorite Christmas movie."

"Yours and everybody else's. I think Fred and I are the only two people in the world who like *Miracle on 34th Street* better. See, Edmund Gwenn, he's Santa Claus, gets committed to Bellevue because he thinks he's Santa Claus, and since there isn't any Santa Claus, he has to be crazy, but he *is* Santa Claus and Fred Gailey, that's John Payne, he's a lawyer in the movie, he decides to have a court hearing to prove it, and—"

"I watch *It's a Wonderful Life* every Christmas. I love the part where Jimmy Stewart and Donna Reed fall into the swimming pool," Cassie said. "What happened to the stapler?"

* * *

They had the dress and it fit, but there was an enormous jam-up at the cash register, and then they couldn't find a hanging bag for it.

"Just put it in a shopping bag," Lauren said, looking anxiously at her watch.

"It'll wrinkle," the clerk said ominously and continued to search for a hanging bag. By the time Lauren convinced her a shopping bag would work, it was already twelve-fifteen. She had hoped she'd have time to look for a present for her sister, but there wasn't going to be time. She still had to run the dress home and mail the Christmas cards.

I can pick up Fred's video, she thought, fighting her way onto the escalator. That wouldn't take much time since she knew what she wanted, and maybe they'd have something with Shirley Maclaine in it she could get her sister. Ten minutes to buy the video, she thought, tops.

It took her nearly half an hour. There was only one copy, which the clerk couldn't find.

"Are you sure you wouldn't rather have *It's a Wonderful Life*?" she asked Lauren. "It's my favorite movie."

"I want *Miracle on 34th Street*," Lauren said patiently. "With Edmund Gwenn and Natalie Wood."

The clerk picked up a copy of *It's a Wonderful Life* off a huge display. "See, Jimmy Stewart's in trouble and he wishes he'd never been born, and this angel grants him his wish—"

"I know," Lauren said. "I don't care. I want *Miracle on 34th Street.*"

"Okay!" the clerk said, and wandered off to look for it, muttering, "Some people don't have any Christmas spirit."

She finally found it, in the M's of all places, and then insisted on giftwrapping it.

By the time Lauren made it back to her apartment, it was a quarter to one. She would have to forget lunch and mailing the Christmas cards, but she could at least take them with her, buy the stamps, and put the stamps on at work.

She took the video out of the shopping bag and set it on the coffee table next to her purse, picked up the bag and started for the bedroom.

Someone knocked on the door.

"I don't have time for this," she muttered, and opened the door, still holding the shopping bag.

It was a young man wearing a "Save the Whales" T-shirt and khaki pants. He had shoulder-length blond hair and a vague expression that made her think of Southern California.

"Yes? What is it?" she asked.

"I'm here to give you a Christmas present," he said.

"Thank you, I'm not interested in whatever you're selling," she said, and shut the door.

He knocked again immediately. "I'm not selling anything," he said through the door. "Really."

I don't have *time* for this, she thought, but she opened the door again.

"I'm not a salesguy," he said. "Have you ever heard of the Maharishi Ram Dras?"

A religious nut.

"I don't have time to talk to you." She started to say, "I'm late for work," and then remembered you weren't supposed to tell strangers your apartment was going to be empty. "I'm very busy," she said and shut the door, more firmly this time.

The knocking commenced again, but she ignored it. She started into the bedroom with the shopping bag, came back and pushed the deadbolt across and put the chain on, and then went in to hang up her dress. By the time she'd extricated it from the tissue paper and found a hanger, the knocking had stopped. She hung up the dress, which looked just as deadly now that she had it home, and went back in the living room.

The young man was sitting on the couch, messing with her TV remote. "So, what do you want for Christmas? A yacht? A pony?" He punched buttons on the remote, frowning. "A new TV?"

"How did you get in here?" Lauren said squeakily. She looked at the door. The deadbolt and chain were both still on.

"I'm a spirit," he said, putting the remote down. The TV suddenly blared on. "The Spirit of Christmas Present."

"Oh," Lauren said, edging toward the phone. "Like in *A Christmas Carol.*"

"No," he said, flipping through the channels. She looked at the remote. It was still on the coffee table. "Not Christmas Present. Christmas *Present*. You *know*, Barbie dolls, ugly ties, cheese logs, the stuff people give you for Christmas."

"Oh, Christmas *Present*. I see," Lauren said, carefully picking up the phone.

"People *always* get me confused with him, which is really insulting. I mean, the guy obviously has a really high cholesterol level. Anyway, I'm the Spirit of Christmas Present, and your sister sent me to—"

Lauren had dialed nine one. She stopped, her finger poised over the second one. "My sister?"

"Yeah," he said, staring at the TV. Jimmy Stewart was sitting in the guard's room wrapped in a blanket. "Oh, wow! *It's a Wonderful Life.*"

My sister sent you, Lauren thought. It explained everything. He was not a Moonie or a serial killer. He was this year's version of the crystal pyramid mate selector. "How do you know my sister?"

"She channeled me," he said, leaning back against the sofa. "The Maharishi Ram Dras was instructing her in trance-meditation, and she accidentally channeled my spirit out of the astral plane." He pointed at the screen. "I love this part where the angel is trying to convince Jimmy Stewart he's dead."

"I'm not dead, am I?"

"No. I'm not an angel. I'm a spirit. The Spirit of Christmas Present. You can call me Chris for short. Your sister sent me to give you what you really want for Christmas. You know, your heart's desire. So what is it?"

For my sister not to send me any more presents, she thought. "Look, I'm really in a hurry right now. Why don't you come back tomorrow and we can talk about it then?"

"I hope it's not a fur coat," he said as if he hadn't heard her. "I'm opposed to the killing of endangered species." He picked up Fred's present. "What's this?"

"It's a videotape of *Miracle on 34th Street*. I really have to go."

"Who's it for?"

"Fred Hatch. I'm his Secret Santa."

"Fred Hatch." He turned the package over. "You had it gift-wrapped at the store, didn't you?"

"Yes. If we could just talk about this later—"

"This is a great part, too," he said, leaning forward to watch the TV. The angel was explaining to Jimmy Stewart how he hadn't gotten his wings yet.

"I *have* to go. I'm on my lunch hour, and I need to mail my Christmas cards, and I have to get back to work—" She glanced at her watch, "—oh my God, fifteen minutes ago."

He put down the package and stood up. "Gift-wrapped presents," he said, making a "tsk"-ing noise. "Everybody rushing around spending money, rushing to parties, never stopping to have some eggnog or watch a movie. Christmas is an endangered species." He looked longingly back at the screen, where the angel was trying to convince Jimmy Stewart he'd never been alive, and then wandered into the kitchen. "You got any Evian water?"

"No," Lauren said desperately. She hurried after him. "Look, I really have to get to work."

He had stopped at the kitchen table and was holding one of the Christmas cards. "Computer-addressed," he said reprovingly. He tore it open.

"Don't—" Lauren said.

"Printed Christmas cards," he said. "No letter, no quick note, not even a handwritten signature. That's exactly what I'm talking about. An endangered species."

"I didn't have time," Lauren said defensively. "And I don't have time to discuss this or anything else with you. I have to get to work."

"No time to write a few words on a card, no time to think about what you want for Christmas." He slid the card back into the envelope. "Not even on recycled paper," he said sadly. "Do you know how many trees are chopped down every year to send Christmas cards?"

"I am *late* for—" Lauren said, and he wasn't there anymore.

He didn't vanish like in the movies, or fade out slowly. He simply wasn't there.

"—work," Lauren said. She went and looked in the living room.

The TV was still on, but he wasn't there, or in the bedroom. She went in the bathroom and pulled the shower curtain back, but he wasn't there either.

"It was an hallucination," she said out loud, "brought on by stress." She looked at her watch, hoping it had been part of the hallucination, but it still read one-fifteen. "I will figure this out later," she said. "I *have* to get back to work."

She went back in the living room. The TV was off. She went into the kitchen. He wasn't there. Neither were her Christmas cards, exactly.

"You! Spirit!" she shouted. "You come back here this minute!"

* * *

"You're late," Cassie said, filling out a catalog form. "You will not believe who was just here. Scott Buckley. God, he is so cute." She looked up "What happened?" she said, "Didn't they hold the dress?"

"Do you know anything about magic?" Lauren said.

"What *happened?*"

"My sister sent me her Christmas present," Lauren said grimly. "I need to talk to someone who knows something about magic."

"Fat . . . I mean Fred Hatch is a magician. What did your sister send you?"

Lauren started down the hall to Documentation at a half-run.

"I told Scott you'd be back any minute," Cassie said. "He said he wanted to talk to you."

Lauren opened the door to Documentation and started looking over partitions into the maze of cubicles. They were all empty.

"Anybody here?" Lauren called. "Hello?"

A middle-aged woman emerged from the maze, carrying five rolls of wrapping paper and a large pair of scissors. "You don't have any Scotch tape, do you?" she asked Lauren.

"Do you know where Fred Hatch is?" Lauren asked.

The woman pointed toward the interior of the maze with a roll of reindeer-covered paper. "Over there. Doesn't *anyone* have any tape? I'm going to have to staple my Christmas presents."

Lauren worked her way toward where the woman had pointed,

looking over partitions as she went. Fred was in the center one, leaning back in a chair, his hands folded over his ample stomach, staring at a screen covered with yellow numbers.

"Excuse me," Lauren said, and Fred immediately sat forward and stood up.

"I need to talk to you," she said. "Is there somewhere we can talk privately?"

"Right here," Fred said. "My assistant's on the 800 line in my office placing a catalog order, and everyone else is next door in Graphic Design at a Tupperware party." He pushed a key, and the computer screen went blank. "What did you want to talk to me about?"

"Cassie said you're a magician," she said.

He looked embarrassed. "Not really. The PMS Committee put me in charge of the magic show for the office party last year, and I came up with an act. This year, luckily, they assigned me to play Santa Claus." He smiled and patted his stomach. "I'm the right shape for the part, and I don't have to worry about the tricks not working."

"Oh, dear," Lauren said. "I hoped . . . Do you know any magicians?"

"The guy at the novelty shop," he said, looking worried. "What's the matter? Did PMS assign you the magic show this year?"

"No." She sat down on the edge of his desk. "My sister is into New Age stuff, and she sent me this spirit—"

"Spirit," he said. "A ghost, you mean?"

"No. A person. I mean he looks like a person. He says he's the Spirit of Christmas Present, as in Gift, not Here and Now."

"And you're sure he's not a person? I mean, tricks can sometimes really look like magic."

"There's a Christmas tree in my kitchen," she said.

"Christmas tree?" he said warily.

"Yes. The spirit was upset because my Christmas cards weren't on recycled paper, he asked me if I knew how many trees were chopped down to send Christmas cards, then he disappeared, and when I went back in the kitchen there was this Christmas tree in my kitchen."

"And there's no way he could have gotten into your apartment earlier and put it there?"

"It's *growing* out of the floor. Besides, it wasn't there when we were in the kitchen five minutes before. See, he was watching *It's A Wonderful Life* on TV, which, by the way, he turned on without using the remote, and he asked me if I had any Evian water, and he went in the kitchen and . . . this is ridiculous. You have to think I'm crazy. *I* think I'm crazy just listening to myself tell this ridiculous story. Evian water!" She folded her arms. "People have a lot of nervous breakdowns around Christmas time. Do you think I could be having one?"

The woman with the wrapping paper rolls peered over the cubicle wall. "Have you got a tape dispenser?"

Fred shook his head.

"How about a stapler?"

Fred handed her his stapler, and she left.

"Well," Lauren said when she was sure the woman was gone, "do you think I'm having a nervous breakdown?"

"That depends," he said.

"On what?"

"On whether there's really a tree growing out of your kitchen floor. You said he got angry because your Christmas cards weren't on recycled paper. Do you think he's dangerous?"

"I don't know. He says he's here to give me whatever I want for Christmas. Except a fur coat. He's opposed to the killing of endangered species."

"A spirit who's an animal rights activist!" Fred said delightedly. "Where did your sister get him from?"

"The astral plane," Lauren said. "She was trance-channeling or something. I don't care where he came from. I just want to get rid of him before he decides my Christmas presents aren't recyclable, too."

"Okay," he said, hitting a key on the computer. The screen lit up. "The first thing we need to do is find out what he is and how he got here. I want you to call your sister. Maybe she knows some New Age spell for getting rid of the spirit." He began to type rapidly. "I'll get on the networks and see if I can find someone who knows something about magic."

He swiveled around to face her. "You're sure you want to get rid of him?"

"I have a *tree* growing out of my kitchen floor!"

"But what if he's telling the truth? What if he really can get you what you want for Christmas?"

"What I *wanted* was to mail my Christmas cards, which are now shedding needles on the kitchen tile. Who knows what he'll do next?"

"Yeah," he said. "Listen, whether he's dangerous or not, I think I should go home with you after work, in case he shows up again, but I've got a PMS meeting for the office party—"

"That's okay. He's an animal rights activist. He's not dangerous."

"That doesn't necessarily follow," Fred said. "I'll come over as soon as my meeting's over, and meanwhile I'll check the networks. Okay?"

"Okay," she said. She started out of the cubicle and then stopped. "I really appreciate your believing me, or at least not saying you don't believe me."

He smiled at her. "I don't have any choice. You're the only other person in the world who likes *Miracle on 34th Street* better than *It's a Wonderful Life.* And Fred Gailey believed Macy's Santa Claus was really Santa Claus, didn't he?"

"Yeah," she said. "I don't think this guy is Santa Claus. He was wearing Birkenstocks."

"I'll meet you at your front door," he said. He sat down at the computer and began typing.

Lauren went through the maze of cubicles and into the hall.

"*There* you are!" Scott said. "I've been looking for you all over." He smiled meltingly. "I'm in charge of buying gifts for the office party, and I need your help."

"My help?"

"Yeah. Picking them out. I hoped maybe I could talk you into going shopping with me after work tonight."

"Tonight?" she said. "I can't. I've got—" A Christmas tree growing in my kitchen. "Could we do it tomorrow after work?"

He shook his head. "I've got a date. What about later on tonight? The stores are open till nine. It shouldn't take more than a couple of hours to do the shopping, and then we could go have a late supper somewhere. What say I pick you up at your apartment at six-thirty?"

And have the spirit lying on the couch, drinking Evian water and watching TV? "I can't," she said regretfully.

Even his frown was cute. "Oh, well," he said, and shrugged. "Too bad. I guess I'll have to get somebody else." He gave her another adorable smile and went off down the hall to ask somebody else.

I hate you, Spirit of Christmas Present, Lauren thought, standing there watching his handsome back recede. You'd better not be there when I get home.

A woman came down the hall, carrying a basket of candy canes. "Compliments of the Personnel Morale Special Committee," she said, offering one to Lauren. "You look like you could use a little Christmas spirit."

"No, thanks, I've already got one," Lauren said.

* * *

The door to her apartment was locked, which didn't mean much since the chain and the deadbolt had both been on when he got in before. But he wasn't in the living room, and the TV was off.

He had been there, though. There was an empty Evian water bottle on the coffee table. She picked it up and took it into the kitchen. The tree was still there, too. She pushed one of the branches aside so she could get to the wastebasket and throw the bottle away.

"Don't you know plastic bottles are nonbiodegradable?" the Spirit said. He was standing on the other side of the tree, hanging things on the branches. He was dressed in khaki shorts and a "Save the Rain Forest" T-shirt, and had a red bandanna tied around his head. "You should recycle your bottles."

"It's your bottle," Lauren said. "What are you doing here, Spirit?"

"Chris," he corrected her. "These are organic ornaments," he said. He held one of the brown things out to her. "Handmade by the Yanomamo Indians. Each one is made of natural by-products found in the Brazilian rain forest." He hung the brown thing on the tree. "Have you decided what you want for Christmas?"

"Yes," she said. "I want you to go away."

He looked surprised. "I can't do that. Not until I give you your heart's desire."

"That is my heart's desire. I want you to go away and take this tree and your Yanomamo ornaments with you."

"You know the biggest problem I have as the Spirit of Christmas

Present?" he said. He reached in the back pocket of his shorts and pulled out a brown garland of what looked like coffee beans. "My biggest problem is that people don't know what they want."

"I know what I want," Lauren said. "I don't want to have to write my Christmas cards all over again—"

"You didn't write them," he said, draping the garland over the branches. "They were printed. Do you know that the inks used on those cards contain harmful chemicals?"

"I don't want to be lectured on environmental issues, I don't want to have to fight my way through a forest to get to the refrigerator, and I don't want to have to turn down dates because I have a spirit in my apartment. I want a nice, quiet Christmas with no hassles. I want to exchange a few presents with my friends and go to the office Christmas party and . . ." And dazzle Scott Buckley in my off-the-shoulder black dress, she thought, but she decided she'd better not say that. The Spirit might decide Scott's clothes weren't made of natural fibers or something and turn him into a Yanomamo Indian.

". . . and have a nice, quiet Christmas," she finished lamely.

"Take *It's A Wonderful Life,*" the Spirit said, squinting at the tree. "I watched it this afternoon while you were at work. Jimmy Stewart didn't know what he wanted."

He reached in his pocket again and pulled out a crooked star made of Brazil nuts and twine. "He thought he wanted to go to college and travel and get rich, but what he *really* wanted was right there in front of him the whole time."

He did something, and the top of the tree lopped over in front of him. He tied the star on with the twine, and did something else. The tree straightened up. "You only think you want me to leave," he said.

Someone knocked on the door.

"You're right," Lauren said. "I don't want you to leave. I want you to stay right there." She ran into the living room.

The spirit followed her into the living room. "Luckily, being a spirit, I know what you really want," he said, and disappeared.

She opened the door to Fred. "He was just here," she said. "He disappeared when I opened the door, which is what all the crazies say, isn't it?"

"Yeah," Fred said. "Or else, 'He's right there. Can't you see him?' " He looked curiously around the room. "Where was he?"

"In the kitchen," she said, shutting the door. "Decorating a tree that probably isn't there either." She led him into the kitchen.

The tree was still there, and there were large brownish cards stuck all over it.

"You really do have a tree growing in your kitchen," Fred said, squatting down to look at the roots. "I wonder if the people downstairs have roots sticking out of their ceiling." He stood up. "What are these?" he said, pointing at the brownish cards.

"Christmas cards." She pulled one off. "I told him I wanted mine back." She read the card aloud. " 'In the time it takes you to read this Christmas card, eighty-two harp seals will have been clubbed to death for their fur.' " She opened it up. " 'Happy Holidays.' "

"Cheery," Fred said. He took the card from her and turned it over. " 'This card is printed on recycled paper with vegetable inks and can be safely used as compost.' "

"Did anyone in the networks know how to club a spirit to death?" she asked.

"No. Didn't your sister have any ideas?"

"She didn't know how she got him in the first place. She and her Maharishi were channeling an Egyptian nobleman and he suddenly appeared, wearing a 'Save the Dolphins' T-shirt. I got the idea the Maharishi was as surprised as she was." She sat down at the kitchen table. "I tried to get him to go away this afternoon, but he said he has to give me my heart's desire first." She looked up at Fred, who was cautiously sniffing one of the organic ornaments. "Didn't you find out anything on the networks?"

"I found out there are a lot of loonies with computers. What *are* these?"

"By-products of the Brazilian rain forest." She stood up. "I told him my heart's desire was for him to leave, and he said I didn't know what I really wanted."

"Which is what?"

"I don't know," she said. "I went into the living room to answer the door, and he said that luckily he knew what I wanted because he was a spirit, and I told him to stay right where he was, and he disappeared."

"Show me," he said.

She took him into the living room and pointed at where he'd been standing, and Fred squatted down again and peered at the carpet.

"How does he disappear?"

"I don't know. He just . . . isn't there."

Fred stood up. "Has he changed anything else? Besides the tree?"

"Not that I know of. He turned the TV on without the remote," she said, looking around the room. The shopping bags were still on the coffee table. She looked through them and pulled out the video. "Here. I'm your Secret Santa. I'm not supposed to give it to you till Christmas Eve, but maybe you'd better take it before he turns it into a snowy owl or something."

She handed it to him. "Go ahead. Open it."

He unwrapped it. "Oh," he said without enthusiasm. "Thanks."

"I remember last year at the party we talked about it, and I was afraid you might already have a copy. You don't, do you?"

"No," he said, still in that flat voice.

"Oh, good. I had a hard time finding it. You were right when you said we were the only two people in the world who liked *Miracle on 34th Street*. Everybody else I know thinks *It's A Wonderful Life* is—"

"You bought me *Miracle on 34th Street?*" he said, frowning.

"It's the original black-and-white version. I hate those colorized things, don't you? Everyone has gray teeth."

"Lauren." He held the box out to her so she could read the front. "I think your friend's been fixing things again."

She took the box from him. On the cover was a picture of Jimmy Stewart and Donna Reed dancing the Charleston.

"Oh, no! That little rat!" she said. "He must have changed it when he was looking at it. He told me *It's A Wonderful Life* was his favorite movie."

"Et tu, Brute?" Fred said, shaking his head.

"Do you suppose he changed all my other Christmas presents?"

"We'd better check."

"If he has . . ." she said. She dropped to her knees and started rummaging through them.

"Do you think they look the same?" Fred asked, squatting down beside her.

"*Your* present looked the same." She grabbed a package wrapped in red-and-gold paper and began feeling it. "Cassie's present is okay, I think."

"What is it?"

"A stapler. She's always losing hers. I put her name on it in Magic Marker." She handed it to him to feel.

"It feels like a stapler, all right," he said.

"I think we'd better open it and make sure."

Fred tore off the paper. "It's still a stapler," he said, looking at it. "What a great idea for a Christmas present! Everybody in Documentation's always losing their staplers. I think PMS steals them to use on their Christmas decorations." He handed it back to her. "Now you'll have to wrap it again."

"That's okay," Lauren said. "At least it wasn't a Yanomamo ornament."

"But it might be any minute," Fred said, straightening up. "There's no telling what he might take a notion to transform next. I think you'd better call your sister again, and ask her to ask the Maharishi if *he* knows how to send spirits back to the astral plane, and I'll go see what I can find out from the networks."

"Okay," Lauren said, following him to the door. "Don't take the videotape with you. Maybe I can get him to change it back."

"Maybe," Fred said, frowning. "You're sure he said he was here to give you your heart's desire?"

"I'm sure."

"Then why would he change my videotape?" he said thoughtfully. "It's too bad your sister couldn't have conjured up a nice, straightforward spirit."

"Like Santa Claus," Lauren said.

* * *

Her sister wasn't home. Lauren tried her off and on all evening, and when she finally got her, she couldn't talk. "The Maharishi and I are going to Barbados. They're having a harmonic divergence there on Christmas Eve, so don't worry about getting my present here by Christmas because I won't be back till the day after New Year's," she said and hung up.

"I don't even have her Christmas present bought yet," Lauren said to the couch, "and it's all your fault."

She went in the kitchen and glared at the tree. "I don't even dare go shopping because you might turn the couch into a humpbacked whale while I'm gone," she said, and then clapped her hand over her mouth.

She peered cautiously into the living room and then made a careful circuit of the whole apartment, looking for endangered species. There were no signs of any, and no sign of the spirit. She went back into the living room and turned on the TV. Jimmy Stewart was dancing the Charleston with Donna Reed. She picked up the remote and hit the channel button. Now he was singing, "Buffalo Gals, Won't You Come Out Tonight?"

She hit the automatic channel changer. Jimmy Stewart was on every channel except one. The Ghost of Christmas Present was on that one, telling Scrooge to change his ways. She watched the rest of *A Christmas Carol.* When it reached the part where the Cratchits were sitting down to their Christmas dinner, she remembered she hadn't had any supper and went in the kitchen.

The tree was completely blocking the cupboards, but, by mightily pushing several branches aside she was able to get to the refrigerator. The eggnog was gone. So were the Stouffer's frozen entrees. The only thing in the refrigerator was a half-empty bottle of Evian water.

She shoved her way out of the kitchen and sat back down on the couch. Fred had told her to call if anything happened, but it was after eleven o'clock, and she had a feeling the eggnog had been gone for some time.

A Christmas Carol was over, and the opening credits were starting. "Frank Capra's *It's a Wonderful Life.* Starring Jimmy Stewart and Donna Reed."

* * *

She must have fallen asleep. When she woke up, *Miracle on 34th Street* was on, and the store manager was giving Santa Claus a list of toys he was supposed to push if Macy's didn't have what the children asked Santa for.

"Finally," Lauren said, watching Edmund Gwenn tear the list into pieces, "something good to watch," and promptly fell asleep. When she woke up again, John Payne and Maureen O'Hara were kissing and someone was knocking on the door.

I don't remember anyone knocking on the door, she thought groggily. John Payne told Maureen O'Hara how he'd convinced the State of New York Edmund Gwenn was Santa Claus, and then they both stared disbelievingly at a cane standing in the corner. "The End" came on the screen.

The knocking continued.

"Oh," Lauren said, and answered the door.

It was Fred, carrying a McDonald's sack.

"What time is it?" Lauren said, blinking at him.

"Seven o'clock. I brought you an Egg McMuffin and some orange juice."

"Oh, you wonderful person," she said. She grabbed the sack and took it over to the coffee table. "You don't know what he did." She reached into the sack and pulled out the sandwich. "He transformed the food in my refrigerator into Evian water."

He was looking curiously at her. "Didn't you go to bed last night? He didn't come back, did he?"

"No, I waited for him, and I guess I fell asleep." She took a huge bite of the sandwich.

Fred sat down beside her. "What's that?" He pointed to a pile of dollar bills on the coffee table.

"I don't know," Lauren said.

Fred picked up the bills. Under them was a handful of change and a pink piece of paper. " 'Returned three boxes Christmas cards for refund,' " Lauren said, reading it. " '$22.18.' "

"That's what's here," Fred said, counting the money. "He didn't turn your Christmas cards into a Douglas fir after all. He took them back and got a refund."

"Then that means the tree isn't in the kitchen!" she said, jumping up and running to look. "No, it doesn't." She came back and sat down on the couch.

"But at least you got your money back," Fred said. "And it fits in with what I learned from the networks last night. They think he's a friendly spirit, probably some sort of manifestation of the seasonal spirit. Apparently these are fairly common, variations of Santa Claus being the most familiar, but there are other ones, too. All benign. They think he's probably telling the truth about wanting to give you your heart's desire."

"Do they know how to get rid of him?" she asked, and took a bite.

"No. Apparently no one's ever wanted to exorcise one." He pulled a piece of paper out of his pocket. "I got a list of exorcism books to try, though, and this one guy, Clarence, said the most important thing in an exorcism is to know exactly what kind of spirit it is."

"How do we do that?" Lauren asked with her mouth full.

"By their actions, Clarence said. He said appearance doesn't mean anything because seasonal spirits are frequently in disguise. He said we need to write down everything the spirit's said and done, so I want you to tell me exactly what he did." He took a pen and a notebook out of his jacket pocket. "Everything from the first time you saw him."

"Just a minute." She finished the last bite of sandwich and took a drink of the orange juice. "Okay. He knocked on the door, and when I answered it, he told me he was here to give me a Christmas present, and I told him I wasn't interested, and I shut the door and started into the bedroom to hang up my dress and—my dress!" she gasped and went tearing into the bedroom.

"What's the matter?" Fred said, following her.

She flung the closet door open and began pushing clothes madly along the bar. "If he's transformed this—" She stopped pushing hangers. "I'll kill him," she said and lifted out a brownish collection of feathers and dried leaves. "Benign!?" she said. "Do you call that benign?!"

Fred gingerly touched a brown feather. "What was it?"

"A dress," she said. "My beautiful black, off-the-shoulder, drop-dead dress."

"Really?" he said doubtfully. He lifted up some of the brownish leaves. "I think it still is a dress," he said. "Sort of."

She crumpled the leaves and feathers against her and sank down on the bed. "All I wanted was to go to the office party!"

"Don't you have anything else you can wear to the office party? What about that pretty red thing you wore last year?"

She shook her head emphatically. "Scott didn't even notice it!"

"And that's your heart's desire?" Fred said after a moment. "To have Scott Buckley notice you at the office party?"

"Yes, and he would have, too! It had sequins on it, and it fit perfectly!" She held out what might have been a sleeve. Greenish brown pods dangled from brownish strips of bamboo. "And now he's ruined it!"

She flung the dress on the floor and stood up. "I don't care what this Clarence person says. He is not benign! And he is not trying to get me what I want for Christmas. He is trying to ruin my life!"

She saw the expression on Fred's face and stopped. "I'm sorry," she said. "None of this is your fault. You've been trying to help me."

"And I've been doing about as well as your spirit," he said. "Look, there has to be some way to get rid of him. Or at least get the dress back. Clarence said he knew some transformation spells. I'll go on to work and see what I can find out."

He went out into the living room and over to the door. "Maybe you can go back to the store and see if they have another dress like it." He opened the door.

"Okay." Lauren nodded. "I'm sorry I yelled at you. And you have been a lot of help."

"Right," he said glumly, and went out.

"Where'd you get that dress?" Jimmy Stewart said to Donna Reed.

Lauren whirled around. The TV was on. Donna Reed was showing Jimmy Stewart her new dress.

"Where are you?" Lauren demanded, looking at the couch. "I want you to change that dress back right now!"

"Don't you like it?" the spirit said from the bedroom. "It's completely biodegradable."

She stomped into the bedroom. He was putting the dress on the hanger and making little "tsk"-ing noises. "You have to be careful with natural fibers," he said reprovingly.

"Change it back the way it was. This instant."

"It was handmade by the Yanomamo Indians," he said, smoothing down what might be the skirt. "Do you realize that their natural habitat is being destroyed at the rate of seven hundred and fifty acres a day?"

"I don't care. I want my dress back."

He carried the dress on its hanger over to the chest. "It's so interesting. Donna Reed knew right away she was in love with Jimmy Stewart, but he was so busy thinking about college and his new suitcase, he didn't even know she existed." He hung up the dress. "He practically had to be hit over the head."

"I'll hit you over the head if you don't change that dress back this instant, Spirit," she said, looking around for something hard.

"Call me Chris," he said. "Did you know sequins are made from nonrenewable resources?" he added and disappeared as she swung the lamp.

"And good riddance," she shouted to the air.

* * *

They had the dress in a size three. Lauren put herself through the indignity of trying to get into it and then went to work. The receptionist was watching Jimmy Stewart standing on the bridge in the snow, and weeping into a Kleenex. She handed Lauren her messages.

There were two memos from the PMS Committee—they were having a sleigh ride after work, and she was supposed to bring cheese puffs to the office party. There wasn't a message from Fred.

"Oh!" the receptionist wailed. "This is so sad!"

"I hate *It's a Wonderful Life,*" Lauren said, and went up to her desk. "I hate Christmas," she said to Cassie.

"It's normal to hate Christmas," Cassie said, looking up from the book she was reading. "This book, it's called *Let's Forget Christmas*, says it's because everyone has these unrealistic expectations. When they get presents, they—"

"Oh, that reminds me," Lauren said. She rummaged in her bag and brought out Cassie's present, fingering it quickly to make sure it was still a stapler. It seemed to be. She held it out to Cassie. "Merry Christmas."

"I don't have yours wrapped yet," Cassie said. "I don't even have my wrapping paper bought yet. The book says I'm suffering from an avoidance complex." She picked up the package. "Do I have to open it now? I know it will be something I love, and you won't like what I got you half as well, and I'll feel incredibly guilty and inadequate."

"You don't have to open it now," Lauren said. "I just thought I'd better give it to you before—" She picked her messages up off her desk and started looking through them. "Before I forgot. There haven't been any messages from Fred, have there?"

"Yeah. He was here about fifteen minutes ago looking for you. He said to tell you the networks hadn't been any help, and he was going to try the library." She looked sadly at the present. "It's even wrapped great," she said gloomily. "I went shopping for a dress for the office party last night, and do you think I could find anything off-the-shoulder or with sequins? I couldn't even find anything I'd be caught dead in. Did you know the rate of stress-related illness at Christmas is seven times higher than the rest of the year?"

"I can relate to that," Lauren said.

"No, you can't. You didn't end up buying some awful gray thing with gold chains hanging all over it. At least Scott will notice me. He'll say, 'Hi, Cassie, are you dressed as Marley's ghost?' And there you'll be, looking fabulous in black sequins—"

"No, I won't," Lauren said.

"Why? Didn't they hold it for you?"

"It was . . . defective. Did Fred want to talk to me?"

"I don't know. He was on his way out. He had to pick up his Santa Claus suit. Oh, my God." Her voice dropped to a whisper. "It's Scott Buckley."

"Hi," Scott said to Lauren. "I was wondering if you could go shopping with me tonight." Lauren stared at him, so taken aback she couldn't speak.

"When you couldn't go last night, I decided to cancel my date."

"Uh . . . I . . ." she said.

"I thought we could buy the presents and then have some dinner."

She nodded.

"Great," Scott said. "I'll come over to your apartment around six-thirty."

"No!" Lauren said. "I mean, why don't we go straight from work?"

"Good idea. I'll come up here and get you." He smiled meltingly and left.

"I think I'll kill myself," Cassie said. "Did you know the rate of suicides at Christmas is four times higher than the rest of the year? He is so cute," she said, looking longingly down the hall after him. "There's Fred."

Lauren looked up. Fred was coming toward her desk with a Santa Claus costume and a stack of books. Lauren hurried across to him.

"This is everything the library had on exorcisms and the occult," Fred said, transferring half of the books to her arms. "I thought we could both go through them today, and then get together tonight and compare notes."

"Oh, I can't," Lauren said. "I promised Scott I'd help him pick out the presents for the office party tonight. I'm sorry. I could tell him I can't."

"Your heart's desire? Are you kidding?" He started awkwardly piling the books back on his load. "You go shopping. I'll go through the books and let you know if I come up with anything."

"Are you sure?" she said guiltily. "I mean, you shouldn't have to do all the work."

"It's my pleasure," he said. He started to walk away and then stopped. "You didn't tell the spirit Scott was your heart's desire, did you?"

"Of course not. Why?"

"I was just wondering . . . nothing. Never mind." He walked off down the hall. Lauren went back to her desk.

"Did you know the rate of depression at Christmas is sixteen times higher than the rest of the year?" Cassie said. She handed Lauren a package.

"What's this?"

"It's from your Secret Santa."

Lauren opened it. It was a large book entitled, *It's a Wonderful Life: The Photo Album.* On the cover, Jimmy Stewart was looking depressed.

* * *

"I figure it'll take a half hour or so to pick out the presents," Scott said, leading her past two inflatable palm trees into The Upscale Oasis. "And then we can have some supper and get acquainted." He lay down on a massage couch. "What do you think about this?"

"How many presents do we have to buy?" Lauren asked, looking around the store. There were a lot of inflatable palm trees, and a jukebox, and several life-size cardboard cutouts of Malcolm Forbes and Leona Helmsley. Against the far wall were two high-rise aquariums and a bank of televisions with neon-outlined screens.

"Seventy-two." He got up off the massage couch, handed her the list of employees and went over to a display of brown boxes tied with twine. "What about these? They're handmade Yanomamo Christmas ornaments."

"No," Lauren said. "How much money do we have to spend?"

"The PMS Committee budgeted six thousand and there was five hundred left in the Sunshine Fund. We can spend . . ." He picked up a pocket calculator in the shape of Donald Trump and punched several buttons. "Ninety dollars per person, including tax. How about pet costume jewelry?" He held up a pair of rhinestone earrings for German shepherds.

"We got those last year," Lauren said. She picked up a digital umbrella and put it back down.

"How about a car fax?" Scott said. "No, wait. This, this is it!"

Lauren turned around. Scott was holding up what looked like a gold cordless phone. "It's an investment pager," he said, punching keys. "See, it gives you the Dow Jones, treasury bonds, interest rates. Isn't it perfect?"

"Well," Lauren said.

"See, this is the hostile takeover alarm, and every time the Federal Reserve adjusts the interest rate it beeps."

Lauren read the tag. " 'Portable Plutocrat. $74.99.' "

"Great," Scott said. "We'll have money left over."

"To invest," Lauren said.

He went off to see if they had seventy-two of them, and Lauren wandered over to the bank of televisions.

There was a videotape of *Miracle on 34th Street* lying on top of the

VCR/shower massage. Lauren looked around to see if anyone was watching and then popped the *Wonderful Life* tape out and stuck in *Miracle.*

A dozen Edmund Gwenns dressed as Macy's Santa Claus appeared on the screens, listening to twelve store managers tell them which overstocked toys to push.

Scott came over, lugging four shopping bags. "They come gift wrapped," he said happily, showing her a Portable Plutocrat wrapped in green paper with gold dollar signs. "Which gives us a free evening."

"That's what I've been fighting against for years," a dozen Edmund Gwenns said, tearing a dozen lists to bits, "the way they commercialize Christmas."

* * *

"What I thought," Scott said when they got in the car, "was that instead of going out for supper, we'd take these over to your apartment and order in."

"Order in?" Lauren said, clutching the bag of Portable Plutocrats on her lap to her.

"I know a great Italian place that delivers. Angel hair pasta, wine, everything. Or, if you'd rather, we could run by the grocery store and pick up some stuff to cook."

"Actually, my kitchen's kind of a mess," she said. There is a Christmas tree in it, she thought, with organic by-products hanging on it.

He pulled up outside her apartment building. "Then Italian it is." He got out of the car and began unloading shopping bags. "You like prosciutto? They have a great melon and prosciutto."

"Actually, the whole apartment's kind of a disaster," Lauren said, following him up the stairs. "You know, wrapping presents and everything. There are ribbons and tags and paper all over the floor—"

"Great," he said, stopping in front of her door. "We have to put tags on the presents, anyway."

"They don't need tags, do they?" Lauren said desperately. "I mean, they're all exactly alike."

"It personalizes them," he said, "it shows the gift was chosen especially for them." He looked expectantly at the key in her hand and then at the door.

She couldn't hear the TV, which was a good sign. And every time Fred had come over, the spirit had disappeared. So all I have to do is keep him out of the kitchen, she thought.

She opened the door and Scott pushed past her and dumped the shopping bags on the coffee table. "Sorry," he said. "Those were really heavy." He straightened up and looked around the living room. There was no sign of the spirit, but there were three Evian water bottles on the coffee table. "This doesn't look too messy. You should see my apartment. I'll bet your kitchen's neater than mine, too."

Lauren walked swiftly over to the kitchen and pulled the door shut. "I wouldn't bet on it. Aren't there still some more presents to bring up?"

"Yeah. I'll go get them. Shall I call the Italian place first?"

"No," Lauren said, standing with her back against the kitchen door. "Why don't you bring the bags up first?"

"Okay," he said, smiling meltingly, and went out.

Lauren leaped to the door, put the deadbolt and the chain on, and then ran back to the kitchen and opened the door. The tree was still there. She pulled the door hastily to and walked rapidly into the bedroom. He wasn't there, or in the bathroom. "Thank you," she breathed, looking heavenward, and went back in the living room.

The TV was on. Edmuud Gwenn was shouting at the store psychologist.

"You know, you were right," the spirit said. He was stretched out on the couch, wearing a "Save the Black-Footed Ferret" T-shirt and jeans. "It's not a bad movie. Of course, it's not as good as *It's a Wonderful Life,* but I like the way everything works out at the end."

"What are you doing here?" she demanded, glancing anxiously at the door.

"Watching *Miracle on 34th Street*," he said, pointing at the screen. Edmund Gwenn was brandishing his cane at the store psychiatrist. "I like the part where Edmund Gwenn asks Natalie Wood what she wants for Christmas, and she shows him the picture of the house."

Lauren picked up Fred's video and brandished it at him. "Fine. Then you can change Fred's video back."

"Okay," he said and did something. She looked at Fred's video. It showed Edmund Gwenn hugging Natalie Wood in front of a yellow moon with Santa Claus's sleigh and reindeer flying across it. Lauren put the video hastily down on the coffee table.

"Thank you," she said. "And my dress."

"Natalie Wood doesn't really want a house, of course. What she really wants is for Maureen O'Hara to marry John Payne. The house is just a symbol for what she really wants."

On the TV Edmund Gwenn rapped the store psychologist smartly on the forehead with his cane.

There was a knock on the door. "It's me," Scott said.

"I also like the part where Edmund Gwenn yells at the store manager for pushing merchandise nobody wants. Christmas presents should be something the person wants. Aren't you going to answer the door?"

"Aren't you going to disappear?" she whispered.

"Disappear?" he said incredulously. "The movie isn't over. And besides, I still haven't gotten you what you want for Christmas." He did something, and a bowl of trail mix appeared on his stomach.

Scott knocked again.

Lauren went over to the door and opened it two inches.

"It's me," Scott said. "Why do you have the chain on?"

"I . . ." She looked hopefully at Chris. He was eating trail mix and watching Maureen O'Hara bending over the store psychologist, trying to wake him up.

"Scott, I'm sorry, but I think I'd better take a rain check on supper."

He looked bewildered. And cute. "But I thought . . ." he said.

So did I, she thought. But I have a spirit on my couch who's perfectly capable of turning you into a Yanomamo by-product.

"The Italian take-out sounds great," she said, "but it's kind of late, and we've both got to go to work tomorrow."

"Tomorrow's Saturday."

"Uh . . . I meant go to work on wrapping presents. Tomorrow's

Christmas Eve, and I haven't even started my wrapping. And I have to make cheese puffs for the office party and wash my hair and . . ."

"Okay, okay, I get the message," he said. "I'll just bring in the presents and then leave."

She thought of telling him to leave them in the hall, and then closed the door a little and took the chain off the door.

Go *away!* she thought at the spirit, who was eating trail mix.

She opened the door far enough so she could slide out, and pulled it to behind her. "Thanks for a great evening," she said, taking the shopping bags from Scott. "Good night."

"Good night," he said, still looking bewildered. He started down the hall. At the stairs he turned and smiled meltingly.

I'm going to kill him, Lauren thought, waving back, and took the shopping bags inside.

The spirit wasn't there. The trail mix was still on the couch, and the TV was still on.

"Come back here!" she shouted. "You little rat! You have ruined my dress and my date, and you're not going to ruin anything else! You're going to change back my dress and my Christmas cards, and you are going to get that tree out of my kitchen right *now!"*

Her voice hung in the air. She sat down on the couch, still holding the shopping bags. On the TV, Edmund Gwenn was sitting in Bellevue, staring at the wall.

"At least Scott finally noticed me," she said, and set the shopping bags down on the coffee table. They rattled.

"Oh, no!" she said. "Not the Plutocrats!"

* * *

"The problem is," Fred said, closing the last of the books on the occult, "that we can't exorcise him if we don't know which seasonal spirit he is, and he doesn't fit the profiles of any of these. He must be in disguise."

"I don't want to exorcise him," Lauren said. "I want to kill him."

"Even if we did manage to exorcise him, there'd be no guarantee that the things he's changed would go back to their original state."

"And I'd be stuck with explaining what happened to six thousand dollars' worth of Christmas presents."

"Those Portable Plutocrats cost six thousand dollars?"

"$5,895.36."

Fred gave a low whistle. "Did your spirit say why he didn't like them? Other than the obvious, I mean. That they were non-biodegradable or something?"

"No. He didn't even notice them. He was watching *Miracle on 34th Street,* and he was talking about how he liked the way things worked out at the end and the part about the house."

"Nothing about Christmas presents?"

"I don't remember." She sank down on the couch. "Yes, I do. He said he liked the part where Edmund Gwenn yelled at the store manager for talking people into buying things they didn't want. He said Christmas presents should be something the person wanted."

"Well, that explains why he transformed the Plutocrats then," Fred said. "It probably also means there's no way you can talk him into changing them back. And I've got to have something to pass out at the office party, or you'll be in trouble. So we'll just have to come up with replacement presents."

"Replacement presents?" Lauren said. "How? It's ten o'clock, the office party's tomorrow night, and how do we know he won't transform the replacement presents once we've got them?"

"We'll buy people what they want. Was six thousand all the money you and Scott had?"

"No," Lauren said, rummaging through one of the shopping bags. "PMS budgeted sixty-five hundred."

"How much have you got left?"

She pulled out a sheaf of papers. "He didn't transform the purchase orders or the receipt," she said, looking at them. "The investment pagers cost $5,895.36. We have $604.64 left." She handed him the papers. "That's eight dollars and thirty-nine cents apiece."

He looked at the receipt speculatively and then into the shopping bag. "I don't suppose we could take these back and get a refund from the Upscale Oasis?"

"They're not going to give us $5,895.36 for seventy-two 'Save the Ozone Layer' buttons," Lauren said. "And there's nothing we can buy for eight dollars that will convince PMS it cost sixty-five hundred. And where am I going to get the money to pay back the difference?"

"I don't think you'll have to. Remember when the spirit changed your Christmas cards into the tree? He didn't really. He returned them somehow to the store and got a refund. Maybe he's done the same thing with the Plutocrats and the money will turn up on your coffee table tomorrow morning."

"And if it doesn't?"

"We'll worry about that tomorrow. Right now we've got to come up with presents to pass out at the party."

"Like what?"

"Staplers."

"Staplers?"

"Like the one you got Cassie. Everybody in my department's always losing their staplers, too. And their tape dispensers. It's an office party. We'll buy everybody something they want for the office."

"But how will we know what that is? There are seventy-two people on this list."

"We'll call the department heads and ask them, and then we'll go shopping." He stood up. "Where's your phone book?"

"Next to the tree." She followed him into the kitchen. "How are we going to go shopping? It's ten o'clock at night."

"Bizmart's open till eleven," he said, opening the phone book, "and the grocery store's open all night. We'll get as many of the presents as we can tonight and the rest tomorrow morning, and that still gives us all afternoon to get them wrapped. How much wrapping paper do you have?"

"Lots. I bought it half-price last year when I decided this Christmas was going to be different. A stapler doesn't seem like much of a present."

"It does if it's what you wanted." He reached for the phone.

It rang. Fred picked up the receiver and handed it to Lauren.

"Oh, Lauren," Cassie's voice said. "I just opened your present, and I *love* it! It's exactly what I wanted!"

"Really?" Lauren said.

"It's perfect! I was so depressed about Christmas and the office party and still not having my shopping done. I wasn't even going to open it, but in *Let's Forget Christmas* it said you should open your presents early so they wouldn't ruin Christmas morning, and I did, and it's wonderful! I don't even care whether Scott notices me or not! Thank you!"

"You're welcome," Lauren said, but Cassie had already hung up. She looked at Fred. "That was Cassie. You were right about people liking staplers." She handed him the phone. "You call the department heads. I'll get my coat."

He took the phone and began to punch in numbers, and then put it down. "What exactly did the spirit say about the ending of *Miracle on 34th Street*?"

"He said he liked the way everything worked out at the end. Why?"

He looked thoughtful. "Maybe we're going about this all wrong."

"What do you mean?"

"What if the spirit really does want to give you your heart's desire, and all this transforming stuff is some roundabout way of doing it? Like the angel in *It's a Wonderful Life.* He's supposed to save Jimmy Stewart from committing suicide, and instead of doing something logical, like talking him out of it or grabbing him, he jumps in the river so Jimmy Stewart has to save *him.*"

"You're saying he turned seventy-two Portable Plutocrats into 'Save the Ozone Layer' buttons to help me?"

"I don't know. All I'm saying is that maybe you should tell him you want to go to the office party in a black sequined dress with Scott Buckley and see what happens."

"See what happens? After what he did to my dress? If he knew I wanted Scott, he'd probably turn him into a Brazilian rain forest by-product." She put on her coat. "Well, are we going to call the department heads or not?"

* * *

The Graphic Design department wanted staplers, and so did Accounts Payable. Accounts Receivable, which was having an outbreak of stress-related Christmas colds, wanted Puffs Plus and cough drops. Document Control wanted scissors.

Fred looked at the list, checking off Systems and the other departments they'd called. "All we've got left is the PMS Committee," he said.

"I know what to get them," Lauren said. "Copies of *Let's Forget Christmas.*"

They got some of the things before Bizmart closed, and Fred was back at nine Saturday morning to do the rest of it. At the bookstore they ran into the woman who had been stapling presents together the day Lauren enlisted Fred's help.

"I completely forgot my husband's first wife," she said, looking desperate, "and I don't have any idea of what to get her."

Fred handed her the videotape of *It's a Wonderful Life* they were giving the receptionist. "How about one of these?" he said.

"Do you think she'll like it?"

"Everybody likes it," Fred said.

"Especially the part where the bad guy steals the money, and Jimmy Stewart races around town trying to replace it," Lauren said.

* * *

It took them most of the morning to get the rest of the presents and forever to wrap them. By four they weren't even half done.

"What's next?" Fred asked, tying the bow on the last of the staplers. He stood up and stretched.

"Cough drops," Lauren said, cutting a length of red paper with Santa Clauses on it.

He sat back down. "Ah, yes. Accounts Receivable's heart's desire."

"What's your heart's desire?" Lauren asked, folding the paper over the top of the cough drops and taping it. "What would you ask for if the spirit inflicted himself on you?"

Fred unreeled a length of ribbon. "Well, not to go to an office party, that's for sure. The only year I even had a remotely good time was last year, talking to you."

"I'm serious," Lauren said. She taped the sides and handed the package to Fred. "What do you really want for Christmas?"

"When I was eight, I asked for a computer for Christmas. Home computers were new then and they were pretty expensive, and I wasn't sure I'd get it. I was a lot like Natalie Wood in *Miracle on 34th*

Street. I didn't believe in Santa Claus, and I didn't believe in miracles, but I really wanted it."

He cut off the length of ribbon, wrapped it around the package, and tied it in a knot.

"Did you get the computer?"

"No," he said, cutting off shorter lengths of ribbon. "Christmas morning I came downstairs, and there was a note telling me to look in the garage." He opened the scissors and pulled the ribbon across the blade, making it curl. "It was a puppy. The thing was, a computer was too expensive, but there was an outside chance I'd get it, or I wouldn't have asked for it. Kids don't ask for stuff they *know* is impossible."

"And you hadn't asked for a puppy because you knew you couldn't have one?"

"No, you don't understand. There are things you don't ask for because you know you can't have them, and then there are things so far outside the realm of possibility, it would never even occur to you to want them." He made the curled ribbon into a bow and fastened it to the package.

"So what you're saying is your heart's desire is something so far outside the realm of possibility you don't even know what it is?"

"I didn't say that," he said. He stood up again. "Do you want some eggnog?"

"Yes, thanks. If it's still there."

He went in the kitchen. She could hear forest-thrashing noises and the refrigerator opening. "It's still here," he said.

"It's funny Chris hasn't been back," she called to Fred. "I keep worrying he must be up to something."

"Chris?" Fred said. He came back into the living room with two glasses of eggnog.

"The spirit. He told me to call him that," she said. "It's short for Spirit of Christmas Present." Fred was frowning. "What's wrong?" Lauren asked.

"I wonder . . . nothing. Never mind." He went over to the TV. "I don't suppose *Miracle on 34th Street*'s on TV this afternoon?"

"No, but I made him change your video back." She pointed. "It's there, on top of the TV."

He turned on the TV, inserted the video, and hit play. He came and sat down beside Lauren. She handed him the wrapped box of cough drops, but he didn't take it. He was watching the TV. Lauren looked up. On the screen, Jimmy Stewart was walking past Donna Reed's house, racketing a stick along the picket fence.

"That isn't *Miracle*," Lauren said. "He told me he changed it back." She snatched up the box. It still showed Edmund Gwenn hugging Natalie Wood. "That little sneak! He only changed the box!"

She glared at the TV. On the screen Jimmy Stewart was glaring at Donna Reed.

"It's all right," Fred said, taking the package and reaching for the ribbon. "It's not a bad movie. The ending's too sentimental, and it doesn't really make sense. I mean, one minute everything's hopeless, and Jimmy Stewart's ready to kill himself, and then the angel convinces him he had a wonderful life, and suddenly everything's okay." He looked around the table, patting the spread-out wrapping paper. "But it has its moments. Have you seen the scissors?"

Lauren handed him one of the pairs they'd bought. "We'll wrap them last."

On the TV Jimmy was sitting in Donna Reed's living room, looking awkward. "What I have trouble with is Jimmy Stewart's being so self-sacrificing," she said, cutting a length of red paper with Santa Clauses on it. "I mean, he gives up college so his brother can go, and then when his brother has a chance at a good job, he gives up college *again.* He even gives up committing suicide to save Clarence. There's such a thing as being too self-sacrificing, you know."

"Maybe he gives up things because he thinks he doesn't deserve them."

"Why wouldn't he?"

"He's never gone to college, he's poor, he's deaf in one ear. Sometimes when people are handicapped or overweight they just assume they can't have the things other people have."

The telephone rang. Lauren reached for it and then realized it was on TV.

"Oh, hello, Sam," Donna Reed said, looking at Jimmy Stewart.

"Can you help me with this ribbon?" Fred said.

"Sure," Lauren said. She scooted closer to him and put her finger on the crossed ribbon to hold it taut.

Jimmy Stewart and Donna Reed were standing very close together, listening to the telephone. The voice on the phone was saying something about soybeans.

Fred still hadn't tied the knot. Lauren glanced at him. He was looking at the TV, too.

Jimmy Stewart was looking at Donna Reed, his face nearly touching her hair. Donna Reed looked at him and then away. The voice from the phone was saying something about the chance of a lifetime, but it was obvious neither of them was hearing a word. Donna Reed looked up at him. His lips almost touched her forehead. They didn't seem to be breathing.

Lauren realized she wasn't either. She looked at Fred. He was holding the two ends of ribbon, one in each hand, and looking down at her.

"The knot," she said. "You haven't tied it."

"Oh," he said. "Sorry."

Jimmy Stewart dropped the phone with a clatter and grabbed Donna Reed by both arms. He began shaking her, yelling at her, and then suddenly she was wrapped in his arms, and he was smothering her with kisses.

"The knot," Fred said. "You have to pull your finger out."

She looked blankly at him and then down at the package. He had tied the knot over her finger, which was still pressing against the wrapping paper.

"Oh. Sorry," she said, and pulled her finger free. "You were right. It does have its moments."

He yanked the knot tight. "Yeah," he said. He reached for the spool of ribbon and began chopping off lengths for the bow. On the screen Donna Reed and Jimmy Stewart were being pelted with rice.

"No. You were right," he said. "He is too self-sacrificing." He waved the scissors at the screen. "In a minute he's going to give up his honeymoon to save the building and loan. It's a wonder he ever asked Donna Reed to marry him. It's a wonder he didn't try to fix her up with that guy on the phone."

The phone rang. Lauren looked at the screen, thinking it must be in the movie, but Jimmy Stewart was kissing Donna Reed in a taxicab.

"It's the phone," Fred said.

Lauren scrambled up and reached for it.

"Hi," Scott said.

"Oh, hello, Scott," Lauren said, looking at Fred.

"I was wondering about the office party tonight," Scott said. "Would you like to go with me? I could come get you and we could take the presents over together."

"Uh . . . I . . ." Lauren said. She put her hand over the receiver. "It's Scott. What am I going to tell him about the presents?"

Fred motioned her to give him the phone. "Scott," he said. "Hi. It's Fred Hatch. Yeah, Santa Claus. Listen, we ran into a problem with the presents."

Lauren closed her eyes.

"We got a call from the Upscale Oasis that investment pagers were being recalled by the Federal Safety Commission."

Lauren opened her eyes. Fred smiled at her. "Yeah. For excessive cupidity."

Lauren grinned.

"But there's nothing to worry about," Fred said. "We replaced them. We're wrapping them right now. No, it was no trouble. I was happy to help. Yeah, I'll tell her." He hung up. "Scott will be here to take you to the office party at seven-thirty," he said. "It looks like you're going to get your heart's desire after all."

"Yeah," Lauren said, looking at the TV. On the screen, the building and loan was going under.

* * *

They finished wrapping the last pair of scissors at six-thirty, and Fred went back to his apartment to change clothes and get his Santa Claus costume. Lauren packed the presents in three of the Upscale Oasis shopping bags, said sternly, "Don't you dare touch these," to the empty couch, and went to get ready.

She showered and did her hair, and then went into the bedroom to see if the spirit had biodegraded her red dress, or, by some miracle, brought the black off-the-shoulder one back. He hadn't.

She put on the red dress and went back in the living room. It was only a little after seven. She turned on the TV and put Fred's video in the VCR. She hit play. Edmund Gwenn was giving the doctor the X-ray machine he'd always wanted.

Lauren picked up one of the shopping bags and felt the top pair of scissors to make sure they weren't Yanomamo ornaments. There was an envelope stuck between two of the packages. Inside was a check for $5,895.36. It was made out to the Children's Hospital fund.

She shook her head, smiling, and put the check back in the envelope.

On TV Maureen O'Hara and John Payne were watching Natalie Wood run through an empty house and out the back door to look for her swing. They looked seriously at each other. Lauren held her breath. John Payne moved forward and kissed Maureen O'Hara.

Someone knocked on the door. "That's Scott," Lauren said to John Payne, and waited till Maureen O'Hara had finished telling him she loved him before she went to open the door.

It was Fred, carrying a foil-covered plate. He was wearing the same sweater and pants he'd worn to wrap the presents. "Cheese puffs," he said. "I figured you couldn't get to your stove." He looked seriously at her. "I wouldn't worry about not having your black dress to dazzle Scott with."

He went over and set the cheese puffs on the coffee table. "You need to take the foil off and heat them in a microwave for two minutes on high. Tell PMS to put the presents in Santa's bag, and I'll be there at eleven-thirty."

"Aren't you going to the party?"

"Office parties are your idea of fun, not mine," he said. "Besides, *Miracle on 34th Street*'s on at eight. It may be the only chance I have to watch it."

"But I wanted you—"

There was a knock on the door. "That's Scott," Lauren said.

"Well," Fred said, "if the spirit doesn't do something in the next fifteen seconds, you'll have your heart's desire in spite of him." He opened the door. "Come on in," he said. "Lauren and the presents are all ready." He handed two of the shopping bags to Scott.

"I really appreciate your helping Lauren and me with all this," Scott said.

Fred handed the other shopping bag to Lauren. "It was my pleasure."

"I wish you were coming with us," she said.

"And give up a chance of seeing the real Santa Claus?" He held the door open. "You two had better get going before something happens."

"What do you mean?" Scott said, alarmed. "Do you think these presents might be recalled, too?"

Lauren looked hopefully at the couch and then the TV. On the screen Jimmy Stewart was standing on the bridge in the snow, getting ready to kill himself.

"Afraid not," Fred said.

* * *

It was snowing by the time they pulled into the parking lot at work. "It was really selfless of Fred to help you wrap all those presents," Scott said, holding the lobby door open for Lauren. "He's a nice guy."

"Yes," Lauren said. "He is."

"Hey, look at that!" Scott said. He pointed at the security monitor. "*It's a Wonderful Life*. My favorite movie!"

On the monitor Jimmy Stewart was running through the snow, shouting, "Merry Christmas!"

"Scott," Lauren said, "I can't go to the party with you."

"Just a minute, okay?" Scott said, staring at the screen. "This is my favorite part." He set the shopping bags down on the receptionist's desk and leaned his elbows on it. "This is the part where Jimmy Stewart finds out what a wonderful life he's had."

"You have to take me home," Lauren said.

There was a gust of cold air and snow. Lauren turned around.

"You forgot your cheese puffs," Fred said, holding out the foil-covered plate to Lauren.

"There's such a thing as being too self-sacrificing, you know," Lauren said.

He held the plate out to her. "That's what the spirit said."

"He came back?" She shot a glance at the shopping bags.

"Yeah. Right after you left. Don't worry about the presents. He said he thought the staplers were a great idea. He also said not to worry about getting a Christmas present for your sister."

"My sister!" Lauren said, clapping her hand to her mouth. "I completely forgot about her."

"He said since you didn't like it, he sent her the Yanomamo dress."

"She'll love it," Lauren said.

"He also said it was a wonder Jimmy Stewart ever got Donna Reed, he was so busy giving everybody else what they wanted," he said, looking seriously at her.

"He's right," Lauren said. "Did he also tell you Jimmy Stewart was incredibly stupid for wanting to go off to college when Donna Reed was right there in front of him?"

"He mentioned it."

"What a great movie!" Scott said, turning to Lauren. "Ready to go up?"

"No," Lauren said. "I'm going with Fred to see a movie." She took the cheese puffs from Fred and handed them to Scott.

"What am I supposed to do with these?"

"Take the foil off," Fred said, "and put them in a microwave for two minutes."

"But you're my date," Scott said. "Who am I supposed to go with?"

There was a gust of cold air and snow. Everyone turned around.

"How do I look?" Cassie said, taking off her coat.

"Wow!" Scott said. "You look terrific!"

Cassie spun around, her shoulders bare, the sequins glittering on her black dress. "Lauren gave it to me for Christmas," she said happily. "I love Christmas, don't you?"

"I *love* that dress," Scott said.

"He also told me," Fred said, "that his favorite thing in *Miracle on 34th Street* was Santa Claus's being in disguise—"

"He wasn't in disguise," Lauren said. "Edmund Gwenn told everybody he was Santa Claus."

Fred held up a correcting finger. "He told everyone his name was Kris Kringle."

"Chris," Lauren said.

"Oh, I love this part," Cassie said.

Lauren looked at her. She was standing next to Scott, watching Jimmy Stewart standing next to Donna Reed and singing "Auld Lang Syne."

"He makes all sorts of trouble for everyone," Fred said. "He turns Christmas upside down—"

"Completely disrupts Maureen O'Hara's life," Lauren said.

"But by the end, everything's worked out, the doctor has his X-ray machine, Natalie Wood has her house—"

"Maureen O'Hara has Fred—"

"And no one's quite sure how he did it, or if he did anything."

"Or if he had the whole thing planned from the beginning." She looked seriously at Fred. "He told me I only thought I knew what I wanted for Christmas."

Fred moved toward her. "He told me just because something seems impossible doesn't mean a miracle can't happen."

"What a great ending!" Cassie said, sniffling. "*It's a Wonderful Life* is my favorite movie."

"Mine, too," Scott said. "Do you know how to heat up cheese puffs?" He turned to Lauren and Fred. "Cut that out, you two, we'll be late for the party."

"We're not going," Fred said, taking Lauren's arm. They started for the door. "*Miracle*'s on at eight."

"But you can't leave," Scott said. "What about all these presents? Who's going to pass them out?"

There was a gust of cold air and snow. "Ho ho ho," Santa Claus said.

"Isn't that your costume, Fred?" Lauren said.

"Yes. It has to be back at the rental place by Monday morning," he said to Santa Claus. "And no changing it into rain forest by-products."

"*Mer*ry Christmas!" Santa Claus said.

"I like the way things worked out at the end," Lauren said.

"All we need is a cane standing in the corner," Fred said.

"I have no idea what you're talking about," Santa Claus said. "Where are all these presents I'm supposed to pass out?"

"Right here," Scott said. He handed one of the shopping bags to Santa Claus.

"Plastic shopping bags," Santa Claus said, making a "tsk"-ing sound. "You should be using recycled paper."

"Sorry," Scott said. He handed the cheese puffs to Cassie and picked up the other two shopping bags. "Ready, Cassie?"

"We can't go yet," Cassie said, gazing at the security monitor. "Look, *It's a Wonderful Life* is just starting." On the screen Jimmy Stewart's brother was falling through the ice. "This is my favorite part," she said.

"Mine, too," Scott said, and went over to stand next to her.

Santa Claus squinted curiously at the monitor for a moment and then shook his head. "*Miracle on 34th Street*'s a much better movie, you know," he said reprovingly. "More realistic."

A Foreigner's Christmas in China

Maureen F. McHugh

I don't usually drink, maybe a couple of times a year. I warn you, a couple of wine coolers, a little sleep deprivation at a convention like this, and I'll bore anyone to death. But since everybody is telling about weird experiences. . . . My one paranormal experience was in China, and it could have been a stress reaction.

Let me preface my story by stating that in my estimation the People's Republic of China is not a particularly mystical place. Granted, I came to China because I thought it would change me, would make me into something more than I had been before, but I foresaw this change to be purely an experience of character. I wanted experience to make me wise. *Not* spiritual wisdom, not the New Age *Tao of Kites* and union of souls pseudo-wisdom. I wasn't looking for ancient Eastern secrets; I'm biased against most of that kind of thing anyway. And in my limited experience, mysticism and spiritualism seem more particularly debased in China than they are even in the U.S. When any of my many Chinese friends launched into a description of paranormal experiences, I got the same uncomfortable feeling I do when someone in the U.S. tells me about the time they saw a UFO. I nodded and tried to appear to take them very seriously, because they were usually confiding something they felt slightly embarrassed about, but which was very real to them, namely about miracles of kung fu and the magic psychic healing powers of people that a friend of theirs knew.

I do try to keep an open mind. For example there's a lot of herbal medicine in China, and although my preference is for antibiotics I am willing to concede that seven thousand years of pharmaceutical experience has probably discovered things that Eli Lily hasn't yet had time to research and get past the FDA. So when my translator came down with persistent diarrhea I was interested in his remedy, a kind of tea brewed out of something that the college infirmary gave him that looked more like tree bark and grass clippings than it did my estimation of controlled medication. But Xiao Wong was 5'9" and 120 odd pounds and he didn't have enough body mass to lose much weight or fluid, so when three days later he was still excusing himself abruptly in the middle of conversations I gave him two days' worth of little white pills out of my own hoard or prescription medication, and his problem cleared up within six hours and did not manifest itself again.

So let me begin by way of apology by saying that I do not place much stock in the metaphysical.

I was the only foreigner on staff at my college. I lived in Shijiazhuang, which is a city about the size of Kansas City, located about five hours south of Beijing, in a place where two railway lines cross.

Shijiazhuang was a sere place less than four hundred miles from the edge of the Gobi Desert. It was cold in the winter, hot in the summer, dusty and windy and ugly all the time.

Christmas in China is hard.

The Chinese don't celebrate Christmas, although they have heard of it the way we have heard of Chinese New Year, and they know it is a big deal. Christmas fell on a Thursday, which meant I taught British and American Culture and History. I dedicated the class that day to Christmas.

So much of Christmas is the build-up. I bought gifts in Beijing; a tea set for my mother, cloisonne for friends, a tiny jade horse for my sister; but I had sent the gifts off in October. My family sent chocolate chip cookies, but there wasn't any reason to wait until the twenty-fifth to open the cookies, they'd just be more stale. My sister sent me a new white sweater; a white sweater in Shijiazhuang was so inappropriate I almost cried. By the end of a day anything I was wearing had a ring of gray dirt at the neck and cuffs. But the college decided to have a Christmas Eve party and to invite all the foreigners—there were twelve Americans and Canadians in a city of over a million—so I went and wore the sweater.

Chinese parties usually involve speeches, and then everybody has to sing a song or something. The most successful song I have ever done was "Oh Lord, Won't You Buy Me a Mercedes Benz," sung a la Janis Joplin (the only impression I can do), but that was for students. At the Christmas party there were teachers and administrators, so I sang "Silent Night" badly, but in English. Singing in English is so foreign to most Chinese that it is like watching a dancing bear, it is not that it is done well, but that it is done at all.

I was tired so I left just after the Mitchells. The Mitchells were retired, and they came to China sponsored by their church. They taught English using Bible stories, but could not openly proselytize because it is against Chinese law. Anyway, they tended to leave early, and I had yet another cold, so I left early, too. There are no streetlights, and very few lights in the windows. China is dark in the winter, and this close to Beijing it's about ten degrees colder than New York City in the winter.

I thought maybe I'd get a beer, a kind of Christmas present. I liked the local beer, and a bottle would make me sleepy. I walked out the back gate and up Red Flag Road, watching for bicyclists coming out of the dark.

I usually bought my beer at a place made out of the carcass of a bus. Sheet metal was welded over the wheel wells and there was a narrow counter where the driver's window would be. They had bootleg electricity from an apartment building and a little refrigerator where they kept pork sausage and a bottle of beer for me. (The Chinese don't drink cold beverages, they believe it causes stomach cancer.) The electricity meant that it was dimly golden in the bus, almost the same frail light as some of the other stalls lit only by kitchen candles. Most nights the proprietor or his very pregnant wife were there until about eleven—and it wasn't a holiday for them so I assumed they'd be open—but halfway up the street I could see that the bus was dark.

I was tempted to just sit down on the road except that it was

China, and China was so foreign, and I was so tired of its relentless foreignness. It was Christmas and I wanted to be home, but I was between homes, and when I left China I didn't precisely know where I was going. A cold winter night in China, standing in the street where I could see the window of my apartment and it was as dark as anything else here and I was lost.

A Chinese girl stopped and said, *"Tongshi."* (Comrade.)

It was dark and she couldn't make out my face. She was about to ask me directions, it had happened before. *"Wo shi weiguoren"* (I'm a foreigner), I said and added that I didn't speak Mandarin.

"Miss," she said in English. "I have come looking for you."

A student, or a friend of a student. I was tired from my cold and I didn't want to be polite to this girl in the middle of Red Flag Road. "Yes," I said, without enthusiasm.

"You must come with me," she said.

"I'm sorry, it's very late and I have to teach tomorrow."

"No," she said. "It is Christmas, and I have come for you."

A party, I thought, feeling sick. They do that, make plans and don't tell you until the last minute, and it is rude not to go along.

"No," she said. "I am your Christmas spirit."

The beer was supposed to be my Christmas spirit. "I don't understand," I said. "That isn't clear in English. Do you mean you are going to wish me good spirits?"

"No, no. I am your Christmas spirit," she said. "Like a ghost." I could not really see her face in the dark, just a pale oval turned toward me. The rest of her was shapeless, buried under the interminable layers of sweaters and coats that we all wore. She was only as tall as my shoulder.

"Ahh," I said, as if I had a clue. "I am sorry, but it is very late and I am sure you must be going on your way, and I have a cold, I have to go to bed."

"Come with me," she said firmly and took my hand. I was going to pull away, but something happened. Something . . . happened. I know I said that, I am trying to explain it, but there is a space where the thoughts should be, no exact memory, just the sense that something happened.

And then.

We were in a large unheated room full of people in coats. The people were all standing in rows, their backs to me, rows of Chinese overcoats, women with hair permed in the precise curls of those old Toni perms from the fifties and sixties (home perms had just hit China the way they did the U.S. in the fifties) and men with their hair shining a little, because in China in the winter the heat isn't on very long and no one wants to wash their hair.

Someone was murmuring.

I was standing at the back of the room, next to the girl from the road. A blackout. A seizure of some sort. And a deep, cowardly relief, that this was serious, and it meant that I could go home. I was stunned at the enormity of my relief. A blackout, brain tumor, neurological disease—who cared. I wanted to go home, to run from being here. I realized that the tiredness I was carrying was a kind of despair.

I wondered what time it was, how far we were from my apartment, and how long it would take to get back there.

The people all murmured together, a long muttered response in unison. "It's a church," I whispered. I don't know why I said it out loud, but a person who has had a blackout has a right to be disoriented.

The girl from the road nodded. "A Catholic church."

Christmas Mass. A sad dispirited Christmas Mass. Being Catholic is a hard thing in China. I had one Catholic girl in my third-year class, and she was almost mute, her voice inaudible when she answered questions, silenced by the pressure of being a Chinese girl and a Catholic.

"Christmas is a celebration," I said.

The girl from the road shrugged. What was she supposed to say? I supposed she was Catholic, too, and had brought me here thinking that being in a Catholic church would console me.

I had not been in a church in years, only went for weddings and funerals. When my father died, I went to church for the funeral and my strongest memory was of an altar boy holding a white candle. The candle tilted and wax ran onto his hand. He sucked in his breath but made no noise, because a funeral mass is a solemn thing. No altar boys in white here, plastic flowers on a makeshift altar.

I wondered how she had gotten me here during the space of my blackout, had I seemed normal? One of those multiple personalities that no one notices?

"Are you Catholic?" I whispered.

At that moment people turned and smiled and offered each other their hands to shake. I almost shut my eyes when they turned, somebody would see me, notice the foreigner, and then all of a sudden everyone would fuss.

No one offered their hand to me, no one noticed me. So strange not to be noticed; everywhere I went I was noticed. I walked down the street and people hissed to each other, *weiguoren*, "foreigner," tapping their companions to get their attention, "look, a foreigner." I caused bicycle accidents. Buses nearly hit people, the whole row at the window turning their heads to watch me, in a flannel shirt and jeans and four months without a haircut, waiting to cross the street. But here in this church, no one looked at me. No one saw.

I went still, thinking that perhaps they just hadn't noticed me. I wanted them to have just not noticed me.

"I'm not Catholic," said the girl from the road, her voice normal and therefore loud among these whispering people. No one blinked. It was as if I wasn't there.

My Christmas Spirit looked at me and I willed her not to say anything.

Sick with apprehension. I was losing my mind. My Christmas Spirit had a sidelong look, a face with smooth heavy eyelids and long eyes, an ancient face. Not civilized ancient, primitive ancient. Bone-old, faintly green in the shadows under her eyes, like oxidized copper. She was waiting and expectant. Expecting something from me. Willing to wait.

I had always wanted to be invisible in China. You don't know the strain of doing everything under the public eye, of having every purchase, even my choice of toothpaste or laundry soap, discussed in front of me.

I thought I was dead. There was no explanation. And I would spend eternity like this, haunting China.

Shaken. I did not know if I would ever go home.

We stood through the Mass. There was a closing hymn, plainsong in Chinese. It took me a moment to hear it through the strangeness, but they were singing "Oh, Come All Ye Faithful." Was I brought here to reprimand me for having given up on the church? My Christmas Spirit said she wasn't Catholic, then what was she?

They filed out, looking through my Christmas Spirit and me as if we were not there. Middle-aged women in cloth coats, middle-aged women with tired eyes. Why is church a woman's thing? They didn't look saved, they looked alienated and cold and subdued. It still looked strange to see Catholics in China.

And then the little room was empty. My Christmas Spirit still looked at me. I didn't know what to say.

She shrugged again. "Come," she said, and something . . . happened.

* * *

A Chinese flat, four rooms, concrete floor, walls painted blue to waist height and then white the rest of the way. Comfortably-off people if they had four rooms. A Chinese man with an unruly shock of thick hair came out of the kitchen. He was wearing a white T-shirt despite the chill and smoking a cigarette and I knew him.

It was Liu Liming, cook for the special dining room and therefore, most of the time, only me. He was an alcoholic and a cynic, and a dealmaker, and I liked him very much. We were the same age. He spoke almost no English, I spoke pidgin Mandarin, and yet we were friends because, somehow, we were. I got his jokes; we shared a sense of irony.

But I had never been to his apartment. Never expected to. I knew a little about him—China is a place for gossip.

He stood there for a moment looking at his wife. Their son was asleep on the couch, head thrown back. He was still wearing his glasses. The little boy was four, and he had an eye that crossed inward and it made him shy. His father was hard on him, always a little angry because the boy was not a charmer, not like his father.

Liming's wife was watching television.

"Why don't you put him in bed," Liming said and I understood.

Which was the other thing I always wished for, to understand what was going on around me. Be careful what you wish for. Liming wasn't aware that I was standing in his apartment and although I understood Liming better than I did most people who spoke Chinese, I had never had this easy, conversational understanding.

His wife didn't answer, pretending not to hear. She was the daughter of the president of the college and she was a shrew. He was a clever country boy who had seduced an upper-class girl and expected to live happily ever after.

He made a little sound of disgust, a very faint aiyah, and I could see in her face that she heard him but she wouldn't admit it. So he went back into the kitchen and came out with a bottle of the clear sorghum liquor the Chinese drink. It's about 120 proof and smells like fingernail polish. He poured it into a little Chinese drinking cup and tossed it back, *gang bei,* bottom's up. It was for her benefit.

She refused to look at him.

Awful little scene, I thought.

"Are you going to raise the second one like this, too?" he asked.

They had been granted permission to have a second child, because of the first boy's inward turning eye.

"Are you going to see Xiling?" she said.

His best friend's wife. There were rumors about them, but most people seemed to think neither of them would really have an affair.

He looked at her with hatred. "I am going to bed."

I shook my head.

The Christmas Spirit watched me.

"They don't have to live this way," I said.

She shrugged. "What should they do?"

"Divorce," I said. "It's not against the law. People in China do."

"Where will he live?" she asked. "The work unit has a waiting list for housing."

"He can rent a room," I said. "Some people do. That's not what's stopping him."

"What's stopping him?" she asked.

A thousand things. The fact that he would have to either share a single room with another unmarried man, or pay for a room. The fact that she was the reason he had a good job. That in China, divorce was the moral equivalent of bankruptcy.

"Why did you bring me here?" I asked.

"To show you his choice," she said.

And took my hand and I closed my eyes.

* * *

She took me to the girls dormitories where my students lived eight to a room, building curtains around their bunk beds to hide themselves and make themselves a little space. I saw Lizhi, a girl from the third-year class who had stopped showing up. She was lying on the bed, unable to sleep. Her grades had plummeted before she left and she told me she had headaches and insomnia and she couldn't concentrate and she was sad all the time. But China doesn't treat depression. During the Cultural Revolution it was decided that depression was a sign of an unhealthy society, and mental illness shouldn't exist in a socialist country. So people like Lizhi were self-indulgent.

I had come to visit her twice in the dorm, had talked to her and held her hand, but I hadn't really done anything for her. Hadn't spent any real time on her. I had almost eighty students, and I convinced myself that she wasn't my problem, that I wasn't equipped to help her. But no one was equipped to help her and I was at least aware that talking to her would help her feel less alone.

What would happen to her? She would kill herself. She had talked about dying the last time. Or like many people who suffered from depression, she would get better, have bouts of it for the rest of her life. And unless China made antidepressant drugs available, she would live a kind of half-life, never knowing when she would be swallowed up. I could see her on her bunk, curled on her side, her eyes open, while the other girls slept. I could see the pearl of the whites of her eyes.

My Christmas Spirit stood next to me.

I understood depression, had spent some nights awake and alone. Had walked at two in the morning just to feel the movement, hoping to be tired enough to sleep when I got back, hoping maybe something would happen to me, then it wouldn't be my problem anymore, something would have happened and everything would be changed.

And I remembered getting better. I remember the moment, walking to class, when I looked up at a great beech tree whose roots grew through a stone wall and reached down to uproot the sidewalk, and saw pale new green leaves against the white wood and through the tree saw the intense blue of the sky and I realized I had not looked for beauty for over a year.

I remembered choosing at that moment to look for beauty. And I remembered that it had not happened overnight, but that slowly, the world had come back to me.

When had I stopped looking again? How had I come to China? I had come to China to make something happen, the way I had gone on those 2:00 a.m. walks, hoping something monumental would happen. There are people for whom depression is an indescribable force. For someone like Lizhi, there was no choice, her depression was an illness, rooted in the chemistry of her body, as inescapable as cancer. But then there are people like me, who walk a sort of cliff and who can look into the abyss and know that it is down there, and who have to maintain their balance. I had learned how to balance, I thought.

When had I stopped trying?

"Choose," said my Christmas Spirit, standing in the black dorm room. I could see the half-lit face of my Christmas Spirit in the little bit of light from the window at the end of the room, barely make out the ancient shape of her head, her heavy lidded eyes. Lizhi did not stir, did not hear, the whites of her eyes like pearls.

"I choose beauty," I said, thinking of the pale tree and the green leaves and the intense blue sky.

And something happened.

I was alone on the road outside the college. I was chilled to the bone. A person on a bicycle swerved as if I had just appeared on the road in front of him, and maybe I had.

Of course, this is just a ghost story, a travel story. I should stop now, tell you only that I finished my year in China, during which time I made many close friends, and declined the college's offer to teach another year. That I came home, and went back to writing. That I sold a novel and a couple of short stories.

But I want to say something about why I went abroad. No one

goes abroad to go to something. Everybody goes abroad to flee something. One of the people I knew in Shijiazhuang was in remission for lymphatic cancer and had been for three years. He was hiding from death in China, and that year, in January, in the city of Kunming, China, 150 kilometers north of the Vietnam border, seven of us foreigners working together got him on a plane to Beijing so he could fly from there to the Mayo Clinic. The things you flee find you, even in China. But that is another story.

It's old-fashioned to have morals for stories, but indulge me. I was trying to escape myself, trying to become someone else, someone wise. Maybe I had a sort of blackout on Red Flag Road, or maybe I met an old Chinese spirit. I am telling you now, I don't know. But some things you must choose. Choose a bad marriage, choose a bad life, or choose to look around you and see.

Household Words; Or, The Powers-That-Be

Howard Waldrop

"His theory of life was entirely wrong. He thought men ought to be buttered up, and the world made soft and accommodating for them, and all sorts of fellow have turkey for their Christmas dinner . . ."
—Thomas Carlyle

"He was the first to find out the immense spiritual power of the Christmas turkey."
—Mrs. Oliphant

Under a deep cerulean November sky, the train stopped on a turn near the road one half-mile outside the town of Barchester.

Two closed carriages waited on the road. Passengers leaned out the train windows and watched as a small man in a suit as brown as a Norfolk biffin stepped down from the doorway at the end of the third railcar.

Men waved their hats, women their scarves. "Hurray, Charlie!" they yelled. "Hoorah, Mr. Dickens! Hooray for Boz!"

The small man, accompanied by two others, limped across the cinders to a group of men who waited, hats in hand, near the carriages. He turned, doffed his stovepipe hat to the train and waved to the cheering people.

Footmen loaded his traveling case and the trunk of props from the train into the last carriage.

The train, with barely a lurch, moved smoothly on down the tracks toward the cathedral tower of the town, hidden from view by trees. There a large crowd, estimated at more than three thousand, would be waiting for the author, to cheer him and watch him alight.

The welcoming committee had met him here to obviate that indignity, and to take him by a side street to his hotel, avoiding the crowds.

When the men were all in, the drivers at the fronts of the carriages released their brakes, and the carriages made their way quickly down the road toward town.

* * *

Promptly at 8:00 p.m. the lights in the Workingman's Hall came up to full brilliance.

On stage were three deep magenta folding screens, the center one parallel to the audience, the two wings curved in slightly toward them. The stage curtains had been drawn in to touch the wings of the screen. Directly in front of the center panel stood a waist-high, four-legged small table. At the audience's right side of the desk was a raised wooden block; at its left, on a small lower projection, stood a glass and a sweating carafe of ice water; next to the water was an ivory letter opener and a white linen handkerchief. The top of the table was covered with a fringed magenta cloth that hung below the tabletop only an inch or so.

Without preamble, Charles Dickens walked with a slight limp in from the side of the stage and took his place behind the desk, carrying in his hand a small octavo volume. When he stood behind the thin-legged table his whole body, except for the few inches across his waist, was fully visible to the audience.

There came a thunderous roar of applause, wave alter wave, then as one the audience rose to its feet, joyed for the very sight of the man who had brought so much warmth and wonder to their heater-sides and hearths.

He stood unmoving behind the desk, looking over them with his bright brown eyes above the now-familiar (due to the frontispiece by Mr. Frith in his latest published book, *Pip's Expectations*) visage with its high balding forehead, the shock of brownish hair combed to the left, the large pointed beard and connected thick mustache. He wore a brown formal evening suit, the jacket with black velvet lapels worn open showing his vest and watch-chain. His shirt was white, with an old-fashioned neck-stock in place of the new button-on collars, and he wore an even more old-fashioned bow tie, with two inches of end hanging down from the bows.

After two full minutes of applause, he nodded to the audience and they slowed, then stopped, sitting down with much clatter of canes and rustle of clothing and scraping of chairs, a scattering of coughs. From far back in the hall came a set of nervous hiccups, quickly shushed.

"My dear readers," said Dickens, "you do me more honor than I can stand. Since it is nearing the holiday season, I have chosen my reading especially, as suits that most Christian of seasons." Murmurs went around the hall. "As I look around me at this fine Barchester crowd, I see many of you in the proud blue and red uniforms of Her Majesty's Power Service, and I must remind you that I was writing in a time, more than two decades gone, when things in our country were neither as Christian as we should have liked, nor as fast and modern as we thought. To mention nothing of a type of weather only the most elderly—and I count myself among them—remember with absolutely no regrets whatsoever." Laughter. "As I read, should you my auditors be moved to express yourselves—in matters of appreciation and applause, tears, or indeed hostility"—more laughter—"please be assured you may do so without distracting or discomfiting me in any adverse way."

He poured a small amount of water from carafe to glass and drank. "Tonight, I shall read to you *The Christmas Garland*."

There were oohs and more applause, the ones who guessed before nodding in satisfaction to themselves and their neighbors.

The house lights dimmed until only Dickens, the desk and the central magenta panel were illuminated.

He opened the book in his hand, and without looking at it said, "*The Christmas Garland*. Holly Sprig the First. 'No doubt about it, Marley was dead as a doorknob . . .' "

* * *

Dickens barely glanced at the prompt-book in his hand as he read. It was the regular edition of *The Christmas Garland,* the pages cut out and pasted in the center of larger bound octavo leaves. There were deletions and underlinings in red, blue and yellow inks—notes to directions for changes of voice, alternate wordings for lines. The whole had been shortened by more than a third, to fit into an hour and half for these paid readings. When he had begun his charity readings more than ten years ago, the edition as printed had gone more than two hours and a half. Through deletions and transpositions, he reduced it to its present length without losing effect or sense.

He moved continually as he read, now using the letter opener as Eben Mizer's quill, then the block of wood—three heavy blows with his left hand—as a doorknocker. He moved his fingers together, the book between them, to simulate Cratchitt's attempts to warm himself at a single glowing coal. His voice was slow, cold and drawn as Eben Mizer; solemnly cheerful as the gentleman from the charity; merry and bright as Mizer's nephew. The audience laughed or drew inward on itself as he read the opening scenes.

* * *

"For I am that Spirit of Christmases Past," said the visitant. "I am to show you things that Were. Take my hand."

Eben Mizer did so, and they were out the window casing and over the night city in a slow movement. They flew slowly into the darkness to the north.

And then they were outside a house and shop, looking through the window at a large man in old-fashioned waistcoat and knee-breeks, with his spectacles pushed back on his forehead.

"Why, old Mr. Fezziwigg, to whom I was 'prenticed!" said Eben Mizer.

"Ho!" said Fezziwigg. "Seven o'clock! Away with your quills! Roll back the carpets! Move those desks against the walls! It's Christmas Eve and no one works! . . ."

* * *

* * *

As Dickens acted out preparations for the party, his eyes going to the prompt-book only twice, he remembered the writing of this, his most famous story. It had been late October of the year 1843. He was halfway through the writing of *Martin Sweezlebugg,* had just, in fact, sent the young hero to America—the place he himself had returned from late in 1842, the place that had become the source of one long squeal of protest when he had published *Notes on the Americans* early in the year. He had gone from triumph to disdain in less than six months. For the first time in his life, the monthly numbers had been a chore for him—he was having troubles with *Sweezlebugg,* and the sales were disappointing. As they had been for *Gabriel Vardon: The Locksmith of London* of two years before. (The Americans who were outraged with his travel book were the same who had named a species of Far Western trout after Gabriel Vardon's daughter.) Between finishing the November number of *Sweezlebugg* on October 18, and having to start the next on November 3, he had taken one of the steam-trains to the opening of the Manchester Institute of that city. Sitting on the platform, waiting his turn to speak, the idea for *The Christmas Garland* had come to him unbidden. He could hardly contain himself, waiting until after the speeches and the banquet to return to the quiet of his hotel to think it through.

And since he had a larger and larger family each year to support, more indigent brothers and sisters, in-laws and his importunate mother and father, he conceived the story as a separate book, to be sold at Christmas as were many of the holiday annuals, keepsakes and books of remembrance. Illustrated, of course, with cuts by John Leech. The whole plan was a fire in his mind that night and all the way back to London the next day. He went straight to Chapman and Hall and presented the notion to them. They agreed with alacrity, and began ordering up stock and writing advertisements.

He had had no wild success since the two books that had made his reputation, *Tales of the Nimrod Club* and *Oliver Twist*, parts of them written simultaneously, in overlapping monthly numbers, six years before. He had envisioned for *The Christmas Garland* sales that would earn him £3,000 or more.

* * *

"Show me no more, no more!" said Eben Mizer. "These are things long past; the alternate miseries and joys of my youth. Those times are all gone. We can no more change them than stop the tides!"

"These are things as they were," said the Spirit of Christmases Past. "These things are unchangeable. They *have* happened."

"I had forgotten both pleasure and heartache," said Mizer. "I had forgotten the firewood, the smoke, the horses."

"In another night, as Marley said, you shall be visited by another, who will show you things as they are now. Prepare," said the Spirit. As with the final guttering of a candle, it was gone. Eben Mizer was back in his bed, in his cold bedchamber, in the dark. He dropped his head to the horsehair pillow, and slept.

* * *

Twenty-two years had gone by since Dickens wrote the words he read. He remembered his disappointment with the sales of *The Christmas Garland*—"Disappointment?! Disappointment!" yelled his friend Macready, the actor, when he had complained. "Disappointment at selling twenty thousand copies in six days! Disappointment, Charlie?" It was not that it had not sold phenomenally, but that it was such a well-made book—red cover, gilt-edged pages, four hand-tinted cuts, the best type and paper and, because of Dickens's insistence that everyone have one, priced far too low—that his half-copyright earnings through January 1844 only came to £347 6s 2p when he had counted on thousands. That had been the disappointment.

Dickens spoke on. This was the ninety-fourth public reading of *The Christmas Garland*; his most popular, next to the trial scene from *The Nimrod Club*, and the death of little Dombey. At home these days he worked on an abridgment of the scenes, including that of the great seastorm, from *The Copperfield Record of the World As It Rolled*, which he thought would make a capital dramatic reading, perhaps to be followed by a short comic scene, such as his reading of Mrs. Gamp, the hit of the otherwise disappointing *Martin Sweezlebugg.*

What a winter that had been . . . the hostile American press, doing the monthly numbers of *Sweezlebugg*, writing and seeing to the publication of *The Christmas Garland* in less than six weeks, preparing his growing family—his wife, an ever-increasing number of children, his sister-in-law Georgina Hogarth, the servants and dogs—for the coming sojourn to Italy, severing his ties with *Bentley's Miscellany*, thinking of starting a daily newspaper of a liberal slant, walking each night through London streets five, ten, fifteen miles because his brain was hot with plans and he could not sleep or rest. He was never to know such energies again.

There was his foot now, for instance. He believed its present pain was a nervous condition brought on by walking twelve miles one night years ago through the snow. The two doctors who had diagnosed it as gout were dismissed; a third was brought in who diagnosed it as a nervous condition brought on by walking through the snow. Before each of his readings, his servant John had to put upon the bare foot a fomentation of the poppy, which allowed him to put on a sock and shoe, and make it the two hours standing up.

He still had a wife, though he had not seen her in six years; they had separated after twenty-three years of marriage and nine children. Some of the living children and Georgina had remained with Dickens, taking his side against the mother and sister. One boy was in the Navy, another in Australia, two others in school. Only one child, Mamie—"young Tinderbox," as Dickens called her—visited freely between the two households, taking neither side.

The separation had of course caused scandal, and Dickens's break with Anthony Trollope. They belonged to the same clubs. Trollope had walked into one; several scandalized members were saying that Dickens had taken his sister-in-law as mistress. "No such thing," said Trollope. "It's a young actress."

So it was; Trollope said he was averting a larger outrageous lie with the truth; Dickens had not seen it that way.

Her name was Ellen Ternan. She and Dickens had performed in charity theatricals together, *The Frozen Deep* and Jonson's *Every Man in His Humour*. She was of a stage family—her mother and two sisters were actresses. Her sister Fanny had married Anthony Trollope's brother Tom in Florence, Italy, where she had gone to be his children's tutor after the death of Tom's wife Theodosia.

The world had been a much more settled place when the young fire-eating Boz had published his first works, and had remained so for some time afterwards. But look at it now.

The Americans had just finished blowing the heads off first themselves, and then their president; had thrown the world in turmoil—which side should we take?—for four years, destroying a large part of their manpower and manufacturing capabilities. What irked Dickens was not their violent war—they had it coming—but that he would not be able to arrange a reading tour there for at least another year. An American had shown up two weeks ago at his publisher's office with an offer of £10,000, cash on the barrelhead, if Dickens would agree to a three-month tour of seventy-five readings. Both his friend Forster and the old actor Macready advised him against it for reasons of his health. Besides his foot, there had been some tightening in his chest for the last year or so, and his bowels had been in straitened circumstances long before that.

Ah, but what a trouper. He found even with his mind wandering he had not lost his place, or missed a change of voice or character; nor given the slightest hint that his whole being was not in the reading being communicated to his forward-leaning, intent auditors.

* * *

Eben Mizer opened his eyes. How long had he slept? Was the Spirit of Christmases Past that bit of undigested potato, that dollop of mustard? he thought.

There came to his bedchamber a slight crackling sound; the air was suffused with a faint blue glow. Mizer reached into the watch-catch above his bed and took down his timepiece. It was 12:00, he saw by the glow, which slowly brightened about his bed. Twelve! Surely not noon! And not the midnight before, when the Spirit of Christmases Past had come. Had he slept the clock round, all through the sham-bug Christmas Day? He grasped the bedclothes to haul himself out onto the cold bare floor. The overall bright glow coalesced in the corner nearest the chair.

The popping became louder, like faraway fireworks over the Thames on Coronation Day, or the ice slowly breaking on a March day. There was a smell of hot metal in the air; the sharp odor before a thunderstorm, but without heat or dampness. And then it was there, in the room behind the chair!

It was a looming figure, far above normal height, shrouded in a gown of copper and mica, and above its head, at its top, glowing green and jagged with purple, was one of Faraday's Needles . . .

* * *

The listeners jerked back, as always. There was a rustle of crinoline and starch as they hunkered back down. Most knew the story as they knew their own hearts, but the effect on them was always the same.

Dickens knew why; for when he had written those words more than two decades before, his own hair had stood on end as if he were in the very presence of the Motility Factor itself.

It was from that moment on in the writing of *The Christmas Garland* that he had never wavered, never slowed down; it was that moment when, overcome by tiredness at his desk, he had flung himself and his hat and cane out into the (in those days) dark London night, and had walked till dawn, out to Holborn, up Duckett Lane, across to Seven Sisters, and back up and down Vauxhall Bridge Road, to come in again just as the household was rising, and throw himself fully clothed across his bed, to sleep for an hour, and then, rising, go back to his ink bottle and quills.

* * *

The crackling sound grew louder as the Spirit shook his raiment, and a spark danced between the Needle and the ceiling, leaving a bright blue spot there to slowly fade as Eben Mizer watched, fascinated as a bird before a snake.

"Know that I am the Spirit of Christmases Current, Eben Mizer. Know that I am in the form that the men who hire your accountancy worship, as you worship the money that flows, like the Motive Force itself, from them to you."

"What do you wish of me?" asked Eben. The Spirit laughed, and a large gust of blue washed over the room, as if day had come and gone in an instant.

"Wish? Nothing. I am only to show you what takes place this Christmas."

"You mean this past day?"

"Past? Oh, very well, as you will!" The Spirit laughed again. "Take my hand."

"I will be vulcanized in an instant!" said Mizer.

"No, you shall not." It held out an empty sleeve. Mizer felt invisible fingers take his. "Come," said the Spirit. "Hold on to me."

There was a feeling of lightness in Mizer's head—he became a point of light, as the flash of a meteor across the heavens, or the dot of a lightning-bug against an American night, and they were outside his nephew's house in the daylight.

"As before, you are neither seen nor heard," said the Spirit of Christmases Current. "Walk through this wall with me." They did, but Mizer had the sensation that instead of walking directly through they had, in a twinkling, gone up the windowpane, across the roof tiles, down the heated air of the chimney, across the ceiling, and into the room just inside the window, too fast to apprehend. The effect was the same, from outside to inside, but Eben Mizer had the memory of doing it the long way . . .

* * *

Dickens's voice became high, thin and merry as he took on the younger tones of Mizer's nephew, his nephew's wife, their in-laws and guests at the party where they were settling in for a game of charades before the Christmas meal.

Actors on the stage of the time said that Dickens was the greatest actor of his age; others thought it beneath his dignity to do the readings—authors should be paid to publish books, not read them for money. Some of his readings he had dropped after they did not have the desired effect—comic or pathetic or terrific—on the audience. Others he had prepared but never given, because they had proved unsatisfying to him. By the time any reading had joined his repertoire, he had rehearsed it twenty-five times before its debut.

He knew that he was a good actor—if he had not gone into journalism, covering the courts and the Parliament when a youth, he would have gone on the stage—but he knew he was not great. He knew it was the words and the acting that had made his readings such a success. No matter how many times they had read and heard them, audiences still responded to them as if they had come newly dry from his pen that very morning.

Dickens paused for another drink from the glass, mopped his brow with the handkerchief that a moment before had been Mizer's nightcap. The audience waited patiently, the slight hum of the fans in the ceiling purring to let the accumulated warmth of fifteen hundred bodies escape into the cold night. The glow from the selenium lights against the magenta screen added nothing to the heat.

He put the glass down, eyes twinkling, and went back to his reading.

* * *

"If only my uncle were here," said his nephew.

"Oh, why bother?" asked his pretty young wife. "He's probably at his office counting out more profits from the Greater Cumberland and Smythe-Jones Motility Factory, or the United Batchford Motive-Force Delivery Service. And no doubt got poor Bob Cratchitt there with him, chained to his stool . . ."

"Hush, please," asked the nephew.

"Well, it's true. A man like Eben Mizer. He does sums for seventeen different power-brokers, yet his office is still lit with candles! He lets poor Cratchitt freeze in the outer office. And poor Bob with the troubles he has at home. Your uncle should be ashamed of what he pays him, of how he himself lives . . ."

"But, after all," said her father the greengrocer, "it is a free market, and he pays what the trade will bear."

"That's wrong too," said the young wife, hands on hips. "How the workingmen are to better themselves if their wages are so low they have to put their children working at such early ages is beyond me. How are they to make ends meet? How are they to advance themselves if there are no better wages in the future, perhaps even lower ones, and they can't live decently now?"

"The Tories won't be happy if women such as yourself get the suffrage," said her father with a laugh. "Neither would anyone on the board of directors of a motive-power company!"

"If I did not love you as a father," said the young wife, "I should be very cross with you."

"Come, come," said her husband the nephew. "It's Christmas Day. Where's your charity?"

"Where's your uncle's?"

"He does as the world wills," said the nephew.

"Only more so," said another guest, and they all laughed, the young wife included.

"Well, I invited him," said Mizer's nephew. "It's up to him to come or no. I should welcome him with all the gladness of the season."

"As would I," said his wife. "Only you might as well wish for Christian charity to be carried on every day, in every way, throughout the year, in every nation on Earth!"

"Why show me this?" asked Eben Mizer of the Spirit. "No love is lost betwixt my nephew's wife and myself. My nephew means very well, but he does not grasp the full principles of business to his bosom. He has done well enough; he *could* do much better."

"Come," said the Spirit of Christmases Current, grabbing Mizer's hand in its unseen own. There was another crackle of blue lightning, and they were away, up a nail, across the roof, down the gutter pipe and off into the day.

* * *

After this reading, Dickens had two more in the provinces, then back to St. James Hall in London for the holiday series. He would read not only *The Christmas Garland* there, but also both *The Chimes* and *The Haunted Man*, his last Christmas book from back in 1848.

In London he would also oversee the Christmas supplement of *Household Words*, his weekly magazine. This year, on a theme superintended by Dickens, and including one short story by him, was the conceit of Christmas at Mugby junction, a station where five railway lines converged. Leaning over the junction would be the bright blue towers of the H.M.P.S., from which the trains drew their force. Wilkie Collins's contribution was the story of a boy, back in London, who proudly wore the crisp blue and red uniform imagining, as he sat on duty with his headset strapped on, Mugby Junction and the great rail lines that he powered, on one of which was coming to London, and to whom he would be introduced on his fortnight off duty, his brother-in-law's cousin, a girl. Dickens had, of course, made Collins rewrite all the precious parts, and bring Father Christmas in for a scratch behind the ears—"else it might as well take place during August Bank Holiday!" said Dickens in a terse note to Collins when the manuscript had caught up with him at his hotel in Aberdeen yesterday.

Just now, the letter opener in his hand had become the cane of old Mr. Jayhew as he walked toward the Cratchitts' door.

* * *

Such a smell, like a bakery and a laundry and a pub all rolled together! The very air was thick with Christmas, so much so that Eben Mizer wondered how he detected the smells, unseen and unheard as he was, as the sputtering blue and purple Spirit stood beside him.

"Where's your father?" asked Mrs. Cratchitt.

"He's just gone to fetch Giant Timmy," said the youngest daughter.

"Your brother's name is Tim," said Mrs. Cratchitt. "It's just the neighbors call him that," she added with a smile.

The door came open without a knock, and there stood Katy, their eldest, laden with baskets and a case, come all the way from Cambridge, where she worked as a nanny.

"Mother!" she said. "Oh, the changes on the trains! I thought I should never reach here!"

"Well," said Mrs. Cratchitt, hugging her, "you're here, that's what matters. Now it will be a very merry Christmas!"

"I must have waited in ten stations," said Katy, taking off her shawl, then hugging her sisters and giving them small presents. "Every line its own train, every one with its own motive-car. Absolutely nothing works right on Christmas Eve!" She looked around. "Where's father? Where's Tim?"

"Your father's off fetching him . . . and his pay," said Mrs. Cratchitt.

"When can I go to work, mumsy?" asked Bobby, pulling at his pinafore.

"Not for a long time yet," said Mrs. Cratchitt. "Perhaps you'll be the first one in the family goes to University."

"Don't tease him so," said Katy.

"Well, it's possible," said his mother.

"Not with what Mr. Mizer pays father, and what I can send when I can, nor even with Tim's pay," said Katy. "And unless I am mistaken, his rates have gone down."

"All of them are down," said Mrs. Cratchitt, "what with the Irish and the potato blight. The streets here are full of red hair and beards, all looking for work."

There was a sound outside in the street, and the door came open, Mr. Cratchitt's back appearing as he turned. "This way. No, no, this way." He tugged twice, and then was followed.

Behind Mr. Cratchitt came Tim. He weighed fifteen stone though he was but twelve years old. He wore a white shapeless smock, with the name *Wilborn Mot. Ser.* written in smudged ink across the left chest, and white pants. His skin was translucent, as if made of waxed parchment, and his head had taken on a slight pearlike appearance, not helped by the short bowl-shape into which his hair had been cut. There were two round notches in the bowl-cut, just above the temples, and small bruised and slightly burnt circles covered the exposed skin there.

But it was the eyes Mizer noticed most—the eyes, once blue-green like his father's, had faded to whitish grey; they seemed both starting from their sockets in amazement, and to be taking in absolutely nothing, as if they were white china doorknobs stuck below his brows.

"Tim!" yelled Katy. She ran to him and hugged him as best she could. He slowly lifted one of his arms to wrap around her shoulders.

"Oh! You're hurting!" she said, and pulled away.

"Here, sit here, Tim," said Bob Cratchitt, making motions towards the largest chair. It groaned as the boy sat down.

"There is a small bonus for Christmas," said Mr. Cratchitt. "Not much." He patted the corner of the pay envelope in his pocket. "Not enough to equal even the old pay rates, but something. They've been working especially hard. The paymaster at Wilborn's was telling me they've been hired as motive power for six new factories in the last month alone."

"Oh, Tim," said Katy. "It's so good to see you and have you home for Christmas, even for just the day."

He looked at her for a long time, then went back to watching the fireplace.

Then there was the steaming sound of a goose coming out of the oven, hissing in its own gravy, and of a pudding going in, and Mr. Cratchitt leapt up and started the gin-and-apple punch, with its pieces of pineapple, and oranges, and a full stick of cinnamon bark.

Halfway through the meal, when healths were going round, and Mr. Mizer's name mentioned, and the Queen's, Giant Timmy sat forward suddenly in the big chair that had been pulled up to the table, and said, "God Bless . . . us all each . . . every . . ." Then he went quiet again, staring at his glass.

"That's right, that's exactly right, Tim," said Bob Cratchitt. "God Bless Us All, Each and Every One!"

Then the Spirit and Eben Mizer were outside in the snow, looking in at the window.

"I have nothing to do with this," said Eben. "I pay Cratchitt as good as he could get, and I have *nothing* to do, whatsoever, with the policies of the companies for whom I do the accounts." He looked at the Spirit of Christmases Current, who said nothing, and in a trice, he was back in his bedchamber, and the blue-purple glow was fading from the air. Exhausted as if he had swum ten miles off Blackpool, he dropped to unconsciousness against his stiff pillow.

* * *

Dickens grew rapidly tired as he read, but he dared not now let down either himself or his audience.

In many ways that younger self who had written the story had been a dreamer, but he had been also a very practical man in business and social matters. That night in Manchester as he waited for Mr. Disraeli to wind down, and as the idea for *The Christmas Garland* ran through his head, he thought he had seen a glimpse of a simple social need, and with all the assurance and arrogance of youth, what needed to be done. If he could strike the hammer blow with a Christmas tale, so much the better.

So he had.

* * *

The Spirit of Christmases Yet to Come was a small implike person, jumping here and there. It wore no mica or copper, only a tight garment and a small cloth skullcap from which stood up only a single wire, slightly glowing at the tip. First the Spirit was behind the chair, then in front, then above the bureau, then at one corner of the bed.

Despite its somewhat comic manner, the Spirit frightened Eben Mizer as the others had not. He drew back, afraid, for the face below the cap was an upturned grin, whether from mirth or in a rictus of pain he did not know. The imp said nothing but held out a gutta-percha covered wand for Mizer to grasp, as if it knew the very touch of its nervous hand would cause instant death, of the kind Mizer had feared from the Spirit before. Mizer took the end of the wand; instantly they were on the ceiling, then out in the hall, back near the chair, then inside something dark, then out into the night.

"I know you are to show me the Christmas Yet to Come, as Marley said. But is it Christmas as it *Will Be*, or only Christmas Yet to Come if I *keep on* this way?"

The imp was silent. They were in the air near the Serpentine, then somewhere off Margate, then back at the confluence of the Thames and Isis, then somewhere over the river near the docks. As Eben Mizer looked down, a slow barge transformed into a sleek boat going an unimaginable speed across the water. As he watched, it went in a long fast circle and crashed into a wharf, spewing bodies like toy soldiers from a bumped table.

He looked out towards the city. London towered up and up and up, till the highest buildings were level with his place in the middle of the air. And above the highest buildings stood giant towers of every kind and shape, humming and glowing blue in the air. Between the tall stone and iron buildings ran aerial railways, level after crossing level of them, and on every one some kind of train; some sleek, some boxlike, moving along their spans. The city was a blaze of light; every corner on every street glowed, all the buildings were lit. Far to the horizon the lights stretched, past all comprehension; lights in a million houses, more lights than all the candles and lamps and new motility-lights in Eben Mizer's world could make if all lit at once. There was no end to the glow—the whole river valley was one blue sheen that hurt his eyes.

Here and there, though, the blue flickered. As he watched, some trains gathered speed on their rails three hundred feet above the ground, and on others higher or lower they stopped completely. Then he and the imp were closer to one of the trains that had come to a halt. The passengers were pressed to the windows of one of the carriages, which had no engines or motive-cars attached, and then in a flash around a building came a spotted snake of light that was another train, and there was a great grinding roar as the two became one. The trains were a wilted salad of metal and wheels, and people flew by like hornet larvae from a nest hit by a shotgun blast. They tumbled without sound down the crevasses between the buildings, and cracked windows and masonry followed them as rails snapped like stretched string.

Something was wrong with the sky, for the blue light flickered on and off, as did the lights of the city, and the top of one of the towers began to glow faint red, as if it were a mulling poker.

Then he and the imp were on the ground, near a churchyard, and as they watched, with a grinding clang that died instantly, a train car from above went through the belfry of the church. Bodies, whose screams grew higher and louder, thudded into the sacred ground, snapping off tombstones, giving statues a clothing of true human skin.

The imp of Christmases Yet to Come drew nearer a wooden cross in the pauper's section, pointing. Eben Mizer stood transfixed, watching the towers of buildings, stone attached to iron, and the twisting cords of the railways above come loose and dangle before breaking off and falling.

With a deafening roar a ground-level railway train came ploughing through the churchyard wall, tearing a great gouge in the earth and, shedding passengers like an otter shakes water, burst through the opposite wall, ending its career further out of sight. It left a huge furrow through the cemetery, and at the cemetery's exact center a quiet, intact railway car in which nothing moved. Here and there in the torn earth a coffin stood on end, or lay cut in two, exactly half an anatomy lesson.

Eben Mizer saw that one of the great towers nearby had its side punched open, as neat a cut as with a knife through a hoop of cheese. From this opening shambled an army, if ever army such as this could be . . .

They were huge, and their heads too were huge, and the sides of their heads smoked; the hair of some was smoldering, which they did not notice, until some quite burst afire, and then those slowly sank back to the ground. Others walked in place, only thinking their thin legs were moving them forward. A higher part of the tower fell on twenty or thirty of them with no effect on the others who were walking before or behind them.

Great fires were bursting out in the buildings overhead. A jagged bolt lanced into the Thames, turning it to steam; a return bolt blew the top from a tower, which fell away from the river, taking two giant buildings with it.

A train shot out of the city a thousand feet up. As it left, the entire valley winked out into a darkness lit only by dim blazes from fires. Mizer heard the train hit in Southwark in the pitch blackness before his night vision came back.

All around there was moaning; the small moanings of people, larger ones of twisted cooling metal, great ones of buildings before they snapped and fell.

He began to make out shapes in the churchyard slowly, here and there. There were fires on bodies of people, on the wooden seats of train benches. A burning chesterfield fell onto the railway car, showering sparks.

The staggering figures came closer; they were dressed in loose clothing. By the light of fires he saw their bulbous shapes. One drew near, and turned towards him.

Its eyes, all their eyes, were like pale doorknobs. They moved towards him. The closest, its lips trying to say words, lifted its arms.

Others joined it, and they came on slowly, their shoulders moving ineffectually back and forth; they shuffled from one foot to the other, getting closer and closer. They lifted their white soft grub-worm fingers towards him—

* * *

WHAP!!! Dickens brought his palm down hard on the wooden block. The whole audience jumped. Men and women both yelped. The nervous laughter ran through the hall.

* * *

Eben Mizer opened the shutter. The boy in the street had another snowball ready to throw when he noticed the man at the window. He turned to run.

"Wait, boy!" Eben Mizer called. "Wait! What day is this?"

"What? Why, sir, it's Christmas Day."

"Bless me," said Eben Mizer. "Of course. The Spirits have done it all in one night. Of course they have. There's still time. Boy! You know that turkey in the shop down the street? . . ."

* * *

His foot was paining him mightily. He shifted his weight to the other leg, his arms drawing the giant shape of the man-sized turkey in the air. He was Eben Mizer, and he was the boy, and he was also the poulterer, running back with the turkey.

* * *

And from that day on, he was a man with a mission, a most Christian one, and he took to his bosom his nephew's family, and that of all mankind, but most especially that of Bob Cratchitt, and that most special case of Giant Timmy—who did not die—and took to his heart those great words, "God Bless . . . us all each . . . every . . ."

* * *

Charles Dickens closed his book and stood bathed in the selenium glow, and waited for the battering love that was applause.

Afterword to:
Household Words; Or, The Powers-That-Be

Here's how I killed *Amazing Stories,* world's oldest SF magazine.

The British Postal Service and I seemed to be about the only two entities in the world who noticed that 1993 was the 150th anniversary of *A Christmas Carol*.

Unfortunately, it took me till late July to realize it. That's normally way too late, since magazines are normally made up anywhere from five months to almost a year ahead of time, the ephemera like book reviews and editorials going in at the very last. Which normally meant I was out of luck, even if I was the only person who noticed.

But . . . a few months before, at Wiscon (In Madison, Wisconsin. In February. What's wrong with this picture?), Kim Mohan, editor of *Amazing*, and I sat down to a beer or something and he told me he'd been astounded that I'd only had half a story in *Amazing* in its and my long career. ("Men of Greywater Station" with George R. R. Martin, March 1976.) And that I should probably do something about it. I told him what I always tell editors: "Sure thing. Soon."

But he'd also told me he was editing only about three months ahead, which meant if I fired off something real quick, and he liked it, there was a chance he could get it into print before Christmas.

So I did two things at once: I fired off a letter to Kim asking if the lead time was still the same *and* I hit Peter Ackroyd's *Dickens* again.

I'd been researching Dickens on and off for five or six years (he's very important to *The Moon World*, if I ever finish *that*) and had read the up-to-then standard biographies: Edgar Johnson's *Charles Dickens: His Tragedy and Triumph* (2 vols.), Hesketh Pearson's *Dickens: His Character, Comedy and Career*, and the volume *Dickens at Work*. But a couple of years before, Ackroyd's book had come out. When I'd read it then, I knew what biographies *should* be.

I went back there to get the details of writing *A Christmas Carol* right. I already knew I was going to set the story in the 1860s, during one of Dickens's reading tours, and that it was going to be a work of memory and reconciliation.

The image of the pylons and Giant Timmy came to me about a week later. I had the "thing" that makes a story fall into place. For what did the Victorians do but give their children to the Empire for service?

On August 15–17 I wrote the first and second drafts, and on the eighteenth express-mailed it to Kim.

Who called me on the twenty-fourth accepting it. It was then he said, all the time he was reading it, the middle spirit should be called Christmas Current. "Do it," I said, and changed it to that in my manuscript.

* * *

Charles Dickens was pretty much a phenomenon, and a cautionary one. Family fallen on hard times; the blacking factory; then, shorthand clerk, court reporter, journalist, novelist, newspaper and magazine editor, philanthropist, reformer, speaker, long distance walker, insomniac, actor; the most famous reader of his own works who ever lived; patriarch of a large family (to paraphrase Carla Tortelli on *Cheers*: they popped out of Mrs. Dickens like a Pez dispenser) and supporter of failed parents, siblings, strangers; involved in scandal the last ten years of his life. Some of his children (and his sister-in-law) stayed with him after the separation from his wife, as against the wife's family.

And those books and stories. Yow! They'll probably last as long as there's readin' and writin'.

Ackroyd's book (and the others) can tell you all that. I wanted to do some of the same things in "Household Words . . ." only in an alternate Dickensian England, with another Scrooge, another Cratchitt, another nephew, but the same fat turkey. And, as I remember (like Mel Torme says of writing "The Christmas Song [Chestnuts Roasting on an Open Fire]") it was written on the hottest day of the year, in Texas, without air-conditioning; a story of a cool England and a remembered older Christmas.

When this was published (more later) I got a nice note (via Michael Moorcock, who'd heard me read it in November and asked for a copy) from Peter Ackroyd. Yow! At that same reading, David

Hartwell came up and said he wanted it for his *Christmas Magic* paperback, which appeared in December 1994.

Back to *Amazing*. The story was supposed to be out in the December 1993 issue. I went haring off, on an existential adventure, to be Writer in the Classroom in Telluride, Colorado (the two days after I'd read the story were spent driving one thousand miles to arrive at the hell-hole of Telluride just at dusk the second day), for six weeks (I'm *not* a skier, I'm a fisherman, and the San Miguel froze slowly over, day by day) from November 10 to December 17 of 1993.

In the middle of teaching hellbound seventh graders (and a good class of high school seniors) some ways of expressing themselves not involving knives, a package arrived from home: *Amazing*, with a great illo for the story. Only instead of December 1993 it said Winter 1994.

Uh oh.

You guessed it. That was the last one. Sixty-eight years, and it took me to kill it.

Sorry, Kim. If it's any consolation, I have killed, by having a story in the very last of each, the following things: *Vertex, Galaxy, Crawdaddy* (twice!), *Eternity SF, New Dimensions, Shayol.* But I admit it, it took some *doing* to kill the very first, oldest SF magazine.

Waldrop: The Legend Continues.

Classic Tales of Christmas Science Fiction, Fantasy and Whimsy

The Christmas story as a concept is as old as the holiday itself and at least tangentially related to both fantasy and science fiction.

(After all, the Christian tradition of the savior's birth is directly related to a prophecy—a prediction for the future, an obvious science fiction concept—heralding a divine birth of the son of God, a familiar fantasy trope from various mythologies, pagan and otherwise.)

Not wishing to negate the religious significance of the occasion, I believe it is fair to say that the more secular aspects of the holiday always seem to get more attention, and when it comes to holiday poster boys, Santa Claus has ruled the roost for well over a hundred years.

From Baum to Harte to Powell and McCaffrey, it is obvious that he will continue to enjoy his down home popularity for years to come.

A Kidnapped Santa Claus

L. Frank Baum

Santa Claus lives in the Laughing Valley, where stands the big, rambling castle in which his toys are manufactured. His workmen, selected from the ryls, knooks, pixies and fairies, live with him, and every one is as busy as can be from one year's end to another.

It is called the Laughing Valley because everything there is happy and gay. The brook chuckles to itself as it leaps rollicking between its green banks; the wind whistles merrily in the trees; the sunbeams dance lightly over the soft grass; and the violets and wild flowers look smilingly up from their green nests. To laugh one needs to be happy; to be happy one needs to be content. And throughout the Laughing Valley of Santa Claus contentment reigns supreme.

On one side is the mighty Forest of Burzee. At the other side stands the huge mountain that contains the Caves of the Daemons. And between them the Valley lies smiling and peaceful.

One would think that our good old Santa Claus, who devotes his days to making children happy, would have no enemies on all the earth; and, as a matter of fact, for a long period of time he encountered nothing but love wherever he might go.

But the Daemons who live in the mountain caves grew to hate Santa Claus very much, and all for the simple reason that he made children happy.

The Caves of the Daemons are five in number. A broad pathway leads up to the first cave, which is a finely arched cavern at the foot of the mountain, the entrance being beautifully carved and decorated. In it resides the Daemon of Selfishness. Back of this is another cavern inhabited by the Daemon of Envy. The cave of the Daemon of Hatred is next in order, and through this one passes to the home of the Daemon of Malice—situated in a dark and fearful cave in the very heart of the mountain. I do not know what lies beyond this. Some say there are terrible pitfalls leading to death and destruction, and this may very well be true. However, from each one of the four caves mentioned there is a small, narrow tunnel leading to the fifth cave—a cozy little room occupied by the Daemon of Repentance. And as the rocky floors of these passages are well worn by the track of passing feet, I judge that many wanderers in the Caves of the Daemons have escaped through the tunnels to the abode of the Daemon of Repentance, who is said to be a pleasant sort of fellow who gladly opens for one a little door admitting you into fresh air and sunshine again.

Well, these Daemons of the Caves, thinking they had great cause to dislike old Santa Claus, held a meeting one day to discuss the matter.

"I'm really getting lonesome," said the Daemon of Selfishness. "For Santa Claus distributes so many pretty Christmas gifts to all the children that they become happy and generous, through his example, and keep away from my cave."

"I'm having the same trouble," rejoined the Daemon of Envy. "The little ones seem quite content with Santa Claus, and there are few, indeed, that I can coax to become envious."

"And that makes it bad for me!" declared the Daemon of Hatred. "For if no children pass through the Caves of Selfishness and Envy, none can get to MY cavern."

"Or to mine," added the Daemon of Malice.

"For my part," said the Daemon of Repentance, "it is easily seen that if children do not visit your caves they have no need to visit mine; so that I am quite as neglected as you are."

"And all because of this person they call Santa Claus!" exclaimed the Daemon of Envy. "He is simply ruining our business, and something must be done at once."

To this they readily agreed; but what to do was another and more difficult matter to settle. They knew that Santa Claus worked all through the year at his castle in the Laughing Valley, preparing the gifts he was to distribute on Christmas Eve; and at first they resolved to try to tempt him into their caves, that they might lead him on to the terrible pitfalls that ended in destruction.

So the very next day, while Santa Claus was busily at work, surrounded by his little band of assistants, the Daemon of Selfishness came to him and said:

"These toys are wonderfully bright and pretty. Why do you not keep them for yourself? It's a pity to give them to those noisy boys and fretful girls, who break and destroy them so quickly."

"Nonsense!" cried the old graybeard, his bright eyes twinkling merrily as he turned toward the tempting Daemon. "The boys and girls are never so noisy and fretful after receiving my presents, and if I can make them happy for one day in the year I am quite content."

So the Daemon went back to the others, who awaited him in their caves, and said:

"I have failed, for Santa Claus is not at all selfish."

The following day the Daemon of Envy visited Santa Claus. Said he: "The toy shops are full of playthings quite as pretty as those you are making. What a shame it is that they should interfere with your business! They make toys by machinery much quicker than you can make them by hand; and they sell them for money, while you get nothing at all for your work."

But Santa Claus refused to be envious of the toy shops.

"I can supply the little ones but once a year—on Christmas Eve," he answered; "for the children are many, and I am but one. And as my work is one of love and kindness I would be ashamed to receive money for my little gifts. But throughout all the year the children must be amused in some way, and so the toy shops are able to bring much happiness to my little friends. I like the toy shops, and am glad to see them prosper."

In spite of the second rebuff, the Daemon of Hatred thought he would try to influence Santa Claus. So the next day he entered the busy workshop and said:

"Good morning, Santa! I have bad news for you."

"Then run away, like a good fellow," answered Santa Claus. "Bad news is something that should be kept secret and never told."

"You cannot escape this, however," declared the Daemon; "for in the world are a good many who do not believe in Santa Claus, and these you are bound to hate bitterly, since they have so wronged you."

"Stuff and rubbish!" cried Santa.

"And there are others who resent your making children happy and who sneer at you and call you a foolish old rattlepate! You are quite right to hate such base slanderers, and you ought to be revenged upon them for their evil words."

"But I don't hate 'em!" exclaimed Santa Claus positively. "Such people do me no real harm, but merely render themselves and their children unhappy. Poor things! I'd much rather help them any day than injure them."

Indeed, the Daemons could not tempt old Santa Claus in any way. On the contrary, he was shrewd enough to see that their object in visiting him was to make mischief and trouble, and his cheery laughter disconcerted the evil ones and showed to them the folly of such an undertaking. So they abandoned honeyed words and determined to use force.

It was well known that no harm can come to Santa Claus while he is in the Laughing Valley, for the fairies, and ryls, and knooks all protect him. But on Christmas Eve he drives his reindeer out into the big world, carrying a sleighload of toys and pretty gifts to the children; and this was the time and the occasion when his enemies had the best chance to injure him. So the Daemons laid their plans and awaited the arrival of Christmas Eve.

The moon shone big and white in the sky, and the snow lay crisp and sparkling on the ground as Santa Claus cracked his whip and sped away out of the Valley into the great world beyond. The roomy sleigh was packed full with huge sacks of toys, and as the reindeer dashed onward our jolly old Santa laughed and whistled and sang for very joy. For in all his merry life this was the one day in the year when he was happiest—the day he lovingly bestowed the treasures of his workshop upon the little children.

It would be a busy night for him, he well knew. As he whistled and shouted and cracked his whip again, he reviewed in mind all the towns and cities and farmhouses where he was expected, and figured that he had just enough presents to go around and make every child happy. The reindeer knew exactly what was expected of them, and dashed along so swiftly that their feet scarcely seemed to touch the snow-covered ground.

Suddenly a strange thing happened: a rope shot through the moonlight and a big noose that was in the end of it settled over the arms and body of Santa Claus and drew tight. Before he could resist or even cry out he was jerked from the seat of the sleigh and tumbled head foremost into a snowbank, while the reindeer rushed onward with the load of toys and carried it quickly out of sight and sound.

Such a surprising experience confused old Santa for a moment, and when he had collected his senses he found that the wicked Daemons had pulled him from the snowdrift and bound him tightly with many coils of the stout rope. And then they carried the kidnapped Santa Claus away to their mountain, where they thrust the prisoner into a secret cave and chained him to the rocky wall so that he could not escape.

"Ha, ha!" laughed the Daemons, rubbing their hands together with cruel glee. "What will the children do now? How they will cry and scold and storm when they find there are no toys in their stockings and no gifts on their Christmas trees! And what a lot of punishment they will receive from their parents, and how they will flock to our Caves of Selfishness, and Envy, and Hatred, and Malice! We have done a mighty clever thing, we Daemons of the Caves!"

Now it so chanced that on this Christmas Eve the good Santa Claus had taken with him in his sleigh Nuter the Ryl, Peter the Knook, Kilter the Pixie, and a small fairy named Wisk—his four favorite assistants. These little people he had often found very useful in helping him to distribute his gifts to the children, and when their master was so suddenly dragged from the sleigh they were all snugly tucked underneath the seat, where the sharp wind could not reach them.

The tiny immortals knew nothing of the capture of Santa Claus until some time after he had disappeared. But finally they missed his cheery voice, and as their master always sang or whistled on his journeys, the silence warned them that something was wrong.

Little Wisk stuck out his head from underneath the seat and found Santa Claus gone and no one to direct the flight of the reindeer.

"Whoa!" he called out, and the deer obediently slackened speed and came to a halt.

Peter and Nuter and Kilter all jumped upon the seat and looked back over the track made by the sleigh. But Santa Claus had been left miles and miles behind.

"What shall we do?" asked Wisk anxiously, all the mirth and mischief banished from his wee face by this great calamity.

"We must go back at once and find our master," said Nuter the Ryl, who thought and spoke with much deliberation.

"No, no!" exclaimed Peter the Knook, who, cross and crabbed though he was, might always be depended upon in an emergency. "If we delay, or go back, there will not be time to get the toys to the children before morning; and that would grieve Santa Claus more than anything else."

"It is certain that some wicked creatures have captured him," added Kilter thoughtfully, "and their object must be to make the children unhappy. So our first duty is to get the toys distributed as carefully as if Santa Claus were himself present. Afterward we can search for our master and easily secure his freedom."

This seemed such good and sensible advice that the others at once resolved to adopt it. So Peter the Knook called to the reindeer, and the faithful animals again sprang forward and dashed over hill and valley, through forest and plain, until they came to the houses wherein children lay sleeping and dreaming of the pretty gifts they would find on Christmas morning.

The little immortals had set themselves a difficult task; for although they had assisted Santa Claus on many of his journeys, their master had always directed and guided them and told them exactly what he wished them to do. But now they had to distribute the toys according to their own judgment, and they did not understand children as well as did old Santa. So it is no wonder they made some laughable errors.

Mamie Brown, who wanted a doll, got a drum instead; and a drum is of no use to a girl who loves dolls. And Charlie Smith, who delights to romp and play out of doors, and who wanted some new rubber boots to keep his feet dry, received a sewing box filled with colored worsteds and threads and needles, which made him so provoked that he thoughtlessly called our dear Santa Claus a fraud.

Had there been many such mistakes the Daemons would have accomplished their evil purpose and made the children unhappy. But the little friends of the absent Santa Claus labored faithfully and intelligently to carry out their master's ideas, and they made fewer errors than might be expected under such unusual circumstances.

And, although they worked as swiftly as possible, day had begun to break before the toys and other presents were all distributed; so for the first time in many years the reindeer trotted into the Laughing Valley, on their return, in broad daylight, with the brilliant sun peeping over the edge of the forest to prove they were far behind their accustomed hours.

Having put the deer in the stable, the little folk began to wonder how they might rescue their master; and they realized they must discover, first of all, what had happened to him and where he was.

So Wisk the Fairy transported himself to the bower of the Fairy Queen, which was located deep in the heart of the Forest of Burzee; and once there, it did not take him long to find out all about the naughty Daemons and how they had kidnapped the good Santa Claus to prevent his making children happy. The Fairy Queen also promised her assistance, and then, fortified by this powerful support, Wisk flew back to where Nuter and Peter and Kilter awaited him, and the four counseled together and laid plans to rescue their master from his enemies.

It is possible that Santa Claus was not as merry as usual during the night that succeeded his capture. For although he had faith in the judgment of his little friends he could not avoid a certain amount of worry, and an anxious look would creep at times into his kind old eyes as he thought of the disappointment that might await his dear little children. And the Daemons, who guarded him by turns, one after another, did not neglect to taunt him with contemptuous words in his helpless condition.

When Christmas Day dawned the Daemon of Malice was guarding the prisoner, and his tongue was sharper than that of any of the others.

"The children are waking up, Santa!" he cried. "They are waking up to find their stockings empty! Ho, ho! How they will quarrel, and wail, and stamp their feet in anger! Our caves will be full today, old Santa! Our caves are sure to be full!"

But to this, as to other like taunts, Santa Claus answered nothing. He was much grieved by his capture, it is true; but his courage did not forsake him. And, finding that the prisoner would not reply to his jeers, the Daemon of Malice presently went away, and sent the Daemon of Repentance to take his place.

This last personage was not so disagreeable as the others. He had gentle and refined features, and his voice was soft and pleasant in tone.

"My brother Daemons do not trust me overmuch," said he, as he entered the cavern; "but it is morning, now, and the mischief is done. You cannot visit the children again for another year."

"That is true," answered Santa Claus, almost cheerfully; "Christmas Eve is past, and for the first time in centuries I have not visited my children."

"The little ones will be greatly disappointed," murmured the Daemon of Repentance, almost regretfully; "but that cannot be helped now. Their grief is likely to make the children selfish and envious and hateful, and if they come to the Caves of the Daemons today I shall get a chance to lead some of them to my Cave of Repentance."

"Do you never repent, yourself?" asked Santa Claus, curiously.

"Oh, yes, indeed," answered the Daemon. "I am even now repenting that I assisted in your capture. Of course it is too late to remedy the evil that has been done; but repentance, you know, can come only after an evil thought or deed, for in the beginning there is nothing to repent of."

"So I understand," said Santa Claus. "Those who avoid evil need never visit your cave."

"As a rule, that is true," replied the Daemon; "yet you, who have done no evil, are about to visit my cave at once; for to prove that I sincerely regret my share in your capture I am going to permit you to escape."

This speech greatly surprised the prisoner, until he reflected that it was just what might be expected of the Daemon of Repentance. The fellow at once busied himself untying the knots that bound Santa Claus and unlocking the chains that fastened him to the wall. Then he led the way through a long tunnel until they both emerged in the Cave of Repentance.

"I hope you will forgive me," said the Daemon pleadingly. "I am not really a bad person, you know; and I believe I accomplish a great deal of good in the world."

With this he opened a back door that let in a flood of sunshine, and Santa Claus sniffed the fresh air gratefully.

"I bear no malice," said he to the Daemon, in a gentle voice; "and I am sure the world would be a dreary place without you. So, good morning, and a Merry Christmas to you!"

With these words he stepped out to greet the bright morning, and a moment later he was trudging along, whistling softly to himself, on his way to his home in the Laughing Valley.

Marching over the snow toward the mountain was a vast army, made up of the most curious creatures imaginable. There were numberless knooks from the forest, as rough and crooked in appearance as the gnarled branches of the trees they ministered to. And there were dainty ryls from the fields, each one bearing the emblem of the flower or plant it guarded. Behind these were many ranks of pixies, gnomes and nymphs, and in the rear a thousand beautiful fairies floated along in gorgeous array.

This wonderful army was led by Wisk, Peter, Nuter, and Kilter, who had assembled it to rescue Santa Claus from captivity and to punish the Daemons who had dared to take him away from his beloved children.

And, although they looked so bright and peaceful, the little immortals were armed with powers that would be very terrible to those who had incurred their anger. Woe to the Daemons of the Caves if this mighty army of vengeance ever met them!

But lo! coming to meet his loyal friends appeared the imposing form of Santa Claus, his white beard floating in the breeze and his bright eyes sparkling with pleasure at this proof of the love and veneration he had inspired in the hearts of the most powerful creatures in existence.

And while they clustered around him and danced with glee at his safe return, he gave them earnest thanks for their support. But Wisk, and Nuter, and Peter, and Kilter, he embraced affectionately.

"It is useless to pursue the Daemons," said Santa Claus to the army. "They have their place in the world, and can never be destroyed. But that is a great pity, nevertheless," he continued musingly.

So the fairies, and knooks, and pixies, and ryls all escorted the good man to his castle, and there left him to talk over the events of the night with his little assistants.

Wisk had already rendered himself invisible and flown through the big world to see how the children were getting along on this bright Christmas morning; and by the time he returned, Peter had finished telling Santa Claus of how they had distributed the toys.

"We really did very well," cried the fairy, in a pleased voice; "for I found little unhappiness among the children this morning. Still, you must not get captured again, my dear master; for we might not be so fortunate another time in carrying out your ideas."

He then related the mistakes that had been made, and which he had not discovered until his tour of inspection. And Santa Claus at once sent him with rubber boots for Charlie Smith, and a doll for Mamie Brown; so that even those two disappointed ones became happy.

As for the wicked Daemons of the Caves, they were filled with anger and chagrin when they found that their clever capture of Santa Claus had come to naught. Indeed, no one on that Christmas Day appeared to be at all selfish, or envious, or hateful. And, realizing that while the children's saint had so many powerful friends it was folly to oppose him, the Daemons never again attempted to interfere with his journeys on Christmas Eve.

How Santa Claus Came to Simpson's Bar

Bret Harte

It had been raining in the valley of the Sacramento. The North Fork had overflowed its banks, and Rattlesnake Creek was impassable. The few boulders that had marked the summer ford at Simpson's Crossing were obliterated by a vast sheet of water stretching to the foothills. The upstage was stopped at Granger's; the last mail had been abandoned in the tules, the rider swimming for his life. "An area," remarked the *Sierra Avalanche,* with pensive local pride, "as large as the State of Massachusetts is now under water."

Nor was the weather any better in the foothills. The mud lay deep on the mountain road; wagons that neither physical force nor moral objurgation could move from the evil ways into which they had fallen encumbered the track, and the way to Simpson's Bar was indicated by broken-down teams and hard swearing. And further on, cut off and inaccessible, rained upon and bedraggled, smitten by high winds and threatened by high water, Simpson's Bar, on the eve of Christmas Day, 1862, clung like a swallow's nest to the rocky entablature and splintered capitals of Table Mountain, and shook in the blast.

As night shut down on the settlement, a few lights gleamed through the mist from the windows of cabins on either side of the highway, now crossed and gullied by lawless streams and swept by marauding winds. Happily most of the population were gathered at Thompson's store, clustered around a red-hot stove, at which they silently spat in some accepted sense of social communion that perhaps rendered conversations unnecessary. Indeed, most methods of diversion had long since been exhausted on Simpson's Bar; high water had suspended the regular occupations on gulch and on river, and a consequent lack of money and whiskey had taken the zest from most illegitimate recreation. Even Mr. Hamlin was fain to leave the Bar with fifty dollars in his pocket—the only amount actually realized of the large sums won by him in the successful exercise of his arduous profession. "Ef I was asked," he remarked somewhat later—"ef I was asked to pint out a purty little village when a retired sport as didn't care for money could exercise hisself, frequent and lively, I'd say Simpson's Bar; but for a young man with a large family depending on his exertions, it don't pay." As Mr. Hamlin's family consisted mainly of female adults, this remark is quoted rather to show the breadth of his humor than the exact extent of his responsibilities.

Howbeit, the unconscious objects of this satire sat that evening in the listless apathy begotten of idleness and lack of excitement. Even the sudden splashing of hoofs before the door did not arouse them. Dick Bullen alone paused in the act of scraping out his pipe, and lifted his head, but no other one of the group indicated any interest in, or recognition of, the man who entered.

It was a figure familiar enough to the company, and known in Simpson's Bar as "The Old Man." A man of perhaps fifty years; grizzled and scant of hair, but still fresh and youthful of complexion. A face full of ready but not very powerful sympathy, with a chameleon-like aptitude for taking on the shade and color of contiguous moods and feelings. He had evidently just left some hilarious companions, and did not at first notice the gravity of the group, but clapped the shoulder of the nearest man jocularly, and threw himself into a vacant chair.

"Jest heard the best thing out, boys! Ye know Smiley, over yar—Jim Smiley—funniest man in the Bar? Well, Jim was jest tellin the richest yarn about—"

"Smiley's a—fool," interrupted a gloomy voice.

"A particular—skunk," added another in sepulchral accents.

A silence followed these positive statements. The Old Man

glanced quickly around the group. Then his face slowly changed. "That's so," he said reflectively, after a pause, "certainly a sort of a skunk and suthin' of a fool. In course." He was silent for a moment, as in painful contemplation of the unsavoriness and folly of the unpopular Smiley. "Dismal weather, ain't it?" he added, now fully embarked on the current of prevailing sentiment. "Mighty rough papers on the boys, and no show for money this season. And tomorrow's Christmas."

There was a movement among the men at this announcement, but whether of satisfaction or disgust was not plain. "Yes," continued the Old Man in the lugubrious tone he had within the last few moments unconsciously adopted,—"yes, Christmas, and tonight's Christmas Eve. Ye see, boys, I kinder thought—that is, I sorter had an idee, jest passin' like, you know—that maybe ye'd all like to come over to my house tonight and have a sort of tear round. But I suppose, now, you wouldn't? Don't feel like it, maybe?" he added with anxious sympathy, peering into the faces of his companions.

"Well, I don't know," responded Tom Flynn with some cheerfulness. "P'r'aps we may. But how about your wife, Old Man? What does *she* say to it?"

The Old Man hesitated. His conjugal experience had not been a happy one, and the fact was known to Simpson's Bar. His first wife, a delicate, pretty little woman, had suffered keenly and secretly from the jealous suspicions of her husband, until one day he invited the whole Bar to his house to expose her infidelity. On arriving, the party found the shy, petite creature quietly engaged in her household duties, and retired abashed and discomfited. But the sensitive woman did not easily recover from the shock of this extraordinary outrage. It was with difficulty she regained her equanimity sufficiently to release her lover from the closet in which he was concealed, and escape with him. She left a boy of three years to comfort her bereaved husband. The Old Man's present wife had been his cook. She was large, loyal, and aggressive.

Before he could reply, Joe Dimmick suggested with great directness that it was the "Old Man's house," and that, invoking the Divine Power, if the case were his own, he would invite whom he pleased, even if in so doing he imperiled his salvation. The Powers of Evil, he further remarked, should contend against him vainly. All this delivered with a terseness and vigor lost in this necessary translation.

"In course. Certainly. Thet's it," said the Old Man with a sympathetic frown. "Thar's no trouble about thet. It's my own house, built every stick on it myself. Don't you be afeard o' her, boys. She *may* cut up a trifle rough—ez wimmin do—but she'll come round." Secretly the Old Man trusted to the exaltation of liquor and the power of courageous example to sustain him in such an emergency.

As yet, Dick Bullen, the oracle and leader of Simpson's Bar, had not spoken. He now took his pipe from his lips. "Old Man, how's that yer Johnny gettin' on? Seems to me he didn't look so peart last time I seed him on the bluff heavin' rocks at Chinamen. Didn't seem to take much interest in it. Thar was a gang of 'em by yar yesterday—drownded out up the river—and I kinder thought o' Johnny, and how he'd miss 'em! Maybe now, we'd be in the way ef he wus sick?"

The father, evidently touched not only by this pathetic picture of Johnny's deprivation, but by the considerate delicacy of the speaker, hastened to assure him that Johnny was better, and that a "little fun might 'liven him up." Whereupon Dick arose, shook himself, and saying, "I'm ready. Lead the way, Old Man: here goes," himself led the way with a leap, a characteristic howl, and darted out into the night. As he passed through the outer room he caught up a blazing brand from the hearth. The action was repeated by the rest of the party, closely following and elbowing each other, and before the astonished proprietor of Thompson's grocery was aware of the intention of his guests, the room was deserted.

The night was pitchy dark. In the first gust of wind their temporary torches were extinguished, and only the red brands dancing and flitting in the gloom like drunken will-o'-the-wisps indicated their whereabouts. Their way led up Pine Tree Canyon, at the head of which a broad, low, bark-thatched cabin burrowed in the mountain-side. It was the home of the Old Man, and the entrance to the tunnel in which he worked when he worked at all. Here the crowd paused for a moment, out of delicate deference to their host, who came up panting in the rear.

"P'r'aps ye'd better hold on a second out yer, whilst I go in and see that things is all right," said the Old Man, with an indifference he was far from feeling. The suggestion was graciously accepted, the door opened and closed on the host, and the crowd, leaning their backs against the wall and cowering under the eaves, waited and listened.

For a few moments there was no sound but the dripping of water from the eaves and the stir and rustle of wrestling boughs above them. Then the men became uneasy, and whispered suggestion and suspicion passed from the one to the other. "Reckon she's caved in his head the first lick!" "Decoyed him inter the tunnel and barred him up, likely." "Got him down and sittin' on him." "Prob'ly biling suthin' to heave on us; stand clear the door, boys!" For just then the latch clicked, the door slowly opened, and a voice said, "Come in out o' the wet."

The voice was neither that of the Old Man nor of his wife. It was the voice of a small boy, its weak treble broken by that preternatural hoarseness which only vagabondage and the habit of premature self-assertion can give. It was the face of a small boy that looked up at theirs—a face that might have been pretty, and even refined, but that it was darkened by evil knowledge from within, and dirt and hard experience from without. He had a blanket around his shoulders, and had evidently just risen from his bed. "Come in," he repeated, "and don't make no noise. The Old Man's in there talking to mar," he continued, pointing to an adjacent room which seemed to be a kitchen, from which the Old Man's voice came in deprecating accents. "Let me be," he added querulously to Dick Bullen, who had caught him up, blanket and all, and was affecting to toss him into the fire, "let go o' me, you d—d old fool, d'ye hear?"

Thus adjured, Dick Bullen lowered Johnny to the ground with a smothered laugh, while the men, entering quietly, ranged themselves around a long table of rough boards which occupied the center of the room. Johnny then gravely proceeded to a cupboard and brought out several articles, which he deposited on the table. "Thar's whiskey. And crackers. And red herons. And cheese." He took a bite of the latter on his way to the table. "And sugar." He scooped up a mouthful en route with a small and very dirty hand. "And terbacker. That's dried appils too on the shelf, but I don't admire 'em. Appils is swellin'. Thar," he concluded, "now wade in, and don't he afeard. *I* don't mind the old woman. She don't b'long to *me*. S'long."

He had stepped to the threshold of a small room, scarcely larger than a closet, partitioned off from the main apartment, and holding in its dim recess a small bed. He stood there a moment looking at the company, his bare feet peeping from the blanket, and nodded.

"Hello, Johnny! You ain't goin' to turn in agin, are ye?" said Dick.

"Yes, I are," responded Johnny decidedly.

"Why, wot's up, old fellow?"

"I'm sick."

"How sick?"

"I've got a fevier. And childblains. And roomatiz," returned Johnny, and vanished within. After a moment's pause, he added in the dark, apparently from under the bedclothes—"And biles!"

There was an embarrassing silence. The men looked at each other and at the fire. Even with the appetizing banquet before them, it seemed as if they might again fall into the despondency of Thompson's grocery, when the voice of the Old Man, incautiously lifted, came deprecatingly from the kitchen.

"Certainly! Thet's so. In course they is. A gang o' lazy, drunken loafers, and that ar Dick Bullen's the ornariest of all. Didn't hev no more *sabe* than to come round yar with sickness in the house and no provision. Thet's what I said: 'Bullen,' sez I, 'it's crazy drunk you are, or a fool,' sez I, 'to think o' such a thing.' 'Staples,' I sez, 'be you a man, Staples, and 'spect to raise h—ll under my roof and invalids lyin' round?' But they would come—they would. Thet's wot you must 'spect o' such trash as lays round the Bar."

A burst of laughter from the men followed this unfortunate exposure. Whether it was overheard in the kitchen, or whether the Old Man's irate companion had just then exhausted all other modes of expressing her contemptuous indignation, I cannot say, but a back door was suddenly slammed with great violence. A moment later and the Old Man reappeared, haply unconscious of the cause of the late hilarious outburst, and smiled blandly.

"The old woman thought she'd jest run over to Mrs. MacFadden's for a sociable call," he explained with jaunty indifference, as he took a seat at the board.

Oddly enough it needed this untoward incident to relieve the embarrassment that was beginning to be felt by the party, and their natural audacity returned with their host. I do not propose to record the convivialities of that evening. The inquisitive reader will accept the statement that the conversation was characterized by the same intellectual exaltation, the same cautious reverence, the same fastidious delicacy, the same rhetorical precision, and the same logical and coherent discourse somewhat later in the evening, which distinguish similar gatherings of the masculine sex in more civilized localities and under more favorable auspices. No glasses were broken in the absence of any; no liquor was uselessly spilt on the floor or table in the scarcity of that article.

It was nearly midnight when the festivities were interrupted. "Hush," said Dick Bullen, holding up his hand. It was the querulous voice of Johnny from his adjacent closet: "O Dad!"

The Old Man arose hurriedly and disappeared in the closet. Presently he reappeared. "His rheumatiz is coming on agin bad," he explained, "and he wants rubbin'." He lifted the demijohn of whiskey from the table and shook it. It was empty. Dick Bullen put down his tin cup with an embarrassed laugh. So did the others. The Old Man examined their contents and said hopefully, "I reckon that's enough; he don't need much. You hold on all o' you for a spell, and I'll be back," and vanished in the closet with an old flannel shirt and the whiskey. The door closed but imperfectly, and the following dialogue was distinctly audible:

"Now, sonny, whar does she ache worst?"

"Sometimes over yar and sometimes under yer; but it's more powerful from yer to yer. Rub yer, Dad."

A silence seemed to indicate a brisk rubbing. Then Johnny:

"Hevin' a good time out yer, Dad?"

"Yes, sonny."

"Tomorrer's Chrismiss—ain't it?"

"Yes, sonny. How does she feel now?"

"Better. Rub a little furder down. Wot's Chrismiss, anyway? Wot's it all about?"

"Oh, it's a day."

This exhaustive definition was apparently satisfactory, for there was a silent interval of rubbing. Presently Johnny again:

"Mar sez that everywhere else but yer everybody gives things to everybody Chrismiss, and then she jist waded inter you. She sez thar's a man they call Sandy Claws, not a white man, you know, but a kind o' Chinemin, comes down the chimbley night afore Chrismiss and gives things to chillern—boys like me. Put 'em in their butes! Thet's what she tried to play upon me. Easy now, Pop, whar are you rubbin' to—thet's a mile from the place. She jest made that up, didn't she, jest to aggrewate me and you? Don't rub thar . . . Why, Dad!"

In the great quiet that seemed to have fallen upon the house the sigh of the near pines and the drip of leaves without was very distinct. Johnny's voice, too, was lowered as he went on, "Don't you take on now, for I'm gettin' all right fast. Wot's the boys doin' out thar?"

The Old Man partly opened the door and peered through. His guests were sitting there sociably enough, and there were a few silver coins and a lean buckskin purse on the table. "Bettin' on suthin'—some little game or 'nother. They're all right," he replied to Johnny, and recommenced his rubbing.

"I'd like to take a hand and win some money," said Johnny reflectively after a pause.

The Old Man glibly repeated what was evidently a familiar formula, that if Johnny would wait until he struck it rich in the tunnel he'd have lots of money, etc., etc.

"Yes," said Johnny, "but you don't. And whether you strike it or I win it, it's about the same. It's all luck. But it's mighty cur'o's about Chrismiss—ain't it? Why do they call it Chrismiss?"

Perhaps from some instinctive deference to the overhearing of his guests, or from some vague sense of incongruity, the Old Man's reply was so low as to be inaudible beyond the room.

"Yes," said Johnny, with some slight abatement of interest, "I've heard o' *him* before. Thar, that'll do, Dad. I don't ache near so bad as I did. Now wrap me tight in this yer blanket. So. Now," he added in a muffled whisper, "sit down yer by me till I go asleep." To assure himself of obedience, he disengaged one hand from the blanket, and grasping his father's sleeve, again composed himself to rest.

For some moments the Old Man waited patiently. Then the unwonted stillness of the house excited his curiosity, and without moving from the bed he cautiously opened the door with his disengaged hand, and looked into the main room. To his infinite surprise it was dark and deserted. But even then a smoldering log on the hearth broke, and by the upspringing blaze he saw the figure of Dick Bullen sitting by the dying embers.

"Hello!"

Dick started, rose, and came somewhat unsteadily toward him.

"Whar's the boys?" said the Old Man.

"Gone up the canyon on a little *pasear.* They're coming back for me in a minit. I'm waitin' round for 'em. What are you starin' at, Old Man?" he added, with a forced laugh; "do you think I'm drunk?"

The Old Man might have been pardoned the supposition, for Dick's eyes were humid and his face flushed. He loitered and lounged back to the chimney, yawned, shook himself, buttoned up his coat, and laughed. "Liquor ain't so plenty as that, Old Man. Now don't you git up," he continued, as the Old Man made a movement to release his sleeve from Johnny's hand. "Don't you mind manners. Sit jest whar you be; I'm goin' in a jiffy. Thar, that's them now."

There was a low tap at the door. Dick Bullen opened it quickly, nodded "good night" to his host, and disappeared. The Old Man would have followed him but for the hand that still unconsciously grasped his sleeve. He could have easily disengaged it: it was small, weak, and emaciated. But perhaps because it *was* small, weak, and emaciated he changed his mind, and drawing his chair closer to the bed, rested his head upon it. In this defenseless attitude the potency of his earlier potations surprised him. The room flickered and faded before his eyes, reappeared, faded again, went out, and left him—asleep.

Meantime Dick Bullen, closing the door, confronted his companions. "Are you ready?" said Staples. "Ready," said Dick; "what's the time?" "Past twelve," was the reply; "can you make it?—it's nigh on fifty miles, the round trip hither and yon." "I reckon," returned Dick shortly. "Whar's the mare?" "Bill and Jack's holdin' her at the crossin'." "Let 'em hold on a minit longer," said Dick.

He turned and re-entered the house softly. By the light of the guttering candle and dying fire he saw that the door of the little room was open. He stepped toward it on tip-toe and looked in. The Old Man had fallen back in his chair, snoring, his helpless feet thrust out in a line with his collapsed shoulders, and his hat pulled over his eyes. Beside him, on a narrow wooden bedstead, lay Johnny, muffled tightly in a blanket that hid all save a strip of forehead and a few curls damp with perspiration. Dick Bullen made a step forward, hesitated, and glanced over his shoulder into the deserted room. Everything was quiet. With a sudden resolution he parted his huge mustaches with both hands and stooped over the sleeping boy. But even as he did so a mischievous blast, lying in wait, swooped down the chimney, rekindled the hearth, and lit up the room with a shameless glow from which Dick fled in bashful terror.

His companions were already waiting for him at the crossing. Two of them were struggling in the darkness with some strange misshapen bulk, which as Dick came nearer took the semblance of a great yellow horse.

It was the mare. She was not a pretty picture. From her Roman nose to her rising haunches, from her arched spine hidden by the stiff *machillas* of a Mexican saddle, to her thick, straight bony legs, there was not a line of equine grace. In her half-blind but wholly vicious white eyes, in her protruding underlip, in her monstrous color, there was nothing but ugliness and vice.

"Now then," said Staples, "stand cl'ar of her heels, boys, and up with you. Don't miss your first holt of her mane, and mind ye get your off stirrup *quick*. Ready!"

There was a leap, a scrambling struggle, a bound, a wild retreat of the crowd, a circle of flying hoofs, two springless leaps that jarred the earth, a rapid play and jingle of spurs, a plunge, and then the voice of Dick somewhere in the darkness. "All right!"

"Don't take the lower road back onless you're hard pushed for time! Don't hold her in downhill! We'll be at the ford at five. G'lang! Hoopa! Mula! GO!"

A splash, a spark struck from the ledge in the road, a clatter in the rocky cut beyond, and Dick was gone.

* * *

Sing, O muse, the ride of Richard Bullen! Sing, O Muse, of chivalrous men! the sacred quest, the doughty deeds, the battery of low churls, the fearsome ride and gruesome perils of the Flower of Simpson's Bar! Alack! she is dainty, this Muse! She will have none of this bucking brute and swaggering, ragged rider, and I must fain follow him in prose, afoot!

It was one o'clock, and yet he had only gained Rattlesnake Hill. For in that time Jovita had rehearsed to him all her imperfections and practiced all her vices. Thrice had she stumbled. Twice had she thrown up her Roman nose in a straight line with the reins, and resisting bit and spur, struck out madly across country. Twice had she reared, and rearing, fallen backward; and twice had the agile Dick, unharmed, regained his seat before she found her vicious legs again. And a mile beyond them, at the foot of a long hill, was Rattlesnake Creek. Dick knew that here was the crucial test of his ability to perform his enterprise, set his teeth grimly, put his knees well into her flanks, and changed his defensive tactics to brisk aggression. Bullied and maddened, Jovita began the descent of the hill. Here the artful Richard pretended to hold her in with ostentatious objurgation and well-feigned cries of alarm. It is unnecessary to add that Jovita instantly ran away. Nor need I state the time made in the descent; it is written in the chronicles of Simpson's Bar. Enough that in another moment, as it seemed to Dick, she was splashing on the overflowed banks of Rattlesnake Creek. As Dick expected, the momentum she had acquired carried her beyond the point of balking, and holding her well together for a mighty leap, they dashed into the middle of the swiftly flowing current. A few moments of kicking, wading, and swimming, and Dick drew a long breath on the opposite bank.

The road from Rattlesnake Creek to Red Mountain was tolerably level. Either the plunge in Rattlesnake Creek had dampened her baleful fire, or the art which led to it had shown her the superior wickedness of her rider, for Jovita no longer wasted her surplus energy in wanton conceits. Once she bucked, but it was from force of habit; once she shied, but it was from a new, freshly painted meetinghouse at the crossing of the county road. Hollows, ditches, gravelly deposits, patches of freshly springing grasses, flew from beneath her rattling hoofs. She began to smell unpleasantly, once or twice she coughed slightly, but there was no abatement of her strength or speed. By two o'clock he had passed Red Mountain and begun the descent to the plain. Ten minutes later the driver of the fast Pioneer coach was overtaken and passed by a "man on a pinto hoss,"—an event sufficiently notable for remark. At half-past two Dick rose in his stirrups with a great shout. Stars were glittering through the rifted clouds, and beyond him, out of the plain, rose two spires, a flagstaff, and a straggling line of black objects. Dick jingled his spurs and swung his *riata*, Jovita hounded forward, and in another moment they swept into Tuttleville, and drew up before the wooden piazza of "The Hotel of All Nations."

What transpired that night at Tuttleville is not strictly a part of this record. Briefly I may state, however, that after Jovita had been handed over to a sleepy ostler, whom she at once kicked into unpleasant consciousness, Dick sallied out with the barkeeper for a tour of the sleeping town. Lights still gleamed from a few saloons and gambling houses; but avoiding these, they stopped before several closed shops, and by persistent tapping and judicious outcry roused the proprietors from their beds, and made them unbar the doors of their magazines and expose their wares. Sometimes they were met by curses, but oftener by interest and some concern in their needs, and the interview was invariably concluded by a drink. It was three o'clock before this pleasantry was given over, and with a small waterproof bag of India rubber strapped on his shoulders, Dick returned to the hotel. But here he was waylaid by Beauty—Beauty opulent in charms, affluent in dress, persuasive in speech, and Spanish in accent! In vain she repeated the invitation in "Excelsior," happily scorned by all Alpine-climbing youth, and rejected by this child of the Sierras—a rejection softened in this instance by a laugh and his last gold coin. And then he sprang to the saddle and dashed down the lonely street and out into the lonelier plain, where presently the lights, the black line of houses, the spires, and the flagstaff sank into the earth behind him again and were lost in the distance.

The storm had cleared away, the air was brisk and cold, the outlines of adjacent landmarks were distinct, but it was half-past four before Dick reached the meetinghouse and the crossing of the country road. To avoid the rising grade he had taken a longer and more circuitous road, in whose viscid mud Jovita sank fetlock deep at every bound. It was a poor preparation for a steady ascent of five miles more; but Jovita, gathering her legs under her, took it with her usual blind, unreasoning fury, and a half-hour later reached the long level that led to Rattlesnake Creek. Another half-hour would bring him to the creek. He threw the reins lightly upon the neck of the mare, chirruped to her, and began to sing.

Suddenly Jovita shied with a bound that would have unseated a less practiced rider. Hanging to her rein was a figure that had leaped from the bank, and at the same time from the road before her arose a shadowy horse and rider.

"Throw up your hands," commanded the second apparition, with an oath.

Dick felt the mare tremble, quiver, and apparently sink under him. He knew what it meant and was prepared.

"Stand aside, Jack Simpson. I know you, you d—d thief! Let me pass, or—"

He did not finish the sentence. Jovita rose straight in the air with a terrific bound, throwing the figure from her bit with a single shake of her vicious head, and charged with deadly malevolence down on the impediment before her. An oath, a pistol shot, horse and highway rolled over in the road, and the next moment Jovita was a hundred yards away. But the good right arm of her rider, shattered by a bullet, dropped helplessly at his side.

Without slacking his speed he shifted the reins to his left hand. But a few moments later he was obliged to halt and tighten the saddle girths that had slipped in the onset. This in his crippled condition took some time. He had no fear of pursuit, but looking up he saw that the eastern stars were already paling, and that the distant peaks had lost their ghostly whiteness and now stood out blackly against a lighter sky. Day was upon him. Then completely absorbed in a single idea, he forgot the pain of his wound and mounting again dashed on toward Rattlesnake Creek. But now Jovita's breath came broken by gasps; Dick reeled in his saddle, and brighter and brighter grew the sky.

Ride, Richard; run, Jovita; linger, O day!

For the last few rods there was a roaring in his ears. Was it exhaustion from loss of blood, or what? He was dazed and giddy as he swept down the hill, and did not recognize his surroundings. Had he taken the wrong road, or was this Rattlesnake Creek?

It was. But the brawling creek he had swam a few hours before had risen, more than doubled its volume, and now rolled a swift and resistless river between him and Rattlesnake Hill. For the first time that night Richard's heart sank within him. The river, the mountain, the quickening east, swam before his eyes. He shut them to recover his self-control. In that brief interval, by some fantastic mental process, the little room at Simpson's Bar and the figures of the sleeping father and son rose upon him. He opened his eyes wildly, cast off his coat, pistol, boots, and saddle, bound his precious pack tightly to his shoulders, grasped the bare flanks of Jovita with his bared knees, and with a shout clashed into the yellow water. A cry rose from the opposite bank as the head of a man and horse struggled for a few moments against the battling current, and then were swept away amidst unrooted trees and whirling driftwood.

* * *

The Old Man started and woke. The fire on the hearth was dead, the candle in the outer room flickering in its socket, and somebody was rapping at the door. He opened it, but fell back with a cry before the dripping, half-naked figure that reeled against the doorpost.

"Dick?"

"Hush! Is he awake yet?"

"No; but, Dick—"

"Dry up, you old fool! Get me some whiskey, *quick!*" The Old Man flew and returned with—an empty bottle! Dick would have sworn, but his strength was not equal to the occasion. He staggered, caught at the handle of the door, and motioned to the Old Man.

"Thar's suthin' in my pack yer for Johnny. Take it off. I can't."

The Old Man unstrapped the pack and laid it before the exhausted man.

"Open it, quick."

He did so with trembling fingers. It contained only a few poor toys—cheap and barbaric enough, goodness knows, but bright with paint and tinsel. One of them was broken; another, I fear, was irretrievably ruined by water, and on the third—ah me! there was a cruel spot.

"It don't look like much, that's a fact," said Dick ruefully. . . . "But it's the best we could do. . . . Take 'em, Old Man, and put 'em in his stocking, and tell him—tell him, you know—hold me, Old Man—" The Old Man caught at his sinking figure. "Tell him," said Dick, with a weak little laugh—"tell him Sandy Claus has come."

And even so, bedraggled, ragged, unshaven and unshorn, with one arm hanging helplessly at his side, Santa Claus came to Simpson's Bar and fell fainting on the first threshold. The Christmas dawn came slowly after, touching the remoter peaks with the rosy warmth of ineffable love. And it looked so tenderly on Simpson's Bar that the whole mountain, as if caught in a generous action, blushed to the skies.

A Proper Santa Claus

Anne McCaffrey

Jeremy was painting. He used his fingers instead of the brush because he liked the feel of paint. Blue was soothing to the touch, red was silky, and orange had a gritty texture. Also he could tell when a color was "proper" if he mixed it with his fingers. He could hear his mother singing to herself, not quite on pitch, but it was a pleasant background noise. It went with the rhythm of his fingers stroking color onto the paper.

He shaped a cookie and put raisins on it, big, plump raisins. He attempted a sugar frosting but the white kind of disappeared into the orange of the cookie. So he globbed up chocolate brown and made an icing. Then he picked the cookie out of the paper and ate it. That left a hole in the center of the paper. It was an excellent cookie, though it made his throat very dry.

Critically he eyed the remaining unused space. Yes, there was room enough, so he painted a glass of Coke. He had trouble representing the bubbles that're supposed to bounce up from the bottom of the glass. That's why the Coke tasted flat when he drank it.

It was disappointing. He'd been able to make the cookie taste so good, why couldn't he succeed with the Coke? Maybe if he drew the bubbles in first . . . he was running out of paper.

"Momma, Momma?"

"What is it, honey?"

"Can I have more paper? Please?"

"Honest, Jeremy, you use up more paper . . . Still, it does keep you quiet and out of my hair . . . why, whatever have you done with your paper? What are those holes?"

Jeremy pointed to the round one. "That was a cookie with raisins and choc'late icing. And that was a Coke only I couldn't make the bubbles bounce."

His mother gave him "the look," so he subsided.

"Jeremy North, you use more paper than—than a . . ."

"Newspaperman?" he suggested, grinning up at her. Momma liked happy faces best.

"Than a newspaperman."

"Can you paint on newspaper?"

His mother blinked. "I don't see why not. And there's pictures already. You can color them in." She obligingly rummaged in the trash and came up with several discarded papers. "There you are, love. Enough supplies to keep you in business a while. I hope."

Well, Jeremy hadn't planned on any business, and newsprint proved less than satisfactory. There wasn't enough white space to draw *his* paintings on, and the newspaper soaked up his paints when he tried to follow the already-pictures. So he carefully put the paints away, washed his hands, and went outside to play.

* * *

For his sixth birthday Jeremy North got a real school-type easel with a huge pad of paper that fastened onto it at the top and could be torn off, sheet by sheet. There was a rack of holes for his poster paint pots and a rack for his crayons and chalk and eraser. It was exactly what he wanted. He nearly cried for joy. He hugged his mother, and he climbed into his father's lap and kissed him despite his prickly beard.

"Okay, okay, da Vinci," his father laughed. "Go paint us a masterpiece."

Jeremy did. But he was so eager that he couldn't wait until the paint had completely dried. It smeared and blurred, brushing against his body as he hurried to find his dad. So the effect wasn't quite what Jeremy intended.

"Say, that's pretty good," said his father, casting a judicious eye on the proffered artwork. "What's it supposed to be?"

"Just what you wanted." Jeremy couldn't keep the disappointment out of his voice.

"I guess you're beyond me, young feller me lad. I can dig Andy Warhol when he paints tomato soup, but you're in Picasso's school." His father tousled his hair affectionately and even swung him up high so that, despite his disappointment, Jeremy was obliged to giggle and squeal in delight.

Then his father told him to take his painting back to his room.

"But it's your masterpiece, Daddy. I can fix it . . ."

"No, son. You painted it. You understand it." And his father went about some Sunday errand or other.

Jeremy did understand his painting. Even with the smears he could plainly see the car, just like the Admonsens', which Daddy had admired the previous week. It *had* been a proper car. If only Daddy had *seen* it . . .

His grandmother came, around lunchtime, and brought him a set of pastel crayons with special pastel paper and a simply superior picture book of North American animals and birds.

"Of course, he'll break every one of the pastels in the next hour," he heard his grandmother saying to his mother, "but you said he wants only drawing things."

"I like the book, too, Gramma," Jeremy said politely, but his fingers closed possessively around the pastels.

Gramma glanced at him and then went right on talking. "But I think it's about time he found out what animals really look like instead of those monstrosities he's forever drawing. His teacher's going to wonder about his home life when she sees those nightmares."

"Oh, c'mon, Mother. There's nothing abnormal about Jeremy. I'd far rather he daubed himself all over with paint than ran around like the Reckoffs' kids, slinging mud and sand everywhere."

"If you'd only *make* Jeremy . . ."

"Mother, you can't *make* Jeremy do anything. He slides away from you like . . . like a squeeze of paint."

Jeremy lost interest in the adults. As usual, they ignored his presence, despite the fact that he was the subject of their conversation. He began to leaf through the book of birds and animals. The pictures weren't proper. That brown wasn't a bird-brown. And the red of the robin had too much orange, not enough gray. He kept his criticism to himself, but by the time he'd catalogued the anatomical faults in the sketch of the mustang, he was thoroughly bored with the book. His animals might *look* like nightmares, but they were proper ones for all of that. They worked.

His mother and grandmother were engrossed in discussing the fixative that would have made the pictures "permanent." Gramma said she hadn't bought it because it would be dangerous for him to breathe the fumes. They continued to ignore him. Which was as well. He picked up the pastels and began to experiment. A green horse with pink mane and tail, however anatomically perfect, would arouse considerable controversy.

He didn't break a single one of the precious pastels. He even blew away the rainbow dust from the tray. But he didn't let the horse off the pad until after Gramma and his mother had wandered into the kitchen for lunch.

"I wish . . ."

The horse was lovely.

"I *wish* I had some . . ." Jeremy said.

The horse went cantering around the roam, pink tail streaming out behind him and pink mane flying.

". . . Fixative, Green Horse!" But it didn't work. Jeremy knew it took more than just *wishing* to do it proper.

He watched regretfully as Green Horse pranced too close to a wall and brushed himself out of existence.

* * *

Miss Bradley, his first-grade teacher, evidently didn't find anything untoward about his drawings, for she constantly displayed them on the bulletin boards. She had a habit of pouncing on him when he had just about finished a drawing so that after all his effort, he hadn't much chance to see if he'd done it "proper" after all. Once or twice he managed to reclaim one from the board and use it, but Miss Bradley created so much fuss about the missing artwork that he diplomatically ceased to repossess his efforts.

On the whole he liked Miss Bradley, but about the first week in

October she developed the distressing habit of making him draw to order: "class assignments," she called it. Well, that was all right for the ones who never knew what to draw anyhow, but "assignments" just did not suit Jeremy. While part of him wanted to do hobgoblins, and witches, and pumpkin moons, the other part obstinately refused.

"I'd really looked forward to *your* interpretations of Hallowe'en, Jeremy," Miss Bradley said sadly when he proffered another pedantic landscape with nothing but ticky-tacky houses. "This is very beautiful, Jeremy, but it isn't the assigned project. Now, look at Cynthia's witch and Mark's hobgoblin. I'm certain you could do something just as original."

Jeremy dutifully regarded Cynthia's elongated witch on an outsized broomstick apparently made from 2 x 4s instead of broom reeds, and the hobgoblin Mark had created by splashing paint on the paper and folding, thus blotting the wet paint. Neither creation had any chance of working properly; surely Miss Bradley could see that. So he was obliged to tell her that his landscape was original, particularly if she would *look* at it properly.

"You're not getting the point, Jeremy," Miss Bradley said with unaccustomed sternness.

She wasn't either, but Jeremy thought he might better not say that. So he was the only student in the class who had no Hallowe'en picture for parents to admire on Back-to-School Night.

His parents were a bit miffed since they'd heard that Jeremy's paintings were usually prominently displayed.

"The assignment was Hallowe'en and Jeremy simply refused to produce something acceptable," Miss Bradley said with a slightly forced smile.

"Perhaps that's just as well," his mother said, a trifle sourly. "He used to draw the most frightening nightmares and say he 'saw' them."

"He's got a definite talent. Are either you or Mr. North artistically inclined?"

"Not like he is," Mr. North replied, thinking that if he himself were artistically inclined he would use Miss Bradley as a model. "Probably he's used up all his Hallowe'en inspiration."

"Probably," Miss Bradley said with a laugh.

Actually Jeremy hadn't. Although he dutifully set out trick-or-treating, he came home early. His mother made him sort out his candy, apples, and money for UNICEF, and permitted him to stay up long past his regular bedtime to answer the door for other beggars. But, once safely in his room, he dove for his easel and drew frenetically, slathering black and blue poster paint across clean paper, dashing globs of luminescence for horrific accents. The proper ones took off or crawled obscenely around the room, squeaking and groaning until he released them into the night air for such gambols and aerial maneuvers as they were capable of. Jeremy was impressed. He hung over the windowsill, cheering them on by moonlight. (Around three o'clock there was a sudden shower. All the water solubles melted into the ground.)

For a while after that, Jeremy was not tempted to approach the easel at all, either in school or at home. At first, Miss Bradley was sincerely concerned lest she had inhibited her budding artist by arbitrary assignments. But he was only busy with a chemical garden, lumps of coal and bluing and ammonia and all that. Then she got the class involved in making candles out of plastic milk cartons for Thanksgiving, and Jeremy entered into the project with such enthusiasm that she was reassured.

She ought not to have been.

Three-dimensionality and a malleable substance fascinated Jeremy. He went in search of anything remotely pliable. He started with butter (his mother had a fit about a whole pound melted on his furry rug; he'd left the creature he'd created prancing around his room, but then the heat came up in the radiators). Then he tried mud (which set his mother screaming at him). She surrendered to the inevitable by supplying him with Play-Doh. However, now his creations thwarted him because as soon as the substance out of which the proper ones had been created hardened, they lost their mobility. He hadn't minded the ephemeral quality of his drawings, but he'd begun to count on the fact that sculpture lasted a while.

Miss Bradley introduced him to plasticine. And Christmas.

Success with three-dimensional figures, the availability of plasticine, and the sudden influx of all sorts of Christmas mail order catalogs spurred Jeremy to unusual efforts. This time he did not resist the class assignment of a centerpiece to deck the Christmas festive tables. Actually, Jeremy scarcely heard what Miss Bradley was saying past her opening words.

"Here's a chance for you to create your very own Santa Claus and reindeer, or a sleigh full of presents . . ."

Dancer, Prancer, Donner, Blitzen, and Dasher and Comet and Rudolph of the red nose, took form under his flying fingers. Santa's sack was crammed with full-color advertisements clipped from mail order wish-books. Indeed, the sleigh threatened to crumble on its runners from paper weight. He saved Santa Claus till the last. And once he had the fat and jolly gentleman seated in his sleigh, whip in hand, ready to urge his harnessed team, Jeremy was good and ready to make them proper.

Only they weren't; they remained obdurately immobile. Disconsolate, Jeremy moped for nearly a week, examining and re-examining his handiwork for the inhibiting flaw.

Miss Bradley had been enthusiastically complimentary and the other children sullenly envious of his success when the finished group was displayed on a special table, all red and white, with Ivory Snow snow and little evergreens in proportion to the size of the figures. There was even a convenient chimney for the good Santa to descend. Only Jeremy knew that that was not *his* Santa's goal.

In fact Jeremy quite lost interest in the whole Christmas routine. He refused to visit the Santa on tap at the big shopping center, although his mother suspected that his heart had been set on the Masterpiece Oil Painting Set with its enticing assortment of brushes and every known pigment in life-long-lasting color.

Miss Bradley, too, lost all patience with him and became quite stern with his inattentiveness, to the delight of his classmates.

As so often happens when people concentrate too hard on a problem, Jeremy almost missed the solution, inadvertently provided by the pert Cynthia, now basking in Miss Bradley's favor.

"He's naked, that's what. He's naked and ugly. Everyone knows Santa is red and white. And reindeers aren't gray-yecht. They're brown and soft and have fuzzy tails."

Jeremy had, of course, meticulously detailed the clothing on Santa and the harness on the animals, but they were still plasticine. It hadn't mattered with his other creations that they were the dull gray-brown of plasticine because that's how he'd envisaged them, being products of his imagination. But Santa wasn't, or so he thought.

To conform to a necessary convention was obviously, to Jeremy, the requirement that had prevented his Santa from being a proper one. He fabricated harness of string for the reindeer. And a new sleigh of balsa wood with runners of laboriously straightened bobby pins took some time and looked real tough. A judicious coat of paint smartened both reindeer and sleigh. However, the design and manufacture of the red Santa suit proved far more difficult and occupied every spare moment of Jeremy's time. He had to do it in the privacy of his room at home because, when Cynthia saw him putting harness on the reindeer, she twitted him so unmercifully that he couldn't work in peace at school.

He had had little practice with needle and thread, so he actually had to perfect a new skill in order to complete his project. Christmas was only a few days away before he was satisfied with his Santa suit.

He raced to school so he could dress Santa and make him proper. He was just as startled as Miss Bradley when he slithered to a stop inside his classroom door, and found her tying small gifts to the branches of the class tree. They stared at each other for a long moment, and then Miss Bradley smiled. She'd been so hard on poor Jeremy lately.

"You're awfully early, Jeremy. Would you like to help me . . . Oh! How adorable!" She spotted the Santa suit which he hadn't had the presence of mind to hide from her. "And you did them yourself? Jeremy, you never cease to amaze me." She took the jacket and pants and little hat from his unresisting hand, and examined them carefully. "They are simply beautiful. Just beautiful. But honestly, Jeremy, your Santa is lovely just as he is. No need to gild the lily."

"He isn't a proper Santa without a proper Santa suit."

Miss Bradley looked at him gravely, and then put her hands on his shoulders, making him look up at her.

"A *proper* Santa Claus is the one we have in our own hearts at this time of year, Jeremy. Not the ones in the department stores or on the street corners or on TV. They're just his helpers." You never knew which of your first-graders still did believe in Santa Claus in this cynical age, Miss Bradley thought. "A proper Santa Claus is the spirit of giving and sharing, of good fellowship. Don't let anyone tell you that there isn't a Santa Claus. The proper Santa Claus belongs to all of us."

Then, pleased with her eloquence and restraint, she handed him back the Santa suit and patted his shoulder encouragingly.

Jeremy was thunderstruck. *His* Santa Claus had only been made for Jeremy. But poor Miss Bradley's words rang in his ears. Miss Bradley couldn't know that she had improperly understood Jeremy's dilemma. Once again the blight of high-minded interpretation and ladylike good intentions withered primitive magic.

The little reindeer in their shrinking coats of paint would have pulled the sleigh only to Jeremy's house so that Santa could descend only Jeremy's chimney with the little gifts all bearing Jeremy's name.

There was no one there to tell him that it's proper for little boys and girls of his age to be selfish and acquisitive, to regard Santa as an exclusive property.

Jeremy took the garments and let Miss Bradley push him gently toward the table on which his figures were displayed.

She'd put tinsel about the scene, and glitter, but they didn't shine or glisten in the dull gray light filtering through the classroom windows. They weren't proper snow and icicles anyway.

Critically, he saw only string and the silver cake ornaments instead of harness and sleigh bells. He could see the ripples now in the unbent bobby pins which wouldn't ever draw the sleigh smoothly, even over Ivory Snow snow. Dully, he reached for the figure of his Santa Claus.

Getting on the clothes, he dented the plasticine a bit, but it scarcely mattered now. After he'd clasped Santa's malleable paw around the whip, the toothpick with a bright, thick, nylon thread attached to the top with glue, he stood back and stared.

A proper Santa Claus is the spirit of giving and sharing.

So overwhelming was Jeremy's sense of failure, so crushing his remorse for making a selfish Santa Claus instead of the one that belonged to everyone, that he couldn't imagine ever creating anything properly again.

The Plot Against Santa Claus

James Powell

Rory Bigtoes, Santa's Security Chief, was tall for an elf, measuring almost seven inches from the curly tips of his shoes to the top of his fedora. But he had to stride to keep abreast of Garth Hardnoggin, the quick little Director General of the Toyworks, as they hurried, beards streaming back over their shoulders, through the racket and bustle of Shop Number 5, one of the many vaulted caverns honeycombing the undiscovered island beneath the Polar icecap.

Director General Hardnoggin wasn't pleased. He slapped his megaphone, the symbol of his office (for as a member of the Board he spoke directly to Santa Claus), against his thigh. "A bomb in the Board Room on Christmas Eve!" he muttered with angry disbelief.

"I'll admit that Security doesn't look good," said Bigtoes.

Hardnoggin gave a snort and stopped at a construction site for Dick and Jane Doll dollhouses. Elf carpenters and painters were hard at work, pipes in their jaws and beards tucked into their belts. A foreman darted over to show Hardnoggin the wallpaper samples for the dining room.

"See this unit, Bigtoes?" said Hardnoggin. "Split-level ranch type. Wall-to-wall carpeting. Breakfast nook. Your choice of Early American or French Provincial furnishings. They said I couldn't build it for the price. But I did. And how did I do it?"

"Cardboard," said a passing elf, an old carpenter with a plank over his shoulder.

"And what's wrong with cardboard? Good substantial cardboard for the interior walls!" shouted the Director General striding off again. "Let them bellyache, Bigtoes. I'm not out to win any popularity contests. But I do my job. Let's see you do yours. Find Dirk Crouchback and find him fast."

At the automotive section the new Lazaretto sports cars (1/32 scale) were coming off the assembly line. Hardnoggin stopped to slam one of the car doors. "You left out the *kachunk*," he told an elf engineer in white cover-alls.

"Nobody gets a tin door to go *kachunk*," said the engineer.

"Detroit does. So can we," said Hardnoggin, moving on. "You think I don't miss the good old days, Bigtoes?" he said. "I was a spinner. And a damn good one. Nobody made a top that could spin as long and smooth as Garth Hardnoggin's."

"I was a jacksmith myself," said Bigtoes. Satisfying work, building each jack-in-the-box from the ground up, carpentering the box, rigging the spring mechanism, making the funny head, spreading each careful coat of paint.

"How many could you make in a week?" asked Director General Hardnoggin.

"Three, with overtime," said Security Chief Bigtoes.

Hardnoggin nodded. "And how many children had empty stockings on Christmas morning because we couldn't handcraft enough stuff to go around? That's where your Ghengis Khans, your Hitlers, and your Stalins come from, Bigtoes—children who through no fault of their own didn't get any toys for Christmas. So Santa had to make a policy decision: quality or quantity? He opted for quantity."

Crouchback, at that time one of Santa's right-hand elves, had blamed the decision on Hardnoggin's sinister influence. By way of protest he had placed a bomb in the new plastic machine. The explosion had coated three elves with a thick layer of plastic which had to be chipped off with hammers and chisels. Of course they lost their beards. Santa, who was particularly sensitive about beards, sentenced Crouchback to two years in the cooler, as the elves called it. This meant he was assigned to a refrigerator (one in Ottawa, Canada, as it happened) with the responsibility of turning the light on and off as the door was opened or closed.

But after a month Crouchback had failed to answer the daily roll call which Security made by means of a two-way intercom system. He had fled the refrigerator and become a renegade elf. Then suddenly, three years later, Crouchback had reappeared at the North Pole, a shadowy fugitive figure, editor of a clandestine newspaper, *The Midnight Elf*, which made violent attacks on Director General Hardnoggin and his policies. More recently, Crouchback had become the leader of SHAFT—Santa's Helpers Against Flimsy Toys—an organization of dissident groups including the Anti-Plastic League, and Sons and Daughters of the Good Old Days, the Ban the Toy-Bomb people and the Hippie Elves for Peace . . .

"Santa opted for quantity," repeated Hardnoggin. "And I carried out his decision. Just between the two of us it hasn't always been easy." Hardnoggin waved his megaphone at the Pacification and Rehabilitation section where thousands of toy bacteriological warfare kits (JiffyPox) were being converted to civilian use (The Freckle Machine). After years of pondering Santa had finally ordered a halt to war-toy production. His decision was considered a victory for SHAFT and a defeat for Hardnoggin.

"Unilateral disarmament is a mistake, Bigtoes," said Hardnoggin grimly as they passed through a door marked *Santa's Executive Helpers Only* and into the carpeted world of the front office. "Mark my words, right now the tanks and planes are rolling off the assembly lines at Acme Toy and into the department stores." (Acme Toy, the international consortium of toymakers, was the elves' greatest bugbear.) "So the rich kids will have war toys, while the poor kids won't even have a popgun. That's not democratic."

Bigtoes stopped at a door marked *Security*. Hardnoggin strode on without slackening his pace. "Sticks-and-Stones session at five o'clock," he said over his shoulder. "Don't be late. And do your job. Find Crouchback!"

* * *

Dejected, Bigtoes slumped down at his desk, receiving a sympathetic smile from Charity Nosegay, his little blond blue-eyed secretary. Charity was a recent acquisition and Bigtoes had intended to make a play for her once the Sticks-and-Stones paperwork was out of the way. (Security had to prepare a report for Santa on each alleged naughty boy and girl.) Now that play would have to wait.

Bigtoes sighed. Security looked bad. Bigtoes had even been warned. The night before, a battered and broken elf had crawled into his office, gasped, "He's going to kill Santa," and died. It was Darby Shortribs, who had once been a brilliant doll designer. But then one day he had decided that if war toys encouraged little boys to become soldiers when they grew up, then dolls encouraged little girls to become mothers, contributing to overpopulation. So Shortribs had joined SHAFT and risen to membership on its Central Committee.

The trail of Shortribs's blood had led to the Quality Control lab and the Endurance Machine which simulated the brutal punishment, the bashing, crushing, and kicking that a toy receives at the hands of a four-year-old (or two two-year-olds). A hell of a way for an elf to die!

After Shortribs's warning, Bigtoes had alerted his Security elves and sent a flying squad after Crouchback. But the SHAFT leader had disappeared. The next morning a bomb had exploded in the Board Room.

On the top of Bigtoes's desk were the remains of that bomb. Small enough to fit into an elf's briefcase, it had been placed under the Board Room table, just at Santa's feet. If Owen Brassbottom, Santa's Traffic Manager, hadn't chosen just that moment to usher the jolly old man into the Map Room to pinpoint the spot where, with the permission and blessing of the Strategic Air Command, Santa's sleigh and reindeer were to penetrate the DEW Line, there wouldn't have been much left of Santa from the waist down. Seconds before the bomb went off, Director General Hardnoggin had been called from the room to take a private phone call. Fergus Bandylegs, Vice-President of Santa Enterprises, Inc., had just gone down to the other end of the table to discuss something with Tom Thumbskin, Santa's Creative Head, and escaped the blast. But Thumbskin had to be sent to the hospital with a concussion when his chair—the elves sat on high chairs with ladders up the side like those used by lifeguards—was knocked over backward by the explosion.

All this was important, for the room had been searched before the meeting and found safe. So the bomb must have been brought in by a member of the Board. It certainly hadn't been Traffic Manager Brassbottom, who had saved Santa, and probably not Thumbskin. That left Director General Hardnoggin and Vice-President Bandylegs . . .

"Any luck checking out that personal phone call Hardnoggin received just before the bomb went off?" asked Bigtoes.

Charity shook her golden locks. "The switchboard operator fainted right after she took the call. She's still out cold."

* * *

Leaving the Toyworks, Bigtoes walked quickly down a corridor lined with expensive boutiques and fashionable restaurants. On one wall of Mademoiselle Fanny's Salon of Haute Couture some SHAFT elf had written: *Santa, Si! Hardnoggin, No!* On one wall of the Hotel St. Nicholas some Hardnoggin backer had written: *Support Your Local Director General!* Bigtoes was no philosopher and the social unrest that was racking the North Pole confused him. Once, in disguise he had attended a SHAFT rally in The Underwood, that vast and forbidding cavern of phosphorescent stinkhorn and hanging roots. Gathered beneath an immense picture of Santa were hippie elves with their beards tied in outlandish knots, matron-lady elves in sensible shoes, tweedy elves and green-collar elves.

Crouchback himself had made a surprise appearance, coming out of hiding to deliver his now famous "Plastic Lives!" speech. "Hardnoggin says plastic is inanimate. But I say that plastic lives! Plastic infects all it touches and spreads like crab grass in the innocent souls of little children. Plastic toys make plastic girls and boys!" Crouchback drew himself up to his full six inches. "I say: quality—quality now!" The crowd roared his words back at him. The meeting closed with all the elves joining hands and singing "We Shall Overcome." It had been a moving experience . . .

As he expected, Bigtoes found Bandylegs at the Hotel St.

Nicholas bar, staring morosely down into a thimble mug of ale. Fergus Bandylegs was a dapper, fast-talking elf with a chestnut beard which he scented with lavender. As Vice-President of Santa Enterprises, Inc., he was in charge of financing the entire Toyworks operation by arranging for Santa to appear in advertising campaigns, by collecting royalties on the use of the jolly old man's name, and by leasing Santa suits to department stores.

Bandylegs ordered a drink for the Security Chief. Their friendship went back to Rory Bigtoes's jacksmith days when Bandylegs had been a master sledwright. "These are topsy-turvy times, Rory," said Bandylegs. "First there's that bomb and now Santa's turned down the Jolly Roger cigarette account. For years now they've had this ad campaign showing Santa slipping a carton of Jolly Rogers into Christmas stockings. But not anymore. 'Smoking may be hazardous to your health,' says Santa."

"Santa knows best," said Bigtoes.

"Granted," said Bandylegs. "But counting television residuals, that's a cool two million sugar plums thrown out the window." (At the current rate of exchange there are 4.27 sugar plums to the U.S. dollar.) "Hardnoggin's already on my back to make up the loss. Nothing must interfere with his grand plan for automating the Toyworks. So it's off to Madison Avenue again. Sure I'll stay at the Plaza and eat at the Chambord, but I'll still get homesick."

The Vice-President smiled sadly. "Do you know what I used to do? There's this guy who stands outside Grand Central Station selling those little mechanical men you wind up and they march around. I used to march around with them. It made me feel better somehow. But now they remind me of Hardnoggin. He's a machine, Rory, and he wants to make all of us into machines."

"What about the bomb?" asked Bigtoes.

Bandylegs shrugged. "Acme Toy, I suppose."

Bigtoes shook his head. Acme Toy hadn't slipped an elf spy into the North Pole for months. "What about Crouchback?"

"No," said Bandylegs firmly. "I'll level with you, Rory. I had a get-together with Crouchback just last week. He wanted to get my thoughts on the quality-versus-quantity question and on the future of the Toyworks. Maybe I'm wrong, but I got the impression that a top-level shake-up is in the works with Crouchback slated to become the new Director General. In any event I found him a very perceptive and understanding elf."

Bandylegs smiled and went on, "Darby Shortribs was there, prattling on against dolls. As I left, Crouchback shook my hand and whispered, 'Every movement needs its lunatic fringe, Bandylegs. Shortribs is ours.'" Bandylegs lowered his voice. "I'm tired of the grown-up ratrace, Rory. I want to get back to the sled shed and make Blue Streaks and High Flyers again. I'll never get there with Hardnoggin and his modern ideas at the helm."

Bigtoes pulled at his beard. It was common knowledge that Crouchback had an elf spy on the Board. The reports on the meetings in *The Midnight Elf* were just too complete. Was it his friend Bandylegs? But would Bandylegs try to kill Santa?

That brought Bigtoes back to Hardnoggin again. But cautiously. As Security Chief, Bigtoes had to be objective. Yet he yearned to prove Hardnoggin the villain. This, as he knew, was because of the beautiful Carlotta Peachfuzz, beloved by children all around the world. As the voice of the Peachy Pippin Doll, Carlotta was the most envied female at the North Pole, next to Mrs. Santa. Girl elves followed her glamorous exploits in the press. Male elves had Peachy Pippin Dolls propped beside their beds so they could fall asleep with Carlotta's sultry voice saying: "Hello, I'm your talking Peachy Pippin Doll. I love you. I love you. I love you . . ."

But once it had just been Rory and Carlotta, Carlotta and Rory—until the day Bigtoes had introduced her to Hardnoggin. "You have a beautiful voice, Miss Peachfuzz," the Director General had said. "Have you ever considered being in the talkies?" So Carlotta had dropped Bigtoes for Hardnoggin and risen to stardom in the talking-doll industry. But her liaison with Director General Hardnoggin had become so notorious that a dutiful Santa—with Mrs. Santa present—had had to read the riot act about executive hanky-panky. Hardnoggin had broken off the relationship. Disgruntled, Carlotta had become active with SHAFT, only to leave after a violent argument with Shortribs over his anti-doll position.

Today Bigtoes couldn't care less about Carlotta. But he still had that old score to settle with the Director General.

* * *

Leaving the fashionable section behind, Bigtoes turned down Apple Alley, a residential corridor of modest, old-fashioned houses with thatched roofs and carved beams. Here the mushrooms were in full bloom—the stropharia, inocybe, and chanterelle—dotting the corridor with indigo, vermilion, and many yellows. Elf householders were out troweling in their gardens. Elf wives gossiped over hedges of gypsy pholiota. Somewhere an old elf was singing one of the ancient work songs, accompanying himself on a concertina. Until Director General Hardnoggin discovered that it slowed down production, the elves had always sung while they worked, beating out the time with their hammers; now the foremen passed out song sheets and led them in song twice a day. But it wasn't the same thing.

Elf gardeners looked up, took their pipes from their mouths, and watched Bigtoes pass. They regarded all front-office people with suspicion—even this big elf with the candy-stripe rosette of the Order of Santa, First Class, in his buttonhole.

Bigtoes had won the decoration many years ago when he was a young Security elf, still wet behind his pointed ears. Somehow on that fateful day, Billy Roy Scoggins, President of Acme Toy, had found the secret entrance to the North Pole and appeared suddenly in parka and snowshoes, demanding to see Santa Claus. Santa arrived, jolly and smiling, surrounded by Bigtoes and the other Security elves. Scoggins announced he had a proposition "from one hard-headed businessman to another."

Pointing out the foolishness of competition, the intruder had offered Santa a king's ransom to come in with Acme Toy. "Ho, ho, ho," boomed Santa with jovial firmness, "that isn't Santa's way." Scoggins—perhaps it was the "ho, ho, ho" that did it—turned purple and threw a punch that floored the jolly old man. Security sprang into action.

Four elves had died as Scoggins flayed at them, a snowshoe in one hand and a rolled up copy of *The Wall Street Journal* in the other. But Bigtoes had crawled up the outside of Scoggins's pantleg. It had taken him twelve karate chops to break the intruder's kneecap and send him crashing to the ground like a stricken tree. To this day the President of Acme Toy walks with a cane and curses Rory Bigtoes whenever it rains.

As Bigtoes passed a tavern—The Bowling Green, with a huge horse mushroom shading the door—someone inside banged down a thimble-mug and shouted the famous elf toast: "My Santa, right or wrong! May he always be right, but right or wrong, my Santa!" Bigtoes sighed. Life should be so simple for elves. They all loved Santa—what did it matter that he used blueing when he washed his beard, or liked to sleep late, or hit the martinis a bit too hard—and they all wanted to do what was best for good little girls and boys. But here the agreement ended. Here the split between Hardnoggin and Crouchback—between the Establishment and the revolutionary—took over.

Beyond the tavern was a crossroads, the left corridor leading to the immense storage areas for completed toys, the right corridor to The Underwood. Bigtoes continued straight and was soon entering that intersection of corridors called Pumpkin Corners, the North Pole's bohemian quarter. Here, until his disappearance, the SHAFT leader Crouchback had lived with relative impunity, protected by the inhabitants. For this was SHAFT country. A special edition of *The Midnight Elf* was already on the streets denying that SHAFT was involved in the assassination attempt on Santa. A love-bead vendor, his beard tied in a sheepshank, had *Hardnoggin Is a Dwarf* written across the side of his pushcart. *Make love, not plastic* declared the wall of The Electric Carrot, a popular discotheque and hippie hangout.

The Electric Carrot was crowded with elves dancing the latest craze, the Scalywag. Until recently, dancing hadn't been popular with elves. They kept stepping on their beards. The hippie knots effectively eliminated that stumbling block.

Buck Withers, leader of the Hippie Elves for Peace, was sitting in a corner wearing a *Santa Is Love* button. Bigtoes had once dropped a first-offense drug charge against Withers and three other elves caught nibbling on morning-glory seeds. "Where's Crouchback, Buck?" said Bigtoes.

"Like who's asking?" said Withers. "The head of Hardnoggin's Gestapo?"

"A friend," said Bigtoes.

"Friend, like when the news broke about Shortribs, he says 'I'm next, Buck.' Better fled than dead, and he split for parts unknown."

"It looks bad, Buck."

"Listen, friend," said Withers, "SHAFT's the wave of the future. Like Santa's already come over to our side on the disarmament thing. What do we need with bombs? That's a bad scene, friend. Violence isn't SHAFT's bag."

As Bigtoes left The Electric Carrot a voice said, "I wonder, my dear sir, if you could help an unfortunate elf." Bigtoes turned to find a tattered derelict in a filthy button-down shirt and greasy gray-flannel suit. His beard was matted with twigs and straw.

"Hello, Baldwin," said Bigtoes. Baldwin Redpate had once been the head of Santa's Shipping Department. Then came the Slugger Nolan Official Baseball Mitt Scandal. The mitt had been a big item one year, much requested in letters to Santa. Through some gigantic snafu in Shipping, thousands of inflatable rubber ducks had been sent out instead. For months afterward, Santa received letters from indignant little boys, and though each one cut him like a knife he never reproached Redpate. But Redpate knew he had failed Santa. He brooded, had attacks of silent crying, and finally took to drink, falling so much under the spell of bee wine that Hardnoggin had to insist he resign.

"Rory, you're just the elf I'm looking for," said Redpate. "Have you ever seen an elf skulking? Well, I have."

Bigtoes was interested. Elves were straightforward creatures. They didn't skulk.

"Last night I woke up in a cold sweat and saw strange things, Rory," said Redpate. "Comings and goings, lights, skulking." Large tears rolled down Redpate's cheeks. "You see, I get these nightmares, Rory. Thousands of inflatable rubber ducks come marching across my body and theirs eyes are Santa's eyes when someone's let him down." He leaned toward Bigtoes confidentially. "I may be a washout. Occasionally I may even drink too much. But I don't skulk!" Redpate began to cry again.

His tears looked endless. Bigtoes was due at the Sticks-and-Stones session. He slipped Redpate ten sugar plums. "Got to go, Baldwin."

Redpate dabbed at the tears with the dusty end of his beard. "When you see Santa, ask him to think kindly of old Baldy Redpate," he sniffed and headed straight for The Good Gray Goose, the tavern across the street—making a beeline for the bee wine, as the elves would say. But then he turned. "Strange goings-on," he called. "Storeroom Number 14, Unit 24, Row 58. Skulking."

* * *

"Hardnoggin's phone call was from Carlotta Peachfuzz," said Charity, looking lovelier than ever. "The switchboard operator is a big Carlotta fan. She fainted when she recognized her voice. The thrill was just too much."

Interesting. In spite of Santa's orders, were Carlotta and Hardnoggin back together on the sly? If so, had they conspired on the bomb attempt? Or had it really been Carlotta's voice? Carlotta Peachfuzz impersonations were a dime a dozen.

"Get me the switchboard operator," said Bigtoes and returned to stuffing Sticks-and-Stones reports into his briefcase.

"No luck," said Charity, putting down the phone. "She just took another call and fainted again."

* * *

Vice-President Bandylegs looked quite pleased with himself and threw Bigtoes a wink. "Don't be surprised when I cut out of Sticks-and-Stones early, Rory," he smiled. "An affair of the heart. All of a sudden the old Bandylegs charm has come through again. He nodded down the hall at Hardnoggin, waiting impatiently at the Projection Room door. "When the cat's away, the mice will play."

The Projection Room was built like a movie theater. "Come over here beside Santa, Rory, my boy," boomed the jolly old man. So Bigtoes scrambled up into a tiny seat hooked over the back of the seat on Santa's left. On Bigtoes's left sat Traffic Manager Brassbottom, Vice-President Bandylegs, and Director General Hardnoggin. In this way Mrs. Santa, at the portable bar against the wall, could send Santa's martinis to him down an assembly line of elves.

Confident that no one would dare to try anything with Santa's Security Chief present, Bigtoes listened to the Traffic Manager, a red-lipped elf with a straw-colored beard, talk enthusiastically about the television coverage planned for Santa's trip. This year, live and in color via satellite, the North Pole would see Santa's arrival at each stop on his journey. Santa's first martini was passed from Hardnoggin to Bandylegs to Brassbottom to Bigtoes. The Security Chief grasped the stem of the glass in both hands and, avoiding the heady gin fumes as best he could, passed it to Santa.

"All right," said Santa, taking his first sip, "let's roll 'em, starting with the worst."

The lights dimmed. A film appeared on the screen. "Waldo Rogers, age five," said Bigtoes. "Mistreatment of pets, eight demerits." (The film showed a smirking little boy pulling a cat's tail.) "Not coming when he's called, ten demerits." (The film showed Waldo's mother at the screen door, shouting.) "Also, as an indication of his general bad behavior, he gets his mother to buy Sugar Gizmos but he won't eat them. He just wants the boxtops." (The camera panned a pantry shelf crowded with opened Sugar Gizmo boxes.) The elves clucked disapprovingly.

"Waldo Rogers certainly isn't Santa's idea of a nice little boy," said Santa. "What do you think, Mother?" Mrs. Santa agreed.

"Sticks-and-stones then?" asked Hardnoggin hopefully.

But the jolly old man hesitated. "Santa always likes to check the list twice before deciding," he said.

Hardnoggin groaned. Santa was always bollixing up his production schedules by going easy on bad little girls and boys.

A new film began. "Next on the list," said Bigtoes, "is Nancy Ruth Ashley, age four and a half . . ."

Two hours and seven martinis later, Santa's jolly laughter and Mrs. Santa's giggles filled the room. "She's a little dickens, that one," chuckled Santa as they watched a six-year-old fill her father's custom-made shoes with molasses, "but Santa will find a little something for her." Hardnoggin groaned. That was the end of the list and so far no one had been given sticks-and-stones. They rolled the film on Waldo Rogers again. "Santa understands some cats like having their tails pulled," chuckled Santa as he drained his glass. "And what the heck are Sugar Gizmos?"

Bandylegs, who had just excused himself from the meeting, paused on his way up the aisle. "They're a delicious blend of toasted oats and corn," he shouted, "with an energy-packed coating of sparkling sugar. As a matter of fact, Santa, the Gizmo people are thinking of featuring you in their new advertising campaign. It would be a great selling point if I could say that Santa had given a little boy sticks-and-stones because he wouldn't eat his Sugar Gizmos."

"Here now, Fergy," said the jolly old man, "you know that isn't Santa's way."

Bandylegs left, muttering to himself.

"Santa," protested Hardnoggin as the jolly old man passed his glass down the line for a refill, "let's be realistic. If we can't draw the line at Waldo Rogers, where can we?"

Santa reflected for a moment. "Suppose Santa let you make the decision, Garth, my boy. What would little Waldo Rogers find in his stocking on Christmas morning?"

Hardnoggin hesitated. Then he said, "Sticks-and-stones."

Santa looked disappointed. "So be it," he said.

The lights dimmed again as they continued their review of the list. Santa's eighth martini came down the line from elf to elf. As Bigtoes passed it to Santa, the fumes caught him—the smell of gin and something else. Bitter almonds. He struck the glass from Santa's hand.

* * *

Silent and dimly lit, Storeroom Number 14 seemed an immense, dull suburb of split-level, ranch-type Dick and Jane Doll dollhouses. Bigtoes stepped into the papier-mâché shrubbery fronting Unit 24, Row 58 as an elf watchman on a bicycle pedaled by singing "Colossal Carlotta," a current hit song. Bigtoes hoped he hadn't made a mistake by refraining from picking Hardnoggin up.

Bandylegs had left before the cyanide was put in the glass. Mrs. Santa, of course, was above suspicion. So that left Director General Hardnoggin and Traffic Manager Brassbottom. But why would Brassbottom first save Santa from the bomb only to poison him later? So that left Hardnoggin. Bigtoes had been eager to act on this logic, perhaps too eager. He wanted no one to say that Santa's Security Chief had let personal feelings color his judgment. Bigtoes would be fair.

Hardnoggin had insisted that Crouchback was the villain. All right, he would bring Crouchback in for questioning. After all, Santa was now safe, napping under a heavy guard in preparation for his all-night trip. Hardnoggin—if *he* was the villain—could do him no harm for the present.

As Bigtoes crept up the fabric lawn on all fours, the front door of the dollhouse opened and a shadowy figure came down the walk. It paused at the street, looked this way and that, then disappeared into the darkness. Redpate had been right about the skulking. But it wasn't Crouchback—Bigtoes was sure of that.

The Security Chief climbed in through a dining-room window. In the living room were three elves, one on the couch, one in an easy chair, and, behind the bar, Dirk Crouchback, a distinguished-looking elf with a salt-and-pepper beard and graying temples. The leader of SHAFT poured himself a drink and turned. "Welcome to my little ménage-à-trois, Rory Bigtoes," he said with a surprised smile. The two other elves turned out to be Dick and Jane dolls.

"I'm taking you in, Crouchback," said the Security Chief.

The revolutionary came out from behind the bar pushing a .55mm. Howitzer (1/32 scale) with his foot. "I'm sorry about this," he said. "As you know we are opposed to the use of violence. But I'd rather not fall into Hardnoggin's hands just now. Sit over there by Jane." Bigtoes obeyed. At that short range the howitzer's plastic shell could be fatal to an elf.

Crouchback sat down on the arm of Dick's easy chair. "Yes," he said, "Hardnoggin's days are numbered. But as the incidents of last night and today illustrate, the Old Order dies hard. I'd rather not be one of its victims."

Crouchback paused and took a drink. "Look at this room, Bigtoes. This is Hardnoggin's world. Wall-to-wall carpeting. Breakfast nooks. Cheap materials. Shoddy workmanship." He picked up an end table and dropped it on the floor. Two of the legs broke. "Plastic," said

Crouchback contemptuously, flinging the table through the plastic television set. "It's the whole middle-class, bourgeois, suburban scene." Crouchback put the heel of his hand on Dick's jaw and pushed the doll over. "Is this vapid plastic nonentity the kind of grownup we want little boys and girls to become?"

"No," said Bigtoes. "But what's your alternative?"

"Close down the Toyworks for a few years," said Crouchback earnestly. "Relearn our ancient heritage of handcrafted toys. We owe it to millions of little boys and girls as yet unborn!"

"All very idealistic," said Bigtoes, "but—"

"Practical, Bigtoes. And down to earth," said the SHAFT leader, tapping his head. "The plan's all here."

"But what about Acme Toy?" protested Bigtoes. "The rich kids would still get presents and the poor kids wouldn't."

Crouchback smiled. "I can't go into the details now. But my plan includes the elimination of Acme Toy."

"Suppose you could," said Bigtoes. "We still couldn't handcraft enough toys to keep pace with the population explosion."

"Not at first," said Crouchback. "But suppose population growth was not allowed to exceed our rate of toy production?" He tapped his head again.

"But good grief," said Bigtoes, "closing down the Toyworks means millions of children with empty stockings on Christmas. Who could be that cruel?"

"Cruel?" exclaimed Crouchback. "Bigtoes, do you know how a grownup cooks a live lobster? Some drop it into boiling water. But others say, 'How cruel!' They drop it in cold water and then bring the water to a boil slowly. No, Bigtoes, we have to bite the bullet. Granted there'll be no Christmas toys for a few years. But we'd fill children's stockings with literature explaining what's going on and with discussion-group outlines so they can get together and talk up the importance of sacrificing their Christmas toys today so the children of the future can have quality handcrafted toys. They'll understand."

Before Bigtoes could protest again, Crouchback got to his feet. "Now that I've given you some food for thought I have to go," he said. "That closet should hold you until I make my escape."

Bigtoes was in the closet for more than an hour. The door proved stronger than he had expected. Then he remembered Hardnoggin's cardboard interior walls and karate-chopped his way through the back of the closet and out into the kitchen.

* * *

Security headquarters was a flurry of excitement as Bigtoes strode in the door. "They just caught Hardnoggin trying to put a bomb on Santa's sleigh," said Charity, her voice shaking.

Bigtoes passed through to the Interrogation Room where Hardnoggin, gray and haggard, sat with his wrists between his knees. The Security elves hadn't handled him gently. One eye was swollen, his beard was in disarray, and there was a dent in his megaphone. "It was a Christmas present for that little beast, Waldo Rogers," shouted Hardnoggin.

"A bomb?" said Bigtoes.

"It was supposed to be a little fire engine," shouted the Director General, "with a bell that goes clang-clang!" Hardnoggin struggled to control himself. "I just couldn't be responsible for that little monster finding nothing in his stocking but sticks-and-stones. But a busy man hasn't time for last-minute shopping. I got a—a friend to pick something out for me."

"Who?" said Bigtoes.

Hardnoggin hung his head. "I demand to be taken to Santa Claus," he said. But Santa, under guard, had already left his apartment for the formal departure ceremony.

Bigtoes ordered Hardnoggin detained and hurried to meet Santa at the elevator. He would have enjoyed shouting up at the jolly old man that Hardnoggin was the culprit. But of course that just didn't hold water. Hardnoggin was too smart to believe he could just walk up and put a bomb on Santa's sleigh. Or—now that Bigtoes thought about it—to finger himself so obviously by waiting until Bandylegs had left the Sticks-and-Stones session before poisoning Santa's glass.

The villain now seemed to be the beautiful and glamorous Carlotta Peachfuzz. Here's the way it figured: Carlotta phones Hardnoggin just before the bomb goes off in the Board Room, thus making him a prime suspect; Carlotta makes a rendezvous with Bandylegs that causes him to leave Stick-and-Stones, thus again making Hardnoggin Suspect Number One; then when Bigtoes fails to pick up the Director General, Carlotta talks him into giving little Waldo Rogers a present that turns out to be a bomb. Her object? To frame Hardnoggin for the murder or attempted murder of Santa. Her elf spy? Traffic Manager Brassbottom. It all worked out—or seemed to . . .

Bigtoes met Santa at the elevator surrounded by a dozen Security elves. The jolly old eyes were bloodshot, his smile slightly strained. "Easy does it, Billy," said Santa to Billy Briskey, the Security elf at the elevator controls. "Santa's a bit hung over."

Bigtoes moved to the rear of the elevator. So it was Brassbottom who had planted the bomb and then deliberately taken Santa out of the room. So it was Brassbottom who had poisoned the martini with cyanide, knowing that Bigtoes would detect the smell. And it was Carlotta who had gift-wrapped the bomb. All to frame Hardnoggin. And yet . . . Bigtoes sighed at his own confusion. And yet a dying Shortribs had said that someone was going to kill Santa.

As the elevator eased up into the interior of the Polar icecap, Bigtoes focused his mind on Shortribs. Suppose the dead elf had stumbled on your well-laid plan to kill Santa. Suppose you botched Shortribs's murder and therefore knew that Security had been alerted. What would you do? Stage three fake attempts on Santa's life to provide Security with a culprit, hoping to get Security to drop its guard? Possibly. But the bomb in the Board Room could have killed Santa. Why not just do it that way?

The elevator reached the surface and the first floor of the Control Tower building which was ingeniously camouflaged as an icy crag. But suppose, thought Bigtoes, it was important that you kill Santa in a certain way—say, with half the North Pole looking on?

More Security elves were waiting when the elevator doors opened. Bigtoes moved quickly among them, urging the utmost vigilance. Then Santa and his party stepped out onto the frozen runway to be greeted by thousands of cheering elves. Hippie elves from Pumpkin

Corners, green-collar elves from the Toyworks, young elves and old had all gathered there to wish the jolly old man godspeed.

Santa's smile broadened and he waved to the crowd. Then everybody stood at attention and doffed their hats as the massed bands of the Mushroom Fanciers Association, Wade Snoot conducting, broke into "Santa Claus Is Coming to Town." When the music reached its stirring conclusion, Santa, escorted by a flying wedge of Security elves, made his way through the exuberant crowd and toward his sleigh.

Bigtoes's eyes kept darting everywhere, searching for a happy face that might mask a homicidal intent. His heart almost stopped when Santa paused to accept a bouquet from an elf child who stuttered through a tribute in verse to the jolly old man. It almost stopped again when Santa leaned over the Security cordon to speak to some elf in the crowd. A pat on the head from Santa and even Roger Chinwhiskers, leader of the Sons and Daughters of the Good Old Days, grinned and admitted that perhaps the world wasn't going to hell in a handbasket. A kind word from Santa and Baldwin Redpate tearfully announced—as he did every year at that time—that he was off the bee wine for good.

After what seemed an eternity to Bigtoes, they reached the sleigh. Santa got on board, gave one last wave to the crowd, and called to his eight tiny reindeer, one by one, by name. The reindeer leaned against the harness and the sleigh, with Security elves trotting alongside, and slid forward on the ice. Then four of the reindeer were airborne. Then the other four. At last the sleigh itself left the ground. Santa gained altitude, circled the runway once, and was gone. But they heard him exclaim, ere he drove out of sight: "Happy Christmas to all, and to all a good night!"

* * *

The crowd dispersed quickly. Only Bigtoes remained on the windswept runway. He walked back and forth, head down, kicking at the snow. Santa's departure had gone off without a hitch. Had the Security Chief been wrong about the frame-up? Had Hardnoggin been trying to kill Santa after all? Bigtoes went over the three attempts again. The bomb in the Board Room. The poison. The bomb on the sleigh.

Suddenly Bigtoes broke into a run.

He had remembered Brassbottom's pretext for taking Santa into the Map Room.

Taking the steps three at a time, Bigtoes burst into the Control Room. Crouchback was standing over the remains of the radio equipment with a monkey wrench in his hand. "Too late, Bigtoes," he said triumphantly. "Santa's as good as dead."

Bigtoes grabbed the phone and ordered the operator to put through an emergency call to the Strategic Air Command in Denver, Colorado. But the telephone cable had been cut. "Baby Polar bears like to teethe on it," said the operator.

Santa Claus was doomed. There was no way to call him back or to warn the Americans.

Crouchback smiled. "In eleven minutes Santa will pass over the DEW Line. But at the wrong place, thanks to Traffic Manager Brassbottom. The American ground-to-air missiles will make short work of him."

"But why?" demanded Bigtoes.

"Nothing destroys a dissident movement like a modest success or two," said Crouchback. "Ever since Santa came out for unilateral disarmament, I've felt SHAFT coming apart in my hands. So I had to act. I've nothing against Santa personally, bourgeois sentimentalist that he is. But his death will be a great step forward in our task of forming better children for a better world. What do you think will happen when Santa is shot down by American missiles?"

Bigtoes shaded his eyes. His voice was thick with emotion. "Every good little boy and girl in the world will be up in arms. A Children's Crusade against the United States."

"And with the Americans disposed of, what nation will become the dominant force in the world?" said Crouchback.

"So that's it—you're a Marxist-Leninist elf!" shouted Bigtoes.

"No!" said Crouchback sharply. "But I'll use the Russians to achieve a better world. Who else could eliminate Acme Toy? Who else could limit world population to our rate of toy production? And they have agreed to that in writing, Bigtoes. Oh, I know the Russians are grownups too and just as corrupt as the rest of the grownups. But once the kids have had the plastic flushed out of their systems and are back on quality handcrafted toys, I, Dirk Crouchback, the New Santa Claus, with the beautiful and beloved Carlotta Peachfuzz at my side as the New Mrs. Santa, will handle the Russians."

"What about Brassbottom?" asked Bigtoes contemptuously.

"Brassbottom will be Assistant New Santa," said Crouchback quickly, annoyed at the interruption. "Yes," he continued, "the New Santa Claus will speak to the children of the world and tell them one thing: Don't trust anyone over thirty inches tall. And that will be the dawning of a new era full of happy laughing children, where grownups will be irrelevant and just wither away!"

"You're mad, Crouchback. I'm taking you in," said Bigtoes.

"I'll offer no resistance," said Crouchback. "But five minutes after Santa fails to appear at his first pit stop, a special edition of *The Midnight Elf* will hit the streets announcing that he has been the victim of a conspiracy between Hardnoggin and the CIA. The same mob of angry elves that breaks into Security headquarters to tear Hardnoggin limb from limb will also free Dirk Crouchback and proclaim him their new leader. I've laid the groundwork well. A knowing smile here, an innuendo there, and now many elves inside SHAFT and out believe that on his return Santa intended to make me Director General."

Crouchback smiled. "Ironically enough, I'd never have learned to be so devious if you Security people hadn't fouled up your own plans and assigned me to a refrigerator in the Russian Embassy in Ottawa. Ever since they found a CIA listening device in their smoked sturgeon, the Russians had been keeping a sharp eye open. They nabbed me almost at once and flew me to Moscow in a diplomatic pouch. When they thought they had me brainwashed, they trained me in deviousness and other grownup revolutionary techniques. They thought they could use me, Bigtoes. But Dirk Crouchback is going to use them!"

Bigtoes wasn't listening. Crouchback had just given him an idea—one chance in a thousand of saving Santa. He dived for the phone.

* * *

"We're in luck," said Charity, handing Bigtoes a file. "His name is Colin Tanglefoot, a stuffer in the Teddy Bear Section. Sentenced to a year in the cooler for setting another stuffer's beard on fire. Assigned to a refrigerator in the DEW Line station at Moose Landing. Sparks has got him on the intercom."

Bigtoes took the microphone. "Tanglefoot, this is Bigtoes," he said.

"Big deal," said a grumpy voice with a head cold.

"Listen, Tanglefoot," said Bigtoes, "in less than seven minutes Santa will be flying right over where you are. Warn the grownups not to shoot him down."

"Tough," said Tanglefoot petulantly. "You know, old Santa gave yours truly a pretty raw deal."

"Six minutes, Tanglefoot."

"Listen," said Tanglefoot. "Old Valentine Woody is ho-ho-hoing around with that 'jollier than thou' attitude of his, see? So as a joke I tamp my pipe with the tip of his beard. It went up like a Christmas tree."

"Tanglefoot—"

"Yours truly threw the bucket of water that saved his life," said Tanglefoot. "I should have got a medal."

"You'll get your medal!" shouted Bigtoes. "Just save Santa."

Tanglefoot sneezed four times. "Okay," he said at last. "Do or die for Santa. I know the guy on duty—Myron Smith. He's always in here raiding the cold cuts. But he's not the kind that would believe a six-inch elf with a head cold."

"Let me talk to him then," said Bigtoes. "But move—you've got only four minutes."

Tanglefoot signed off. Would the tiny elf win his race against the clock and avoid the fate of most elves who revealed themselves to grownups—being flattened with the first object that came to hand? And if he did, what would Bigtoes say to Smith? Grownups—suspicious, short of imagination, afraid—grownups were difficult enough to reason with under ideal circumstances. But what could you say to a grownup with his head stuck in a refrigerator?

An enormous squawk came out of the intercom, toppling Sparks over backward in his chair. "Hello there, Myron," said Bigtoes as calmly as he could. "My name is Rory Bigtoes. I'm one of Santa's little helpers."

Silence. The hostile silence of a grownup thinking. "Yeah? Yeah?" said Smith at last. "How do I know this isn't some Commie trick? You bug our icebox, you plant a little pinko squirt to feed me some garbage about Santa coming over and then, whammo, you slip the big one by us, nuclear warhead and all, winging its way into Heartland, U.S.A."

"Myron," pleaded Bigtoes. "We're talking about Santa Claus, the one who always brought you and the other good little boys and girls toys at Christmas."

"What's he done for me lately?" said Smith unpleasantly. "And hey! I wrote him once asking for a Slugger Nolan Official Baseball Mitt. Do you know what I got?"

"An inflatable rubber duck," said Bigtoes quickly.

Silence. The profound silence of a thunderstruck grownup. Smith's voice had an amazed belief in it. "Yeah," he said. "Yeah."

* * *

Pit Stop Number One. A December cornfield in Iowa blazing with landing lights. As thousands of elfin eyes watched on their television screens, crews of elves in cover-alls changed the runners on Santa's sleigh, packed fresh toys aboard, and chipped the ice from the reindeer antlers. The camera panned to one side where Santa stood out of the wind, sipping on a hot buttered rum. As the camera dollied in on him, the jolly old man, his beard and eyebrows caked with frost, his cheeks as red as apples, broke into a ho-ho-ho and raised his glass in a toast.

Sitting before the television at Security headquarters, a smiling Director General Hardnoggin raised his thimble-mug of ale. "My Santa, right or wrong," he said.

Security Chief Bigtoes raised his glass. He wanted to think of a new toast. Crouchback was under guard and Carlotta and Brassbottom had fled to The Underwood. But he wanted to remind the Director General that SHAFT and the desire for something better still remained. Was automation the answer? Would machines finally free the elves to handcraft toys again? Bigtoes didn't know. He did know that times were changing. They would never be the same. He raised his glass, but the right words escaped him and he missed his turn.

Charity Nosegay raised her glass. "Yes, Virginia," she said, using the popular abbreviation for another elf toast; "yes, Virginia, there is a Santa Claus."

Hardnoggin turned and looked at her with a smile. "You have a beautiful voice, Miss Nosegay," he said. "Have you ever considered being in the talkies?"

And in Closing . . .

One last thing—

Merry Christmas!

Editor's Note

My father was an avid reader, and he instilled in all of his children a love of literature as entertainment. As a result, whenever times got rough, a good book was always the perfect temporary distraction to provide some relief from the difficulties of day-to-day life.

In the fall of 2000, my father was diagnosed with brain cancer, and though he opted for surgery we all knew that this was only a delaying measure at best.

The surgery allowed us all one last Christmas together, and for that we were grateful.

While traveling back and forth on the railroad to visit him at the Northshore Medical Center, my need for distraction was severe, and reading alone just wasn't cutting it, so I put together a few ideas for some reprint anthologies on various subjects. *A Yuletide Universe* was the first of these completed, so I sent it off to my friend and collaborator Marty Greenberg to work his usual magic, which he did.

Coincidentally, the deal for this volume was completed the following June on the day my father died, one last present from our final Christmas together.

About the Contributors

Neil Gaiman is, quite simply, a world-class fantasist. Whether in his graphic novel series *The Sandman* or in his prose novels or story collections, he shows us—and the world around us—in the slightly skewed perspective that writers from Lord Dunsany to Ray Bradbury to Clive Barker to Terry Prachett favor, and, in truth, his unique voice manages to incorporate just about every major strain of traditional and modern fantasy and yet remain just that, unlike anyone else's. Recent books include *The Day I Swapped My Dad for Two Goldfish, Stardust* and the *New York Times*–bestselling *American Gods.*

William Gibson is the author of eight novels, including his latest, *Pattern Recognition*. He lives in Vancouver, British Columbia, and holds an honorary degree of Doctor of Fine Arts from Parsons School of Design of the New School of Social Research.

Richard Christian Matheson is the author of the popular novel *Created By*, a truly horrifying tale of trendy Hollywood. He's even better known for his short stories in the fields of crime and dark suspense. Winner of the Bram Stoker award for best novel, Matheson has written many hours of television and movie scripts, presenting a view of the Southern California lifestyle in a fresh, genuinely chilling way. His style is both unique and startling. Nobody else approaches fiction in quite the same way.

Donald E. Westlake was born in Brooklyn, New York, on July 12, 1933. He attended Champlain College, Plattsburgh, New York, and Harper College, Binghamton, New York, later Binghamton University. He received an honorary Doctor of Letters from Binghamton University in June 1996. He has published more than forty-five novels, which have been translated in fifteen languages. He has received three Edgar Awards, the major award of the Mystery Writers of America, for best novel, best screenplay and best short story. He has received the Grand Master award from MWA, and has served as their president. He has had five produced screenplays: *Cops and Robbers* (1971), *Hot Stuff* (1976), *The Stepfather* (1986), *Why Me* (1989) and *The Grifters* (1989), for which he was nominated for both an Academy Award and a Writer's Guild of America Award. He serves on the Council for the Writer's Guild of America and on the Board for the International Association of Crime Writers.

There is little Harlan Ellison has not done in the field of writing. He has authored over seventeen hundred short stories, four novels, essays, criticisms, plays and teleplays, and has been a constant force for excellence and experimentation in science fiction and fantasy. His works have pushed and often broken through the borders of what would be considered safe fiction by today's society. Having won just about every award in the fiction field, including multiple Nebulas, Hugos and Writer's Guild of America awards, he shows no sign of slowing down. He has also made his mark in the editing field, having put together the groundbreaking collection *Dangerous Visions*, and following that up with *Again, Dangerous Visions*, both books containing stories that at the time were deemed too controversial to publish elsewhere. Recently his enormous fifty-year retrospective, *The Essential Ellison*, was published to rave reviews.

Among Chet Williamson's novels are *Second Chance* (soon to be reprinted in paperback), *Ash Wednesday, Soulstorm, Lowland Rider, McKain's Dilemma, Murder in Cormyr, Mordenheim, Reign, The Crow: Clash By Night*, the paranormal suspense series *The Searchers* and a new children's book, *Pennsylvania Dutch Night Before Christmas*. Nearly a hundred of his short stories have appeared in *The New Yorker, Playboy, Esquire, Twilight Zone*, and *Magazine of F&SF*, and many other magazines and anthologies. He has been a final nominee for the World Fantasy Award and the Mystery Writers of America's Edgar Award, and a six-time nominee for the Horror Writers Association's Stoker Award.

Brian Thomsen is also the editor of *A Date that Will Live in Infamy* and the forthcoming *The American Fantasy Tradition*. He lives in Brooklyn, New York.

Clive Barker first gained prominence in the horror/dark fantasy genre with the publication of his seminal six-volume short story series *The Books of Blood*. He followed that up with a series of novels, including *Weaveworld, Imajica* and *Sacrament*, which blurred the line between literary fiction, imaginative fantasy and outright horror. He has been honored with British and World Fantasy awards and a nomination for the Booker Prize (one of Britain's highest literary honors). His body of work in film is no less impressive, and includes the classic horror film *Hellraiser, Candyman* and the distinguished semi-autobiographical film about the life of director James Whale, *Gods and Monsters*.

Although generally considered a science fiction writer, Michael Bishop has made a career out of crossing back and forth between the horror, fantasy and science fiction genres. His novels *A Funeral for the Eyes of Fire, The Secret Ascension* and the Nebula Award–winning *No Enemy But Time* deploy the traditional science fiction themes of interplanetary adventure, alternate universes and time travel in stories that pose questions regarding human identity and social responsibility. *Who Made Stevie Cry?* is a darkly comic self-reflexive critique of horror fiction, and *Unicorn Mountain* a moving fantasy parable about coming to terms with terminal illness. In his World Fantasy Award–nominated novel *Brittle Innings*, he reworked the Frankenstein theme against the backdrop of minor league baseball. Some of his best short fiction has been collected in the anthologies *Blooded on Arachne, One Winter in Eden* and *At the City Limits of Fate.*

Connie Willis is a multiple Nebula and Hugo award–winning author, primarily for her short fiction. Her novels include the powerful *Doomsday Book, Uncharted Territory* and *Remake.* Her short fiction has been collected in *Fire Watch, Distress Call, Daisy, In the Sun* and *Impossible Things*. In addition, she had edited *The New Hugo Winners, Vol. III.*

Maureen F. McHugh's latest novel, *Nekropolis* (Eos), is out and she thinks it would be a nifty Christmas present. She once spent Christmas in China, but is happy to say, saw no ghosts.

Recent work from Howard Waldrop includes his short novel *The Search for Tom Purdue* from Subterranean Press, and the collection *Custer's Last Jump and Other Collaborations*, with stories co-written by such authors as Steven Utley, George R. R. Martin, Bruce Sterling and William Saunders. A former advertising copywriter and "auditory research subject," his fiction has garnered the Nebula Award and the World Fantasy Award. He lives in Texas.

L. Frank Baum (1856–1919) is best known as the creator of the Oz books, which eventually spanned more than fifteen novels, and, of course, spawned the world-famous film *The Wizard of Oz.* However, the Oz books overshadow his talents as a writer of poetry, plays and other fiction, most notably the fantasy novels *The Master Key* and *Queen Zixi of Ix*. Readers interested in more Santa Claus stories should look up *The Life and Adventures of Santa Claus*, a lighthearted take on Saint Nick.

Bret Harte (1836–1902) was once the highest-paid short story writer in America. He achieved tremendous popularity because of his talent for capturing the sights, sounds and feel of the Old West, which provided the settings for such stories as "The Luck of Roaring Camp" and "The Outcasts of Poker Flat." He remains one of the great writers on the subject of pioneer California, the state that stole his heart.

Anne McCaffrey was the first woman to win both the Nebula and the Hugo awards for her science fiction. She is best known for her popular "Pern" series, which includes the novels *Dragonsflight, Dragonsquest, The White Dragon* and *Dragonsdawn*. Other novels include *The Crystal Singer, Killashandra, Nerika's Story, The Rowan* and *Damia*. Among her novels for younger readers are *Dragonsong, Dragonsinger* and *Dragondrums*. She lives in Ireland.

Anne McCaffrey has said the following about her life: "The early lessons I learned, generally the hard way, in standing up for myself and my egocentricities, being proud of being 'different,' doing my own thing, gave me the strength of purpose to continue doing so in later life. You have to learn how not to conform, how to avoid labels. But it isn't easy! It's lonely until you realize that you have inner resources that those of the herd mentality cannot enjoy. That's where the mind learns the freedom to think science-fictiony things, and where early lessons of tenacity, pure bullheadedness, can make a difference. Most people prefer to be accepted. I learned not to be." (From "Retrospection," in *Women of Vision*, edited by Denise Du Pont, St. Martin's Press, New York, 1988.)

James Powell was born in Toronto in 1932. After graduating from the University of Toronto he spent three years in France studying and teaching in French high schools. He has worked in educational publishing and for a weekly newspaper in the Midwest and has edited an antiques newspaper in Pennsylvania. He has published over 120 short stories of a mysterious and humorous sort. They have appeared in *Ellery Queen's Mystery Magazine* and *Playboy*, among others, and are reprinted regularly in *The Best Detective Stories of the Year* and *The Year's Best Fantasy and Horror* anthology series. In 1989 the readers of *Ellery Queen's Mystery Magazine* voted his "A Dirge for Clowntown" their favorite story of the year. In 1990 his story collection *A Murder Coming* was published in Canada and he was a co-recipient of the Crime Writers of Canada's Derrick Murdock Award "for making a long Canadian story short." A Canadian citizen, he lives in Marietta, Pennsylvania, with his American wife.

Copyrights and Permissions